# BATTLE FOR THE EARTH

# BATTLE FOR THE EARTH

John P. Gledhill

Book Guild Publishing
Sussex, England

First published in Great Britain in 2011 by
The Book Guild Ltd
Pavilion View
19 New Road
Brighton, BN1 1UF

Copyright © John P. Gledhill 2011

The right of John P. Gledhill to be identified as the author of this work has been asserted by him in accordance with the Copyright, Designs and Patents Act 1988.

All rights reserved. No part of this publication may be reproduced, transmitted, or stored in a retrieval system, in any form or by any means, without permission in writing from the publisher or the author, nor be otherwise circulated in any form of binding or cover other than that in which it is published and without a similar condition being imposed on the subsequent purchaser.

All characters in this publication are fictitious and any resemblance to real people, alive or dead, is purely coincidental.

Typesetting in Meridien by
Nat-Type, Cheshire

Printed in Great Britain by
CPI Antony Rowe

A catalogue record for this book is available from
The British Library.

ISBN 978 1 84624 586 2

# 1

It starts December 20, 2020, 12.00 midnight GMT, D-Day for Earth, in total silence. At a height of three hundred miles above our blue planet, high in our thermosphere, twelve strategically placed EMP charges detonate simultaneously. They make very little noise or explosion, but the effects are no less than devastating for humanity. Each burst of EMP has been amplified and targeted to a specific one-twelfth segment of planet Earth, a bit like peeling an orange and splitting the segments.

EMP, Electro-Magnetic Pulse, travels more or less instantaneously. Anything powered by electricity or has wires, your mobile phone, microwave ovens, your television, computers, light bulbs, street lights, power lines, cars, your home, hospitals, police stations, power stations, your nation's ability to defend you, burnt out and gone beyond repair, all in a heart-beat.

12.10 GMT, fifty miles above our blue planet, the start of space, twelve perfect orbs orbiting in unison begin to release in measured quantities their lethal payload, a fine dust of viral content, very similar in genetic code to the 1918 flu virus h1n1, which at the time killed up to one hundred million people worldwide.

The first victims to succumb to this lethal dust will be the birds flying high in our skies, inhaling the fine particles as gravity unwittingly distributes this horrendous virus worldwide. The virus's ability to jump species will do the rest.

For an explanation of this extraordinary death sentence on mankind, we need to travel back in time, 12,000 years ago.

Near the Chinese and Tibetan border high in the mountains of BayanKara-Ula, a team of archaeologists were conducting a very detailed survey of a series of interlinked caves.

This team was lead by Professor Chi Pu Tei, an expert in his field. What they discovered within these caves were lines of neatly arranged graves which contained oddly shaped skeletons, large head, smallish body. As it was initially thought the caves were occupied by an unknown species of ape, this discovery was exceptionally unusual. Apes are not known to bury themselves.

It was while studying the skeletons that one of the team stumbled on a large, round stone disc, half buried in the dust on the floor of the cave. The best way to describe this object would be a prehistoric gramophone record. There was a hole in the centre and a fine spiral groove radiated to the rim.

Because this was 1938, and a troubled time on planet Earth, this discovery passed more or less unnoticed until a closer examination of the disc showed that the groove was, in fact, a continuous spiralling line of closely written characters. Many experts tried to translate the hieroglyphics in the twenty years the disc languished in Peking, but nobody succeeded.

On further study of the caves, a total of 716 of the grooved discs were uncovered. They became known as

'The Dropas Stones'. By this time any conclusions by Professor Chi Pu Tei had been suppressed by the Peking Academy of Pre-History.

Eventually, in 1965, the professor and four of his colleagues were given permission to reveal their theory. It appeared under the longwinded but mysterious title, 'The Grooved Script concerning Space-Ships which, as recorded on the Discs, crash-landed on Earth 12,000 years ago.'

Apparently, as history dictated, the two space craft were caught up in a horrendous storm: one of the craft suffered a direct lightning strike, which catapulted it into the other craft, downing both heavily, and beyond repair. These space ships and their inhabitants were the trigger for civilisation as we have known it over the years.

Over generations the visitors became known as the Dropas, and in build were not too dissimilar to ourselves – slightly smaller in height, larger cranium, greyish, smoother skin, reproductive organs – but worlds apart in intelligence. They were eventually accepted for their peaceful intentions by the surrounding tribe of the Ham, who were indigenous to that region. Integration, breeding and migration followed. The dice of civilisation were thrown and scattered to the four winds.

Over the next eight thousand years Man's intelligence and knowledge steadily improved, to a time when the Sumerian Dynasty depicted, in around 4,000 BC, the Annunaki as travelling from the twelfth planet – 'The Sumerians counted the sun and Earth's moon as planets' – 432,000 years ago to make slaves of Neanderthal man, and mine for gold.

Gold in its pure state is a critical tool for both the Dropas and the Annunaki, as it is used in its gaseous state for hyper-drives in space travel. It was also used in their filtration and atmospheric conditioning systems on Nibiru, the Annunaki-colonised planet in this galaxy. Then there were the obvious uses: electronics, along with crystals and moissanite used in power-pulse systems and weapons. However, the enslavement of this early species of primitive man proved far more difficult than had been imagined by the Annunaki, especially for the purpose of intense mining.

The solution provided by the Annunaki scientists was to splice the genes of Neanderthal man with the Annunaki gene, making a more intelligent Homo Sapiens, in the hope they could be trained more successfully. However, this was unsuccessful and only created a desire for uprising and new-found freedom: the 'Missing Link' had been born.

The Annunaki were banished after a successful uprising, leaving Homo Sapiens with enhanced intellect, aggression and a growing desire over the centuries for valuable precious metals.

# 2

The tenth planet, Nibiru, or planet X, was home to two warring factions, the Dropas – intelligent, technical, and good engineers – and the Annunaki – aggressive warriors.

Nibiru was first colonised by the Annunaki and the Dropas 750,000 years ago for the purpose of mining its valuable metals and minerals – gold, moissanite – and many more required for their technology. This required the annexing of a normally inhabitable planet. Advanced infrastructures capable of supporting life, and a habitat above and below the planet surface were created and mining began.

For the first 450,000 years things went smoothly, with mining and supply convoys going between Nibiru and the star system Sirius, the home star system of both the Annunaki and the Dropas.

Then the supply convoys slowed in regularity and eventually came to a stop, with rumours of a cataclysmic war and extinction in their home star system. The Dropas and the Annunaki found themselves bound together with a common goal: survival.

This led to an uneasy peace between the two for the next 200,000 years. Although Nibiru was now an extremely advanced society, space to live was becoming a premium and natural resources were all but mined out, a combination of events which would prove to be a recipe for disaster.

Eventually the inevitable war happened. Over the next decade the Dropas were routed from Nibiru and fled as a small group of survivors to seek refuge wherever they could. This happened to be a small blue planet called Earth, deep within the Mariana trench, where the Dropas set up home.

The Mariana trench was an ideal bolthole for the Dropas as it was five miles deep under the Pacific Ocean, and at its deepest point seven miles down, this point being known as the Challenger Deep.

From this sub-vantage point the Dropas were able, over 100,000 thousand years and generations of adaptation, to re-establish themselves as a civilisation, even to the extent of subtle integration with mankind.

This was, of course, at BayanKara-Ula, and later, more meaningfully, Atlantis.

On further visitations to Earth by the Annunaki, a surprising legacy was discovered. Mankind had grown over the centuries to value gold, and to mine and refine it for themselves.

A decision was made by the Annunaki high council, to observe the status quo for the time being, and set a date for the harvesting of all the gold man had been able to mine and refine. This was to be done in one swoop.

Fortunately for mankind, this information was obtained by the Dropas from a high-ranking Annunaki, who had been on a craft which had crashed into the south Pacific Ocean due to mechanical failure.

The interrogation of this high-ranking warrior took place using highly advanced mind-probing technology and was a mine of information for the Dropas. Once all the extracted information had been collated, it was clear to the Dropas that mankind faced extermination on 21 December 2020, the date pre-set to harvest Earth's gold. This left the Dropas with a huge dilemma.

The Dropas had also been totally unaware of the Annunaki intervention with Neanderthal man, and the splicing of genes to create homo-sapian man. This would now involve the Dropas in a long-term study of mankind's evolvement, and any permanent damage done to mankind's genes.

The Dropas thought long and hard over this dilemma, and it was decided that over the progress of mankind's development, specimens would need to be extracted for medical investigations. This would be done in the most benign way possible, using the Dropas' mind-control and memory-replacement technology. This policy worked well with mankind up until the late twentieth century, when these episodes became known as 'abductions'.

The abductions caused confusion between scientists and professors, leading to a general opinion that the Dropas, or 'Greys', as they had been labelled, were the bad guys of the galaxy. This, of course, was not the case.

The second dilemma, and definitely more important, was the extermination of mankind set for 21 December 2020. It was decided in order that Annunaki awareness could be kept to a minimum, the Dropas would introduce their own gene of enlightenment to mankind, making full use of mankind's mental abilities. This gene would lie dormant in around ten per cent of the population, until awakened in the first part of the twenty-first century, allowing enlightened man and the Dropas, years to prepare for the onslaught of the Annunaki on 21/12/2020.

This, they hoped, would not allow the Annunaki time to

advance their plans for mankind's destruction, and the reaping of the harvest of gold. However, this still left the Dropas with one big problem: how to introduce the enlightenment gene to mankind?

The Dropas made the decision that the best policy would be a 'Smoke and Mirrors' campaign. This way mankind would not be overwhelmed with too much information too soon, and the Annunaki would have little or no idea what was going on. Information could also be integrated into the myth and culture of civilisation, century by century. In addition, a limited selection of influential members of human society could be made partially aware of the situation in an endeavour to keep the Dropas covert and secret.

The first stage was to alter the Dropas' genetic code and appearance to a more human appearance, which the Dropas scientists successfully achieved. Then thirteen crystal skulls of knowledge and enlightenment, mini-super advanced computers, and various technological tools were loaded between two space craft. The craft then set off on their mission of Smoke and Mirrors, heading towards the BayanKara-Ula province of China.

# 3

Only on a few occasions in Earth's history had the Annunaki used mass force. After the failed enslavement of Neanderthal man, a long period of calm enveloped the Earth until, in 9600 BC, on a continent, mid-Atlantic, between Africa and the Americas a civilisation of technologically advanced humans, who had the Dropas' gene and nearly three centuries of breeding to thank for their technology and achievements was lost to the world. This was of course Atlantis.

When the Annunaki high council discovered Atlantis and its highly advanced Dropas/human heritage, it drew up plans for Atlantis to be wiped from the face of the planet. This happened in 9600 BC and was carried out in mythical terms: 'In a single day and night of misfortune.'

A battle cruiser was dispatched from Nibiru, and Atlantis was no more, sunk to the depths of the Atlantic Ocean, left only to be a ghost of mythology and the Holy Grail of archaeologists' dreams.

There were, however, survivors from Atlantis, some of whom mysteriously vanished, others who migrated east to Africa and on to Egypt, and west to the Americas. Aware they could not make the same mistakes as Atlantis, they blended more subtly into the background, and over the centuries nudged mankind in the right direction with myth and legend.

\* \* \*

The Dropas now knew that any help or intervention from them in future would have to be covert and top secret, so as not to unleash the wrath of the Annunaki again. The high council decided that it would be too risky to leave all thirteen skulls in the care of one civilisation, so the decision to split them up between numerous civilisations was made.

Each civilisation was given instructions to hide the skulls carefully, so they could be brought together in January 2018 to activate the Dropas gene and enlighten mankind.

The Dropas went to ground after that, and only a fleeting few of mankind were aware of their presence. On the odd occasion one of their craft might be spotted, but this would be put down to myth and conjecture.

Later in the twentieth and twenty-first centuries the sightings had become much more frequent – mankind's technology was in danger of exposing the Dropas worldwide. This was pre-empted at Roswell, New Mexico in 1947. The two surviving Dropas pilots from the shuttle-craft that crashed there brought the American government of the time fully up to date with events. A plan was devised to cover up and explain away any further sighting until 2018.

# 4

Now possessing a point of time reference, the UN Security Council and Dropas representative could bring the skulls together and preparations could begin for the defence of mankind. The seventy-one years from 1947 had been arduous but had served the Dropas well for their preparations. Fortunately mankind at least now had a head start and nearly two years to draw up worldwide plans.

Back in spring 2009, Mexico, and the start of a global pandemic which will transcend all borders and continents. Swine flu H1N1, the pandemic feared for decades by scientists and governments alike. This pandemic moves swiftly round the globe, it is extremely virulent and tenacious, lasting up to two days without a host on virtually any smooth surface, which ensures maximum transmission.

What the general public did not realise was that this was a deliberately manufactured genetic code, introduced by the Dropas, to enable mankind to immunise itself against the Annunaki viral weapon, which would be loosed in 2020.

Ever since Atlantis, the Dropas have been very careful to limit their interaction with mankind, so as not to alert the Annunaki high council to the remaining Dropas' presence on Earth. This is why the main Dropas base was built in the Challenger Deep, seven miles beneath the waves, within the Mariana Trench.

Late in 1949, a covert Dropas advisor joined the newly formed UN Security Council to ensure the thirteen crystal skulls would be brought together in time for the specified date of 1 January 2018, and to prepare and coordinate mankind for the coming Armageddon.

# 5

Monday morning 11.00 GMT. It was a cold but very bright day in London, not an untypical New Year's Day apart from one thing: the date line was now 2018, the climax of the coming together of the thirteen crystal skulls.

The UN Security Council members of the five nations, UK, USA, Russia, China and France, had now arrived at COBRA headquarters in London and were awaiting the arrival of the Dropas advisor to initiate procedures.

The sourcing of the thirteen skulls was a fairly easy process for the Dropas as each skull had its own tracking device. When each skull had been tracked down it was secured and replaced by an exact replica until all thirteen skulls were now safe in the hands of the Dropas, and the Security Council.

Konoco, the Dropas advisor, put the finishing gold nano-wire arrangement to the centre skull, in the centre of the perfect circle of twelve outer skulls. The sense of anticipation in the darkened cabinet room was thick and so dense it was almost physical.

Konoco stood back from the skulls and started to back pace. All eyes in the room were focused on the thirteen skulls.

A low humming noise began to be emitted from the skulls, and the centre skull started to glow, a fine piercing light firing from its centre, around two feet in height and half an inch thick. Konoco made a waving motion with his left hand and pointed to the closest skull with his right hand, slowly rotating his hand till his palm was flat, and facing upwards. The beam of light from the centre skull leapt to the skull Konoco was concentrating on, and connected the two skulls in an eerie light show. The second skull then emitted a flat image in thin air of around three feet square, but with the resolution of an HD LCD television.

Konoco moved his left hand rapidly as if turning the pages in a book, and the image in the air changed accordingly, until Konoco stopped his rapid hand movements.

The members of the Security Council were transfixed.

Suddenly all thirteen skulls lit up and each emitted a beam of light. The low hum had turned into a slow pulsating sound, which was now gaining in speed and volume. All the beams of light met at around three feet in height above the centre skull.

Konoco wafted his left hand again and the image in the air disappeared and a visible pulse was emitted from where the light beams met. The pulse at first seemed to be in slow motion then accelerated at unbelievable speed in all directions.

The pulse expanded exponentially over London, Europe, and then continent to continent. The process of global enlightenment had begun.

The skulls fell silent and dimmed as Konoco turned to face the Security Council.

'My friends, what you have just witnessed is the rebirth of mankind. The pulse emitted from the skulls that you have just seen, is a chronological code for the activation of the Dropas gene, implanted in so many humans and passed from generation to generation over centuries.

'For a long time mankind had been aware we only use around 10 to 12 per cent of our brain power; with the activation of the Dropas gene, that figure has now risen to 70 per cent. Not everybody has the Dropas gene, probably around 10 per cent of the population, but that will be enough to give mankind a fighting chance.'

Even as Konoco spoke, two of the Security Council were already being enlightened, as slowly within the subconscious mind of the Chinese and Russian members, clarity was replacing confusion, knowledge was replacing ignorance and with such a sense of freedom that the rush was visibly overwhelming.

Lee Shingho, the Chinese member, approached Konoco with a soft knowing touch on the back of the Dropas representative and said, 'Thank you, my friend.'

Now was the right time to put plans in place for the survival of mankind. Indeed the skulls were all that been hoped for, not just for the rebirth of mankind, but a vast data base of knowledge, everything from Dropas' history and strategy to technical manuals for spaceships, weapons and power sources. Now with the information and people who understood how to use it the learning, building and training could begin.

# 6

Deep in space in the shadow of the far side of the moon a fleet lies in wait, watching and listening, evaluating our blue planet and the space around it. On the bridge of the Annunaki flag ship, *Nephilimis*, a large looming figure appearing deep in thought suddenly spins and in a tone so low-pitched and rough it makes the hairs on the back of your neck stand on end, barks a command to a subordinate. Standing eight feet tall with an intensely muscular frame and intimidating fire-red eyes, the supreme commander of the Annunaki fleet is truly an awesome and fearful sight.

The Annunaki are completely different from either ourselves or the Dropas, standing over eight feet tall, with greenish reptilian skin, an extremely powerful build, likened to be strong as five men, and extremely aggressive with attitude to match.

December 28. Seven days have now passed since the rout of human civilisation, with no technology left working, and a population severely weakened by viral infection, Tannacha, the supreme commander of the Annunaki fleet, is confident of a swift and decisive victory on arrival at Earth. The fleet now within a few hours of the Earth's orbit is considerable in size. Ten battle cruisers, fifty support and troop vessels, five hundred thousand ground troops and five hundred assault craft.

The mighty prize for this fleet is 100,000 tons of pure gold, held by governments in federal reserves all over the globe.

Tannacha gave the order for the fleet to drop out of hyper-drive. Suddenly the *Nephilimis* lurched, and veered left sharply, as a fireball enveloped the front observation window. Tannacha barked out commands one after another, then finally, 'Full stop.' The supreme commander had realised what happened. As they had dropped out of hyper-drive they had ended up in the middle of a huge meteor storm.

Tannacha ordered damage reports. The news was catastrophic. Four battle cruisers had been totally destroyed, and two badly damaged, but were still serviceable; seven of the support vessels had been destroyed and six badly damaged. Two hundred of the assault craft had been lost between the four destroyed battle cruisers, fifty on each. This was truly a disastrous start to the campaign. Tannacha had a hard decision to make.

The fleet now comprised six battle cruisers, forty-three troop and support vessels, three hundred assault ships and around four hundred thousand ground troops. Tannacha weighed up his options, and decided to carry on and see what damage had been done on Earth. This incident had been extremely damaging and unfortunate, and for the sake of morale it must be put behind them.

As the first of the Annunaki fleet started to take their positions in Earth's orbit, Tannacha redirected the battle cruiser commanders to cover the change of strategy caused by the craft lost in the meteor storm. Finally all the craft came to rest in Earth's orbit.

Earth is silent, the crackle of radio waves are nowhere to be heard. The lights of mankind's civilisation are dim. Indeed, to all intent and purpose the blue planet appears to be comatose, just as the Annunaki intended.

An Annunaki assault vessel flashes past the bridge of the *Nephilimis*, at tremendous speed. It enters Earth's atmosphere and heads directly towards North America's eastern seaboard, travelling at low level, and high speed. All the Annunaki pilot can see is desolation and devastation, abandoned cars, rubbish everywhere, dead or dying bodies dotted around. No threat meets the craft in the air or on the ground. The craft stops, abruptly turns vertically on its axis and rockets spaceward.

The report sent to Tannacha makes him smile.

# 7

Back in April 2018. A mild spring, comparatively speaking. Already a fleet was under construction to complement the countless Dropas vessels already in service. This was thanks to Blue Star Base, named after Rigel, the brightest star in the constellation of Orion.

This well-established Dropas facility on the far side of the moon consisted of manufacturing plants, mining operations, living quarters, defence structures, medical facilities and environmental habitat, in all covering fifty square miles both above and below the moon's barren surface.

The population of this sprawling base was varied: mainly human at around 85 per cent, Dropas roughly 5 per cent, the rest being made up of Androids.

The Androids were extremely technologically advanced and the Dropas trusted them and relied on them absolutely. This brought the total population to sixty thousand in all.

The Dropas had been well prepared for the enlightenment of mankind; after all, they had centuries to prepare, build and plan.

Back on Earth preparations were also well under way. All the enlightened over the age of sixteen had been gathered for work allocation in their countries' capitals, and at key strategic points.

A network of civil defence structures, all protected against EMP and fitted with advanced Dropas filtration and environmental systems, were under construction world wide. In actual fact the Dropas had been secretly working on the structures for decades, using advanced mining technology, in preparation for 2020. The structures were three miles beneath the surface of the Earth and when finished could hold up to seven hundred and fifty thousand people for up to six months in perfect comfort.

Thanks to Dropas mining technology the last of the structures were now being completed in months as opposed to years.

Spring had come and gone and it was the height of summer. Spacecraft of all types were now a common sight and the general public had been made fully aware of the situation mankind was facing.

The Dropas were accepted by everyone as friends who had already been with us a long time. After all we now knew for certain we are not alone, and flying saucers did exist. As for Roswell on July 8, 1947 – as they say, accidents do happen.

Konoco had been in the thick of it all, liaising with world leaders and the Dropas High Security Council. The Blue Star Fleet of the Dropas had all but been rebuilt and manned by units of the newly formed ESG, Earth Security Guard, all enlightened and Dropas trained.

Lee Shingho, the Chinese representative to the Earth Security Council, had been a constant companion and confidant to Konoco over the preceding months and was now standing beside him on the bridge of the Dropas flag-ship, *Katchinas*, in awe of the view below him. Somehow the expression 'blue planet' was underselling Earth's awesome beauty.

Konoco was awaiting the arrival of the Dropas Blue Star Fleet commander, Jumouk. Although so much had already been done in such a short time, Earth was still far from ready. There were only fourteen short months till the Annunaki would be due to set off the first of their devices in Earth's atmosphere.

The *Katchinas* was an extremely impressive sight, a huge spaceship, in the shape of a 4,000-metre rain drop, but with all the style of a classic American sportster – smooth curves, nothing to spoil the lines or contours of the ship, soft greyish in colour and no outward signs of propulsion. There was a total of four of these impressive battle cruisers in the fleet, three of which were at Blue Star Base, leaving the *Katchinas* orbiting a hundred miles above Earth. It was a hub for the activities below.

Lee Shingho was startled when a firm voice behind him exclaimed.

'Beautiful, is it not?'

Lee turned, politely agreed. Konoco bowed and acknowledged his commander.

'I think you will find that the latest shipment from Blue Star Base on the dark side has arrived, Konoco.'

Jumouk then turned to Lee. 'Lee, may I speak with you a moment? I have a concern.'

Konoco made his excuses and left. Jumouk continued, 'I don't like the idea of leaving the Annunaki devices orbiting Earth.'

'I totally agree, but if they are moved the trackers attached to them will alert the Annunaki, which could jeopardise our element of surprise. Besides, I may have an idea that will render them totally safe. Trust me, Jumouk, I won't put anyone at risk unnecessarily.'

Jumouk relented. Lee had been enlightened and had shown the most promise of all enlightened mankind, which made him the natural choice as commander of the Earth Security Guard, and this had already proved to be a good choice. He had mastered the tough training courses the Dropas had introduced, including flight training, easily and within half the normal time.

Konoco studied the latest shipment from the Blue Star Base, a consignment of powerful pulse weapons, destined for ground troops of the Earth Security Guard, based on Earth. These weapons were just entering the strict Dropas quality control area before continuing their journey to Earth.

Konoco moved on to the quality control firing range. He stood and pondered, as he watched the pulse weapons being discharged down the range at the three-dimensional targets. Things appeared to be going well, very well.

Back on Earth things could not be going more smoothly. Already, although only December, enough structures had been built to house all Earth's non-combatants safely, and construction had started on the surface of the planet for the fortification of major cities.

The Dropas had a long time to prepare a strategic defence of Earth and also had an excellent knowledge of Earth's terrain both on land and beneath the seas. After all, they had been traversing them for years as UFOs, and USOs, Unidentified Flying Objects and Unidentified Submerged Objects.

Although the Dropas were not a naturally warring species, they were exceptionally adaptable. Thy were also excellent planners and engineers.

# 8

On Earth there were to be two lines of defence, land based and water based. The first point of the Annunaki attack would be over land, aimed at strategic cities and landmarks. It made sense to have the main fire power defending these points, so a defence pod was designed and put into production on the lunar base.

Two hundred of these fearsome pods had just arrived by transporters in North America. The pods themselves were self-contained, manned by Dropas Androids, and full of EMP-protected technology. The fire power was awesome and devastating, even to the Annunaki craft. These pods would be positioned on approaches to specific targets, two pods for the defence of each of a hundred targets selected.

This defence strategy would be repeated on a continental scale. The pods themselves were made from an energy-absorbing mineral found only deep within the moon's crust which made them extremely resilient to weapons' fire. As far as the Dropas were aware, the Annunaki had no such technology available to them. Even with that said, the pods were, in the scheme of things, made to be expendable, which is why they were manned with Androids, not ESG troopers.

To reinforce the pods, bunkers would be built from the same material and positioned around the pods. These bunkers would be manned by twenty-five ESG troopers and twenty-five Android troopers, all armed to the teeth.

A second line of defence was being planned by the ESG in the form of airborne mines, which could be released from cities and hover above the city anywhere from a hundred feet to a mile high, all remotely controlled by ESG troopers on the ground. The mines themselves were relatively quite small, but could easily disable an Annunaki craft.

Konoco had just been made aware of the arrival of the pods and decided to come to the planet surface to see the installation of one himself.

The departure deck of the *Katchinas* was unusually quiet as Konoco entered a small shuttle to travel down to Earth. The pilot greeted Konoco with a smile and commented, 'Not much going on today sir.'

Konoco nodded in agreement and sat down.

'Sorry for the delay, sir. Just waiting for one more passenger booked on board.'

Konoco sat up abruptly as Lee entered the craft.

'I wasn't expecting you to come along as well, Lee.'

Lee shrugged his shoulders.

'Not much else going on, don't know why it's so quiet.'

They both sat back and relaxed as the shuttle silently left the docking bay.

The flight to area 11, which was called Earth Base Central, took only ten minutes. As Konoco and Lee departed the shuttle, they thanked the pilot and both turned towards the construction site, Lee's jaw dropped in awe. A huge pod towered in front of him. Yes, he had seen the plans for the pods, but this had not prepared him for the sight he was witnessing.

The pod was already in place and was being fine-tuned by technicians from the ESG. The appearance of the pod was gold/green in colour and it stood a good thirty feet high, with a base of around sixty feet square and tapering up pyramid style. No apertures were visible, just hundreds of multi-function pulse weapons.

Lee thought to himself: the Annunaki don't stand a chance against this. Konoco made himself known to the technician in charge and asked if the second pod had been put in position yet. It had and what's more, this pod was just about finished. Lee was still wandering around the pod in disbelief, muttering to himself.

Just a few hundred yards away was a major construction site for the main Earth Base Central; all the Dropas mining and technical know-how were going into this base, and it was progressing well.

Konoco caught up with Lee and put a reassuring arm around his shoulder.

'It couldn't be going better, my friend. I just wonder what's going to go wrong. It can't be this easy, can it?'

Konoco had been in human contact for so long that he had picked up a lot of human idiosyncrasies. Truth be known, he was quietly proud of his human side.

Back on board the *Katchinas*, Jumouk was watching a series of digital displays, wafting his left hand and using a poking motion with his right hand. He seemed particularly interested in one display, which showed a craft rapidly approaching Jupiter, only ten or fifteen minutes at most from Earth. This could be disastrous for the element of surprise against the Annunaki.

Like bolts of lightning two Dropas manned assault craft shot from the shadows of the moon, both on an interception course for the unknown craft. This would be a real test of the new Dropas technology as Dropas and Annunaki had not met in battle in millennia.

Within minutes the craft had indeed been identified as Annunaki. Time was now at a premium. One of the Dropas craft kept dead on course for the Annunaki craft, the other went straight to hyper-drive for a fraction of a second, placing it directly behind the enemy craft, and cutting off any chance of escape.

With lightning reflexes the Dropas assault vessel had spun on its axis, coming out of hyper-space, and with the accuracy of a hawk snatching a field mouse, unleashed a deadly volley from its pulse weapon. The Annunaki pilot didn't stand a chance as his craft disintegrated into particles in space.

Jumouk smiled warmly. This incident had answered two pressing questions for him. How would the new assault ships fair against the Annunaki craft, and were our pilots battle ready? Both questions had now been answered and the prognosis was excellent.

By February 2020 all the land-based fortifications were in place and had been fully tested by the Dropas flight commanders with their assault ships, running a minimum of three raids a day over the fortifications.

The emphasis was now on seaward defence. Fortunately, all around the world the Dropas over the centuries had constructed multiple underwater bases. The particular benefit of these bases are total secrecy and freedom of movement underwater, allowing Dropas USOs to shadow ships and submarines in certain knowledge of not being identified.

These bases could now be used for troop dispersion and

repair stations for damaged Dropas craft. By May 2020 all the required bases had been converted to suit their new purpose: in all seventy-five bases worldwide of all shapes and sizes.

On board the *Katchinas*, Jumouk and Konoco were deep in discussion. Konoco was concerned about the ESG and their readiness for the battle ahead.

'Would it be prudent to increase the training schedules especially for the pilots?'

Jumouk shook his head. 'I don't think so. We are already working them harder than we should, and besides the progress till now has been more than we could have hoped for.'

There was a soft knock at the door.

'Enter.'

Jumouk's day had been long and hard, it showed in his weary voice. The door slid open and Lee entered cautiously. He knew they had been discussing the ESG. Jumouk invited him to sit down.

The conference room was luxurious to say the least, all fitted out in the best of taste, with pile carpets, leather chairs and subdued lighting. Konoco acknowledged Lee, then stood up, made his excuses and left. Jumouk relaxed back in his chair and smiled.

'Everything's fine, Lee. The training by all accounts is going well.'

Lee smiled.

'I think we're going to be ready for them, and it's all thanks to the Dropas, with a little hard work on our part as well.'

There was a glint of pride in Lee's eyes, and a stammer in his voice.

# BATTLE FOR THE EARTH

\* \* \*

Next morning Lee was up early, knowing he was going to have a long day. Blue Star Base had been working at full capacity for sixteen months now. It was time to show some appreciation for the hard work done by all to reach this stage.

The shuttle to the dark side was virtually full. Lee settled down for the twenty-minute flight. The views from the shuttle were spectacular, especially on approach to the Blue Star Base. Although on the dark side of the moon, visibility wasn't bad and the views of the open lunar landscapes were spectacular.

The shuttle glided into the landing hangar and landed gently. As Lee disembarked, he experienced a real sense of why Blue Star Base was so productive: there was activity everywhere.

He took a minute to scan his surroundings. In the whole of the hangar area not one person was standing still and everybody was carrying out some kind of activity. Lee felt a touch on his shoulder. He turned to find it was Terry Summers, Terry was the number two for the ESG on the lunar base, answerable only to Marie Baker, the ESG commander there.

'Why not come with me, Lee. I know a great place that does a mean green tea.'

Lee smiled, Terry and Lee had become good friends over the last twelve months. Terry had spent a lot of time on board the *Katchinas* working with Lee in preparation for the Annunaki assault on Earth.

Musing over a cup of green tea, which happened to be Lee's favourite refreshment, Terry asked, 'Do you think we are ready yet, Lee?'

Lee pondered the question

'To be honest Terry, that's part of the reason why I travelled up here today.'

Terry looked bemused.

'I don't understand, Lee; all our quotas and schedules have been met on time .'

Lee continued.

'No, Terry that's not it. The work that's been done here is fantastic. No, it's Earth. All the construction's finished now, but for a while I've felt there's something missing.'

Terry look quizzically at him.

'Missing?'

Lee took another sip of his green tea, and, taking a deep breath, continued.

'What I mean is, I have five commanders on Earth. When the going gets tough I don't want to, and won't have time, to repeat myself five times. What I need is an overall commander on Earth and I think you're the man for the job.'

There was a pregnant pause. Terry looked uncomfortable.

'What about Marie?'

Lee played with his tea cup.

'Marie is the perfect commander for Blue Star Base. She's great at running this base, but the real action is going to be with the Blue Star Fleet and on Earth. I need you to be my right-hand man and defend Earth while I blast the suckers out of the skies.'

Terry shook Lee's hand and replied, 'OK, sir, done deal. Let's go see Marie.'

In Marie's office the three of them were joined by Ravel, the senior Dropas representative on Blue Star Base. Marie had already congratulated Terry and wished him luck on Earth; Lee greeted Ravel and brought him up to speed on events.

Marie stood up, patted Terry on the back and said, 'Haven't you got a bag to pack, Terry?'

Terry stood up, made his excuses, and left the room.

Marie was an emotionally strong woman, in her early forties, firm but fair and more than capable of making tough decisions. If she did have a weakness in her character, it was a soft spot for Lee, whom she respected and admired enormously.

Lee had recommended Marie in the first instance to the Earth Security Council as commander of Blue Star Base along with Ravel, a recommendation that had been warmly welcomed. Lee was confident that the lunar bases' defences were ready for the coming onslaught and Marie and Ravel could handle anything the Annunaki could throw at them. Marie had already asked Lee if he would like to inspect the base, but Lee declined citing time limitations. After all, the two main purposes for the visit had been to congratulate Marie and Ravel along with their whole team on a job well done, and to persuade Terry to take over command of Earth's defences. Both goals had been successfully achieved and, besides, Lee could never get used to the Androids – they unnerved him, quite a lot as it happened. The thought of relying on emotionless chunks of alloy, no matter how technologically advanced, just didn't seem right.

Terry was already at the landing pad waiting for Lee. He had a small attaché case and a holdall in tow. Lee made his way though the clamour of people, Dropas, human and Android, the latter being avoided as much as possible.

The shuttle from *Katchinas* was just arriving at the landing pad, Lee waved to Terry and shouted for him to get on. A minute later Lee climbed through the entry hatch on the little ten-man shuttle and took his seat beside Terry. Lee relaxed back in his seat only to notice that Terry had a very weird expression on his face. Lee enquired, 'Terry, are you OK?'

Terry turned and looked at Lee. Without speaking a word he nodded in the direction of the flight deck and smiled. Lee followed his gaze and realised his worst nightmare: there was an Android piloting the shuttle. Lee closed his eyes and accepted his fate.

Konoco was on the bridge of the *Katchinas* when Lee and Terry arrived back. Konoco greeted Terry warmly, and asked Lee if they had had a good flight. Lee looked to Terry and grinned, and acknowledging Konoco, he said, 'Yes, Konoco, it was fine thanks, but I did learn a lesson today though. Androids do make good pilots.'

Lee was still thinking about the Androids, wondering whether perhaps he might have underestimated them. OK, they did have limited uses like manning the pods on Earth, or for ongoing repairs on the fleet, which they were particularly suited to as they did not need air and could work underwater and in a vacuum. Lee would definitely need to reconsider their part in the scheme of things.

# 9

Lee had called a special meeting of the Dropas and ESG leadership to discuss the formation of a Tactical Android group. This would involve converting one hundred assault craft to customise them for Android use. It would also involve the reprogramming of two hundred and fifty Androids, the special benefit of which was the unique speed and reflexes of the Androids, along with unprecedented targeting skills.

The idea was unanimously accepted and put into motion. This group would be called the Tactical Android Group or TAG for short, and based at Sub Sea One. Lee was confident in the way things were progressing. The Annunaki were going to be in for one hell of a shock come 21/12/2020.

Back on Earth the defence systems were all but complete, all the craft that comprised the fleet having been brought up to the latest specification by the Android maintenance corps. The last thing to be done would be the camouflage, to consolidate the illusion of a run-down world.

The moon base, Blue Star, was ready, and operations had all been closed down in favour of finishing preparations for defence. Around the base fifteen pods had been installed covering all approaches.

To reinforce this there were two rings of bunkers, one

ring in front of the pods and one behind, a total of one hundred in all. The bunkers comprised fifty ESG troopers, unlike on Earth, where it was a mix of ESG and Androids who manned the bunkers. The reason for the slight difference was a fighter group made up completely of Androids, TAG – one hundred assault craft in all and specially designed for the Androids' special skills.

This brought the total fleet to four battle cruisers, three hundred assault vessels, eighty support craft, and four huge transport ships, each capable of carrying huge amounts of materials, or up to two hundred and fifty thousand people, fifty-five shuttle craft of varying sizes and a total of two million ground troops with support from ten thousand Android troopers.

It was now the end of November 2020. The training of the fighter groups was a spectacular sight, on Earth, in space, and over the desolate lunar landscape. Assault ships were sparring with each other, Dropas against ESG, Dropas against Dropas and ESG against ESG. The sight of the assault ships in action was truly awe-inspiring.

All the camouflage was in place now and the planet surface looked a sorry sight, almost as if the hand of God Himself had come down and laid waste to the planet. Konoco was surveying the planet along with Terry. They were in a two-man assault vessel, silver-grey in colour in the shape of a V or triangle fifty foot long with a span of around a hundred feet.

They were travelling over the bay of San Francisco when Konoco unexpectedly dived, taking the craft deep beneath the waves. This was a relatively new experience for Terry and initially not a pleasant one. Terry had been a wing commander in the USAF, and was still not used to zero G force in the Dropas craft, never mind going underwater with them.

The craft itself handled as well underwater as it did in the air or even space. Konoco did quite a few manoeuvres underwater, most of which Terry felt were completely unnecessary, and were aimed at unsettling him.

Konoco merely smiled as he watched Terry's face. The craft settled into the landing bay in an underwater base.

As Terry and Konoco left the assault craft two Androids from the ACM, Android Core of Maintenance, were already inspecting the craft. Terry was very impressed, Konoco remarked.

'I bet you're wondering where we are?'

Terry nodded. Konoco continued:

'Welcome to Sub Sea One. This base controls all the Sub Sea stations, seventy-five in all. This is where we moved to after leaving Challenger Deep. It's our biggest underwater base, it's also the ACM and TAG main base.'

As they walked along the corridor, Terry couldn't help thinking to himself about all the reported UFO sighting over the years – if only we had known then, what we know now!

His thoughts were rudely interrupted as Konoco stopped suddenly. A message had just come in on his Visi Link, a watch-like communication device, which was beamed directly from a Dropas shuttle, hidden deep inside a small space rubble field orbiting Nibiru. The sight that Konoco could see was blood-curdling. It showed a huge and menacing fleet forming in the upper orbital path of Nibiru.

Konoco showed the images to Terry and passed him his Visi Link. They both stood transfixed for a moment. Then Terry swore.

'Shit! I didn't expect this, not so soon, or as big. How many ships do you think, Konoco? And what are those big bastards?'

Terry looked round, Konoco had already started to retrace his steps to the assault vessel.

Back on board the *Katchinas*, Jumouk and Lee were studying detailed images of the Annunaki fleet that was forming. As Konoco and Terry joined them on the bridge, Jumouk commented:

'Well, it will probably take a while for them to get organised and then get underway.'

'When do you think they will get here?' Lee asked.

'Probably around the 25th or maybe up to 29th December. If it was me, I would give it about a week for the dust to settle.'

'That would make it around December 28th,' Terry added cautiously.

Everyone looked at Terry and nodded in agreement.

It could not be stressed enough that the first strike against the Annunaki must be devastating and a complete surprise – or shock and awe, if you like.

# 10

December 2, 2020. The little Dropas vessel only twenty foot wide and thirty foot long watched silently from within the debris field orbiting Nibiru, as warship after warship joined the Annunaki fleet, all shapes and sizes, so that it seemed to go on for ever. The most worrying craft were the massive battle cruisers, 3,000 feet long and 2,000 feet wide, almost triangular in shape. Even in the vastness of space they were big, and there were seven of them there now, each with a complement of fifty assault craft.

Tukie, the pilot of the shuttle, had been so taken with the sight in front of him, that he had not noticed the proximity alarm on the console to the side of him flashing. This was designed to flash when an object was within 3,000 feet of the shuttle and, unless disabled manually for that specific object, to sound a voice warning at 1,000 feet.

All of a sudden a voice warning barked out of the console. Tukie spun round just in time to see three massive Annunaki battle cruisers bearing down on him through the debris field. The little ten-man shuttle spun frantically as boulders thumped across the hull, akin to the balls on a pool table after a wild break.

The Annunaki battle cruisers simply ploughed through the debris field on course to join the rest of the fleet, not even noticing the tiny shuttle in their path. To them the silent shuttle would have looked just like one of the larger boulders in their way. Tukie picked himself up and made a visual check for damage. Things were a mess but it seemed there was no hull breach. As Tukie looked around, the main problem became apparent. He had been thrown clear of the debris field and was starting to drift into open space. He was acutely aware that if he powered up any main systems he would light up the Annunaki proximity detectors like a Christmas tree.

Back on Earth Konoco was worried. The transmissions from Tukie had stopped twenty-four hours ago, which could only mean one of two things: either Tukie's cover had been blown, and a valued friend had been lost to the Annunaki war machine, or there had been some kind of mechanical failure. Konoco was at a loss. The final information regarding fleet size, and departure, could have been invaluable.

Everything was now ready for the arrival of the coming Annunaki fleet. All the preparations that could have been done, were done. In the next few weeks the population of mankind would become subterranean, and our blue planet would shine a little bit less brightly.

December 20, 2020. Jumouk and Lee were on the *Katchinas*, Konoco and Terry were in Earth Base Central located on the outskirts of Washington, and Marie and Ravel were in the Blue Star Base on the dark side of the moon.

Jumouk gave the order for the Dropas and ESG fleet to form a V-shaped formation, half a mile above Blue Star Base.

All of the control rooms on Earth, the moon, the fleet,

and Sub Sea One had specialised digital, 3D displays fitted, showing a real-time representation of Earth, the moon, and all the surrounding space. This would enable the commanders to make tactical decisions instantly.

The 3D display on the *Katchinas* looked extremely impressive as the craft came together in the V shape, but that was nowhere near as impressive as the view from the lunar surface. The huge fleet above the lunar base seemed to be never ending and filled all those who watched with a new sense of hope, inspiration and pride.

Terry contacted the fleet and with Jumouk's blessing fifty of the newest assault craft broke formation, formed their own V-shaped formation and hurtled towards Earth at fantastic speed. Within ten minutes they were hovering above Terry at Earth Central. An experimental magnetic shroud emanating from the ground covered the craft, bending light itself and making the craft virtually invisible. A similar system was installed on Blue Star Base but on a much larger scale. It was designed to cover not only the base, but the fleet hovering half a mile above as well. Unfortunately it hadn't yet been tested.

Marie was full of trepidation as she stood in front of the console. A lot depended on the shroud working correctly. With a small tap of her finger a confirmation notice was voiced from the console.

'Do you wish the shroud activated.'

Marie spoke with authority.

'Yes.'

The console retorted, 'Authorisation code please.'

Marie quoted, 'Baker, Marie, Alpha, Delta, Beta, one six, one six.'

The electronic console replied, 'Accepted, thank you.'

It seemed as if everybody held their breath at the same time.

A slight shudder could be felt through the base floor and everybody looked to Marie, or at least it seemed that way to Marie.

A small shuttle craft left the lunar surface and sped off towards Earth. About ten miles from the base it came to an abrupt halt. Lee stood up and looked out the front observation window. All there was to be seen was the desolate lunar landscape. So far so good, thought Lee, and set the shuttle craft on an automatic orbit of the moon. As he continued to watch from the window, he couldn't help thinking how beautiful space and the many planets were.

After three orbits Lee reported back favourably. Now he checked the shuttle's proximity indicators and ran a fifty-mile sweep of the area while continuing to orbit the moon. Good, he thought to himself, still nothing showing, to all intents and purposes Blue Star Base and the fleet are invisible.

Much to Marie's relief, Lee reported back that the cloaking had been a complete success. Marie thanked Lee and wished him a successful trip to Sub Sea One. Lee sat back, resumed control of the shuttle and sped towards Earth.

Lee had docked at Sub Sea One and was on the way to the control room. He had never seen so many Androids at one time, certainly not in the last two and a half years he had known about them. The control room was a hive of activity, all run by Androids, and run quite well, he thought.

A meeting had been arranged between Lee and the

principal Android, who was called Thourus. This still unsettled Lee a bit, but he was getting more used to it. Lee went over to the meeting area in the control room, and sat down. Within a couple of minutes Thourus arrived and sat down opposite him. This was the closest Lee had been to an Android and he was fascinated by the look of them. Standing around five feet tall, humanoid in appearance, but expressionless, they were remarkably life-like.

Thourus thanked Lee for coming. His voice was soft and expressionless, strangely almost hypnotic in its monotone.

'Eh, thank you,' Lee stammered.

'It's alright, you know,' said Thourus.

What's alright, thought Lee?

'I know it takes a little bit of getting used to,' Thourus continued. 'Talking to Androids, I mean.'

Lee nodded, thinking to himself: this is my fault. I was picked to do this meeting I shouldn't have been so unsociable to Androids. This is Konoco's idea of payback.

Taking stock, he determined to pull himself together. The meeting was going extremely well and Thourus was brought up to speed with the entire game plan. After four hours of discussion Lee was starting to flag a bit. It was Thourus who suggested they take a break. Lee agreed and thought: Thourus is a pretty considerate guy or however you want to describe him. Thourus immediately became involved in another task, while Lee went to find some refreshment.

Feeling a bit better and a lot more comfortable with Androids, Lee resumed the meeting. He explained to Thourus that, when the Dropas and ESG high councils had planned a strategy, it was decided that the most obvious place the Annunaki would attack first would be North America – this being the biggest threat to them on Earth –

probably the eastern seaboard. From there they could set up a land base and mop up the rest of America, then the world. After a long debate, it was decided the trap would be sprung there. Thourus agreed this would be the most logical course to take and enquired what he and his Androids could do to help. The meeting carried on for another two hours before everything could be concluded. Lee thanked Thourus, and left Sub Sea One feeling a great sense of achievement.

As he guided the shuttle through the depths of San Francisco Bay, Lee had an idea. Why not give Terry a quick visit? After all, he hadn't seen Earth Central since the shroud mag had been turned on.

Lee turned the craft vertical and shot out of the water like a bullet out a gun – no gravity, no G force, inertia a thing of the past. Excellent! His face lit up like a kid in a sweet factory. He loved doing this, but would never admit it.

He levelled off and headed for Earth Central. If he had wanted he could have made it in seconds, but Lee was enjoying himself, a rare feeling nowadays. The shuttle skipped along effortlessly and Lee took in the views; even though the planet surface had been trashed to fool the enemy, it was still beautiful.

It took Lee two hours of leisurely sight-seeing to reach Earth Central.

# 11

Lee's craft landed just outside the main entrance, a desolate-looking suburban house in a street of similar-looking desolate houses. Lee entered the house and lifted the telephone. He spoke an access code into the receiver. The whole floor of the living room descended a level.

Lee entered a corridor and, as he pressed a pad to his left, the living-room floor promptly ascended to its rightful place. Lee carried along the corridor for fifty feet and entered a huge turbo lift guarded by two ESG troopers. The turbo lift went into freefall, at least it felt like it to Lee. Secretly he liked the feeling, it reminded him of the feeling of flying in an F-15 Eagle. That was when gravity counted.

There were only four floors: the living room, the ground floor; the top of the turbo lift, floor one; base command where Lee was going, floor two; munitions and weapons technology, floor three; three miles down, the non-combatants' shelter, floor four. Apart from the living room to the turbo shaft each floor was a mile down.

In all there were five turbo shafts feeding this massive complex.

Arriving at floor two, Lee left the turbo lift and stepped onto a magnetic conveyor system used to traverse the huge complex of corridors. All you had to do was enter your choice of destination, the conveyor system would do the rest. Not bad, he thought. A six-foot-wide by fifteen-foot-long slab of alloy, hovering two inches above the shining metallic floor of the corridor. You had a central hand rail and the control panel with choices of destination. Pick one and away you go.

The journey took Lee about seven minutes. When he entered the control room, Terry looked taken aback.

'I hadn't expected to see you here today, Lee,' he said. 'I thought you had a meeting with some Android?'

Terry smiled, and Lee thought defiantly: Konoco's idea of a joke at my expense.

'Been there, seen it and got the tee shirt.' he said jokingly.

Terry enquired a little more seriously:

'How did it go?'

'Really well, learnt a lot, and brought Thourus right up to speed with the plans.' Lee spoke with a slight sense of self-satisfaction.

'You hungry, Lee? I'm just going to get something to eat,' Terry asked.

'Excellent!' exclaimed Lee.

He was starving. It had been a long day.

Lee was up early next day. He had checked in with Jumouk, and stayed the night at Earth Central.

After a hearty breakfast, Terry had taken him back to the surface. They were both surveying the area around Earth Central's entrance. Terry crossed the road to the houses there, then, carrying on to the back garden of one, suddenly disappeared in a field at the bottom of the garden, Lee followed in his footsteps and likewise disappeared. They had just slipped through the magnetic shroud covering the fifty assault craft sent to Earth Central yesterday. It was an extremely impressive sight, and Lee was impressed by the way the mag shroud was working.

He wandered around the parked craft. They were stacked as if in a multi-story car park, but without the concrete. Sitting there defiantly suspended by their own power, truly a sight to be seen, thought Lee.

The new Dropas assault ships had all been built incorporating the same type of energy-absorbing materials as the defence pods. It was hoped that this would give them a significant advantage over the Annunaki craft.

Terry winked at Lee.

'Fancy a test drive?'

Lee was up for it and they hopped into a two-man assault craft. Terry gestured to Lee, and Lee powered up the Dropas craft. Silently it slipped out of the parked formation and slid through the mag shield.

Lee glanced across to Terry for assurance that everything was OK. Terry nodded.

The assault vessel tore upwards vertically at stupendous speed, levelled off at 30,000 feet and proceeded to circumvent the globe.

Lee and Terry were like kids on their first bikes, both smiling ear to ear, doing moves a jet fighter pilot couldn't even imagine, swapping the controls between them and trying to outdo each other. Still, all good things had to come to an end and they headed back to drop Lee at his shuttle.

With a smile and the word 'superb' somewhere in the conversation, Lee thanked Terry and returned to his shuttle. Meanwhile Terry returned the assault craft to its makeshift parking place within the safety of the mag shield.

JOHN P. GLEDHILL

* * *

Back on board the shuttle Lee was just leaving Earth's atmosphere, feeling quite relaxed. Yesterday had been a really good day and had lifted his spirits. He thought to himself: I hope today's as good. It was probably more to do with the flying than anything else. Lee just loved to fly, and his time with Terry this morning had been a tonic.

The proximity detector on board the shuttle craft could be set on a scale of five feet, to one million miles, roughly four times the distance to the moon, not as much as it sounds in the terms of deep space. Mars our closest planet, after Venus, is roughly thirty-six million miles away depending on time of orbit.

Lee was just having a leisurely cruise back to Blue Star Base, about half an hour on auto pilot.

Jumouk was looking serious as he studied a large display on board the bridge of the *Katchinas*. It was the long-range proximity detector. This was similar to the ones on the shuttles, but much more powerful and with a far greater range.

He had been watching Lee's progress back from Earth, when a small speck on the edge of our solar system caught his attention. At first it looked like a meteor, but when Jumouk enhanced the speck on the display, it showed a faint electronic signature. Jumouk switched the proximity detector to look only for electronic signatures and carried out a maximum scan.

Our part of space around Earth and the moon showed a lot of traffic, but the only other very faint signature was the speck Jumouk had been watching. Jumouk thought for a moment: at least it didn't appear to be the onslaught of the Annunaki fleet.

Lee almost fell off his seat when the message came through. He had been nearly asleep while the auto pilot ferried him back to the moon. Jumouk explained the situation to Lee, and asked if he could investigate, Lee had already dropped out of auto pilot and turned to an intercept course by the time Jumouk had finished speaking.

It hadn't taken Lee long to go from being a back-seat diplomat to a full-blown adventurer.

With a big smile on his face Lee sat back and engaged the shuttle's hyper-drive from a touch pad on his control seat, taking him more or less instantaneously to the outer reaches of our solar system.

# 12

Back on December 2, Tukie was in a bit of a fix. He had to think fast. He was heading for open space. From a standing start the hyper-drive would take twenty seconds to power up, and in that time the Annunaki would have incinerated him. Just at that moment a large piece of debris in the form of a huge boulder spun past his front viewing window.

Tukie reacted instinctively. In a split second a tractor beam shot from the front of the shuttle, latched onto the huge boulder, then pulled the craft to within five feet of the surface.

The discharge from the shuttle was mainly masked by the boulder, Tukie immediately fired up the engines and hyper-drive. The next few seconds were the longest in Tukie's life. Finally the hyper-drive came alive and the shuttle, boulder and all, disappeared in a burst of light.

Onboard the *Nephilimis*, the targeting computers locked onto a small surge of energy just on the outskirts of the debris field.

Tannacha, the Annunaki supreme commander, studied the view screen. A small electronic signature was emanating from a boulder tumbling out of the debris field. It was possible this could be some form of background radiation and Tannacha scrutinised the view screen, then he paced up the deck of the bridge to the viewing window at the front of his magnificent flagship.

Tannacha was not one to leave things to chance and barked the command:

'Fire!'

A shot flashed from one of the smaller banks of weapons on the flagship and cracked into the boulder, just as it disappeared into a ball of light and flame.

On the bridge of the shuttle craft Tukie picked himself up. The boulder had taken most of blast from the flagship and reduced in size by about a third, the remaining part still in the hold of the tractor beam. Tukie checked for damage. There was plenty of it. Up till now Tukie had got off extremely lightly.

The primary concern was the hyper-drive. Sure enough the seals on the hyper-drive containment field had been pushed beyond their limits. The hyper-drive was working, but for how long? Tukie just didn't know.

As the days and hours passed, Tukie had time to reflect. Four years ago there was virtually no direct contact with the humans; everything had been covert, and life had been simpler. Having said that, things had got a lot more exciting in the last four years; after all, look at him now!

Tukie thought back and remembered the sense of pride he had felt when Konoco had personally picked him for this mission. Sure, they had been friends for a long time, but Tukie was sure he had been picked for his piloting abilities, at least he would have liked to think so.

Konoco had stressed how dangerous the mission would be, but also reflected on the huge advantage of a positive outcome. How knowing your enemy's movements and strength would be a great advantage.

Tukie had agreed straightaway to the mission. He had felt that anything he could do to lessen the Annunaki advantage in the coming attack was well worth giving his life for.

That thought was rudely interrupted as his craft shuddered and came out of hyper-drive. Driven now only by momentum and on minimal power, Tukie's future was looking a lot less promising.

# 13

The date was now December 11 and Tukie was trying everything he could think of to get some kind of power back to his instruments. No engines, no guidance, no communication and life support more or less non-existent. If that wasn't bad enough, he didn't even know his position in space.

Tukie had stripped the hyper-drive assembly to the core, the gaseous gold had reverted back to its normal state and lay at the bottom of the drive unit like sand on a golden beach. The matter rods had overheated and been sealed off by the core safety systems, leaving a gelatinous blob of inert matter, Tukie shook his head. There was absolutely nothing salvageable from this mess.

The view from Tukie's front window was mesmerising and very relaxing. Tukie was taking full advantage of this as he relaxed back into his comfortable pilot's chair, watching the stars slowly rotate past the horizon on his soul mate, the boulder.

Nine days had now passed after his inventive escape from the Annunaki. Had it all been for nothing?

Two of those days had been in hyper-drive, and the rest of the time just drifting with a huge boulder in tow. Round and round they tumbled together, like some kind of crazy waltz, making their way through space. The idea had even occurred to Tukie that his boulder could serve as his headstone.

I wonder what inscription should be put on it, he thought?

Several other ideas had already occurred to Tukie, but the one he liked best said it all.

*Here lies Tukie the Dropas who gave his life in friendship with mankind to benefit Dropas and mankind alike. He reached for the stars and the stars took him. Rest in peace.*

All of a sudden a flash to the left-hand side of the craft made Tukie spin round. His first thought was that an Annunaki assault craft had followed him. He knew what he would have to do, he must not be taken alive. He had far too much information for that.

# 14

As Lee came out of hyper-drive, he could see a large boulder on his right-hand side. It almost looked like it had a squashed shuttle craft on its surface, an odd sight at the best of times, he thought.

Lee banked sharply and pulled alongside the shuttle's observation window. To his delight he saw a very relieved, if not embarrassed, Tukie waving at him. Fortunately as Lee's shuttle craft banked, Tukie instantly recognised it as Dropas and had gone to the observation window to watch.

Lee turned his shuttle round and applied his tractor beam to Tukie's shuttle. Slowly he tugged the battered shuttle away from the boulder and repositioned it in a parallel course next to him. He wasn't sure if Tukie's shuttle would stand a few seconds in hyper-drive, and because Tukie had no communicators that worked, he used sign language to communicate his concerns.

Tukie responded that they at least had to try. Before Lee took the chance, he contacted Jumouk to ask his advice and to pass on the good news. Everyone was delighted, especially Konoco. Jumouk agreed with Lee that the chance was worth taking, and wished them both luck.

Lee sat back in his seat and waved over to Tukie, they both smiled and Lee engaged the hyper-drive. Seconds later both craft dropped out of hyper-drive and Lee gave a concerned look in Tukie's direction. Tukie was fine, and waved back at Lee. Lee towed Tukie's craft down to the Blue Star Base on the lunar surface and both of them went off to get debriefed.

Jumouk carried out the debriefing himself and it soon became clear how big a task they were going to face.
 'Ten battle cruisers, you say?' he said, looking concerned. 'Are you quite sure, Tukie?'
 'Definitely,' replied Tukie. 'Remember three of them ran me down, and they have got a lot more besides.'
 Jumouk started to pace the floor of the room.
 'I didn't expect that many, that's two and a half to one. Any ideas, Lee?'
 Lee looked at Jumouk. He knew the awesome power of a battle cruiser, and thought to himself, for the Annunaki to have six more than us is a huge advantage for them, and a major disadvantage for us, no matter how well we have prepared.
 The room fell into a deathly hush. Then Lee stood up suddenly and started to pace up and down the room. Thinking out loud he said:
 'We can't attack them when they come out of hyper-drive. That would spoil all the preparations on Earth. But what if they left hyper-drive, and thought they were encountering some natural disaster?'
 Jumouk looked encouraged, and asked Lee to carry on.
 'Perhaps a meteor shower? Or something similar?'
 'Good,' said Jumouk. 'Let's get some ideas on the table.'
 The idea was simple.
 Place objects of sufficient density and mass in the flight path of the Annunaki fleet, so when they drop out of hyper-

drive, as much damage as possible is done to the fleet. The objects would be natural in origin, and with luck the Annunaki would put this down to meteor strike and extreme misfortune. The proximity detectors on the Annunaki fleet would be useless, as the craft travels faster in hyper-drive than the detectors signal. It would be a bit like putting your hand out a car window at 70mph and feeling it getting blown backwards. Mapping technology had to be used in hyper-drive, not unlike a high-tech shipping lane.

Jupiter's moon Callisto was selected by the Dropas scientists, and the Dropas miners set to work.

Time was now very short, but the miners were very determined. Large pieces of Callisto were mined and transported into the Annunaki orbital approach, then finally Callisto was blown up strategically, and the larger debris was towed and placed at calculated points where the Annunaki would drop out of hyper-drive.

Five days had now passed, it was now December 16. Konoco and Lee were checking the mapping of the approach to Earth.

'It looks good, very good,' Lee commented. 'That should do a bit of damage when they drop out of hyper-drive. With a bit of luck we might get one or two of their cruisers.'

Konoco nodded in agreement and said:

'Lee, that was a brilliant plan you had, let's just hope it works as well as we hope.'

Lee smiled.

'I think under the circumstances we've all done brilliantly.'

Everything was now in place awaiting the imminent arrival of the Annunaki fleet, and Earth was in the hands of its destiny.

# 15

December 20, 2020, 23.15 GMT. Jumouk, Konoco and Lee were in a shuttle craft standing off Earth, in orbit at around 600 miles. They were watching the Annunaki globes orbiting the Earth. Just forty-five short minutes to go and it was game on.

Terry was back on Earth. Everything had been done to ensure minimal damage from the EMP charge. He couldn't help thinking to himself, 'Bring it on.'

There had been so much anticipation of this moment it had been a physical drain on everybody.

Midnight arrived, and sure enough the twelve globes detonated in unison and delivered their devastating pulse. The bright flashes could be seen in the night sky, a few seconds of intense light, dazzling to watch and quite spectacular in their own way.

Ten minutes later the viral orbs released their payload to allow the dust of death to slowly filter into our atmosphere.

Unfortunately for the Annunaki plan, Dropas engineers had surrounded each of the viral orbs in a protective skin, stopping the deadly payload from being dispersed into our atmosphere.

The deadly dust now trapped within their new containment package could be safely collected by a few assault craft, and the twelve packages taken deep into space and destroyed safely by members of the newly formed Tactical Android Group.

This had been the plan from day one, but had been a closely guarded secret. The introduction of the flu virus back in 2009 had just been a back-up in case one of the orbs or protective skins should leak.

Lee engaged the drive on the shuttle and flew it into the upper part of Earth's atmosphere. As he did so they could see one of the protective skins being picked up in a tractor beam from an assault craft, ready to be taken out into deep space.

As far as the Annunaki were concerned everything would be going to plan. Lee circumvented Earth at high speed, scanning for traces of virus as he went.

After six sweeps of Earth's atmosphere, Earth was given a clean bill of health. They all breathed a quiet sigh of relief and returned to Blue Star Base.

Back on the moon base, Marie was waiting for Lee, and as he came into the control room she smiled, a radiant smile with warmth and genuine affection. This had, after all, been one of the trickiest parts of the plan so far. One wrong move and the whole plan could have been exposed, or God forbid, everyone exposed to a lethal virus.

Lee smiled back and said:

'Job well done, Marie. Have you heard anything from Thourus yet regarding the disposal of the virus?'

Marie nodded.

'Yep, just finished talking to him. All the virus has been destroyed by his Androids. You could say the mission was a total success.'

Lee sat down at one of the consoles and let out another

sigh of relief. He looked tired. It had been another long night, but again Marie came to the rescue with a steaming hot cup of green tea. Lee looked bemused as he took the tea from Marie.

'I don't deserve you, do I, Marie?' he said with a weary smile.

Marie just smiled, this time a smile of satisfaction.

Next morning Terry was up bright and early, another two runs had been completed to check for any viral contamination and a complete systems check had been run to check for damage from the EMP discharge. All the checks had come up green, and Earth was good to go.

# 16

Standing on the bridge of his flagship *Nephilimis*, Tannacha looked mighty pleased with himself. Yes, he had suffered losses, but not due to direct action. The date was now December 28 and everything had more or less gone to plan so far, except of course the unfortunate meteor incident. Still, that was all behind them now.

The plan was to take the eastern seaboard of the United States of America first, establish a main base there and then pick off the continents of Earth one by one. Tannacha barked out the command for the routing to begin and a squadron of fifty assault craft sped out of the landing bay on board the *Nephilimis*. This was of course Tannacha's personal guard, the elite of the fleet.

The squadron streaked up the eastern coast of America heading directly for New York. Anything in their path that moved, was annihilated. The lead assault vessel piloted by a particularly vicious Annunaki called Verton, was just arriving over Charlotte, North Carolina, when he began to break left slightly with a group of five other craft, to head directly for Washington DC and the White House. The rest of the squadron would carry on to New York.

Verton had slowed the speed of his six craft down to a minimum and looked downward to his left. They had just entered Virginia, and he could make out the Mill Mountain

Star just ahead of him. With a wry smile on his face he disengaged the auto-targeting system on his console and, selecting the landmark manually, loosed a volley of weapon fire on it.

The Star imploded violently, then erupted into atoms. Verton rolled his craft in a sick victory roll then sped on northward towards his chosen target, the White House. Back on board *Nephilimis*, Tannacha gave the command for a troop transport to be dispatched to New York, and a second troop transport to go to Washington DC. Both transports were to have an escort of six assault craft, which would allow ground bases to be set up and a foothold be gained.

Verton was just passing over Bailey's Crossroads, Fairfax County, Virginia, normal population around thirty thousand, just another wholesome American town. Flying in diamond formation, the six Annunaki craft were preparing their targeting systems for an all-out blitz on the White House, and central Washington. Suddenly and without any warning at all, the craft to Verton's left erupted in a flash of white hot alloy and disintegrated in front of his eyes. Unwittingly, Verton had just flown his wing of six Annunaki assault craft directly over Earth Central.

Deep beneath the suburban streets of Bailey's Crossroads, Terry had been watching Verton's approach and had timed his strike precisely, ordering the two pods to fire at the most opportune second, and with devastating effect. The defence of Earth had begun.

Verton spun his craft into a vertical dive, flipping it over at the same time to allow him to see where he had just come from. The formation had fractured and two more of the Annunaki assault craft were in real trouble from the pods. Verton watched in disbelief as the two craft disintegrated before him. He still couldn't see clearly where the ground fire was coming from. He barked commands to the two remaining craft to follow him. Abruptly and at high speed he shot upwards.

Terry ordered five of the camouflaged ESG assault ships to take up the pursuit, Appearing from nowhere, the ESG vessels sped after the Annunaki craft. Their advanced targeting systems scouring the skies for a lock on the Annunaki targets. A volley of pulse weapons spat out from the first two ESG ships and found their target, a trailing Annunaki craft. The craft spun from the violent explosions on its hull and tore into three pieces, in an inferno of white-hot fire.

The two remaining Annunaki vessels powered their engines to full, and rocketed off to join the safety of the squadron heading to New York. As Verton approached the squadron heading for New York he could tell all was not well. They were just over East Freehold, Monmouth County, New Jersey, and had run into another two of the Dropas pods.

Fifteen of the Annunaki craft had already succumbed to the devastating fire power of the pods, and the other twenty-nine craft were in a desperate struggle for survival. The element of surprise had been well worth all the secrecy and given the Dropas and mankind a huge psychological advantage.

Verton immediately gave the command for all the Annunaki craft to withdraw. He was still physically stunned from what had just happened.

The Annunaki ships sped eastward and down into the depths of the Atlantic ocean, two hundred miles offshore, and on the sea bed Verton took stock.

BATTLE FOR THE EARTH

* * *

On the west coast of America, the calm, shallow waters of San Francisco Bay, just east of Point Blunt Rock, erupted as eighteen Dropas assault ships, piloted by the Tactical Android Group, or TAG, blasted from the waters in a perfect wing-shaped formation.

The leader of this group was Balac, Thourus's right-hand man, so to speak. Thourus had ordered Balac to take the group, three assault wings, eighteen assault vessels in all, and intercept the Annunaki troop transports before they could reach their destinations. Balac spotted the first of the troop transports and its escort. Without hesitation and ignoring the escort vessels, he and the rest of his group tore straight in, releasing a cataclysm of pulse weapons fire at the troop transport.

The troop transports were fairly large, and could carry up to five thousand troops at a time. The two that had been sent to Earth were both full, so that ground bases could be established.

Now the lead transport was taking direct fire from eighteen TAG assault ships. Inside the Annunaki troop transport confusion reigned. No one knew what was happening or who was attacking them.

On the bridge the commander was desperately trying evasive manoeuvres, but nothing seemed to shake his attackers off, there was just too many of them.

Balac watched the explosions rip through the troop transport, as it tried desperately to crash-land, so as to evacuate surviving troops to safety, but one of the Annunaki escort vessels had just taken a direct hit from a TAG craft and was spinning violently towards the bridge of the transport.

The impact was tremendous. The explosion ripped right down the length of the troop transport and ruptured the on-board armoury. The troop transport's nose rose up and its back broke in four places, then it exploded into a thousand flying fragments.

The TAG had already broken off their attack and were now in the process of mopping up the escort craft.

One by one the Annunaki assault vessels fell, some spectacularly and some in a flash and a puff of smoke, but all six fell with no Dropas casualties. Balac was as close to exhilaration as an Android could get. What a result! The wing re-formed, and proceeded to speed off to intercept the surviving troop transport.

# 17

Tannacha stood on the bridge of his flagship. Proximity alarms were sounding everywhere, Annunaki officers were running backwards and forward trying to verify reports, and confusion had replaced the calm of a short hour ago, Tannacha spun round and shouted in his low growling tone, 'Stop!'

Everyone on the bridge came to an abrupt halt.

'Will someone please tell me where these attack vessels have come from and who the hell is behind it?'

'Dropas, sir, we think, but we've got no idea where they're coming from.'

'Find out, then get me our losses so far in this abomination. No excuses, recall everything till I find out what's going on.'

At that moment as Tannacha turned round, the *Nephilimis* banked hard to its right. Several juddering movements followed, the sound of weapons fire spoiled the quiet on the bridge, and smoke started to taint the air.

The *Nephilimis* had been hit by a barrage of pulse weapons and was listing badly to the right. A small number of fires had broken out along its sprawling corridors. Jumouk had ordered an ESG battle cruiser and twenty assault ships from the safety of the shroud on the far side of the moon to attack the *Nephilimis* and destroy it, in the hope that if the

Annunaki flagship was destroyed the Annunaki will to fight on would crumble.

The ESG ships had moved so fast that in the confusion they were on top of the *Nephilimis* before they were even noticed. They had managed to do a considerable amount of damage to the flagship before it turned tail and ran to join two of the other battle cruisers which were orbiting on the far side of Earth.

The ESG ships returned quickly and silently to their lair under the cover of the mag shield on the far side of the moon.

Meanwhile Tannacha had flown into a violent rage and broken the neck of one of his officers for so-called stupidity. This was the officer who was in charge of fleet security and should have noticed the oncoming ESG attack.

Tannacha's rage only grew worse as reports of the losses on Earth started to flood in. Still under the delusion that the ESG attack on his flagship must have come from Earth, he ordered two waves of assault craft to Earth on a search and destroy mission, a total of a hundred craft.

Balac had now got the other troop transport in his sights. It had changed course with its escort and started heading back to the Annunaki fleet which was orbiting the Earth.

The strategy was the same from the TAG craft, apart from now targeting the weakness on the bridge of the troop transport. As all eighteen vessels let loose a horrendous volley of pulse weapons at the bridge area of the troop transport, the whole front section of the troop transport crumbled under a ball of fire to become a flaming inferno. The troop transport fell back on itself and plummeted to

Earth, breaking up into a million pieces as it hit the Georgia landscape.

Two of Balac's TAG pilots were in trouble. Three Annunaki assault ships were chasing them down, while the other three escort craft had retired from the fray and were heading back to the relative safety of their orbiting fleet.

Balac immediately set off in pursuit of the Annunaki vessels which were threatening his attack craft. As he closed in on the first Annunaki craft, the TAG craft it was pursuing appeared to tumble in the air and burst into flames. Balac continued to bear down on the Annunaki craft and opened fire. The Annunaki pilot never knew what had hit him. What had been a short-lived celebration of a kill now became his funeral pyre. The blazing Annunaki craft smashed into the ground without being able to try so much as an evasive manoeuvre.

Balac now turned his attention to the two remaining Annunaki vessels. They were chasing down a TAG pilot who was bravely outmanoeuvring them at every turn, even though he was clearly under severe pressure. Balac slipped in behind the trailing Annunaki craft and opened up with his pulse weapons, landing a glancing blow just to the left-hand side of the pilot. The Annunaki pilot watched in horror as his console went dead in front of his eyes. He tried desperately to steer the craft with his limp, lifeless controls, but nothing was working.

Seizing his opportunity, Balac fired a volley directly at the disabled craft. The outcome was inevitable. The Annunaki vessel disintegrated before his eyes. Balac turned to the right just as the other Annunaki ship was breaking off its pursuit of the TAG craft. It bolted directly upwards at tremendous velocity, its destination the safety of the orbiting Annunaki fleet.

Balac signalled for the wing, now seventeen ships, to return to Sub Sea One. At full speed they took off, flying as low as possible to reduce the risk of detection, over Idaho, then Oregon, passing just above Salem and onto Rabbit Rock and into the blue Pacific waters where they were now invisible.

# 18

Verton had received new orders from Tannacha. He was to join up with the group of a hundred assault vessels, take command and resume the search-and-destroy mission.

Verton and what was left of his wing burst through the choppy Atlantic waves and set off to join up with the main Annunaki group. With Verton and his wing slipping into formation with the group, this was now a sizeable task force, one hundred and thirty-one Assault craft in all, and a major responsibility for Verton. After all, he knew well enough what Tannacha did to failures.

The formation was spectacular. Verton's ship was right at the front, followed closely by four section leaders' vessels, two either side and trailing him, thus creating a V-shape. Following them were seven sections of eighteen ships each, in V formations, creating the wider effect of a giant diamond. They travelled comparatively slowly, looking out for any Dropas or human activity.

Verton couldn't understand it. There was nothing, it was as quiet as the proverbial grave, yet ten minutes ago the skies were full of activity. Below him he could see Andrews Air Force Base. It was totally desolate, abandoned by its inhabitants. Nothing below him or even around him was stirring.

He was not to know, however, that he was being closely watched.

Glued to the console and monitoring Verton's every move, Terry had decided to play the long game. After all they still had the advantage that the Annunaki didn't have a clue where they were or how many they numbered.

Verton was allowed to fly over Washington unchallenged.

Tannacha thought long and hard, Verton and his squadron had not come across any signs of life for the last half an hour, even though they had flown over Washington and New York and the surrounding terrain. It was time to recall Verton and the squadron back to the main fleet. That way they could piece together what little intelligence they had, and at least plan a way forward.

Terry watched closely as the squadron left Earth's atmosphere and joined the main Annunaki fleet, which had now regrouped about six hundred miles above Australia.

Tannacha sat down in the main conference room on board the *Nephilimis*. His chair stood at the head of a large, metallic, rectangular table, almost surgical in appearance. All of his commanders were present and each of them had their own feelings of dread, a shared, total terror of their supreme commander.

Tannacha looked calm enough as he reviewed the screens in front of him, even though they made extremely difficult reading. Nineteen assault vessels, two troop transports and their cargo of ten thousand ground troops lost, and not a sign of the enemy.

Tannacha finished reading and stood up slowly. He began to move round the table, in the direction of an extremely nervous-looking Verton. He stopped behind Verton, bent over his left shoulder and thundered:

'How can you disrespect me like this, Verton? I don't understand you. I gave you one simple task, and you screwed it up completely.'

Turning to the rest of the commanders he shouted:

'Where are they? How are they doing this?'

Tannacha returned to his seat. He was well aware two major mistakes had now been made, both mainly down to complacency. He looked at each of his commanders in turn. All of them were quiet and unresponsive, desperately fearful of provoking a savage attack from Tannacha, aware also that so far he had acted out of character by not simply slaughtering someone in response to the initial defeat.

Tannacha stood up again and, shaking his head, glared at Verton.

'I'm going to give you one last chance, Verton. Take seven assault ships and a troop transport with one thousand troops, and find out where that ground fire came from. Eliminate it and set up a safe ground base. Fail me and you will wish you were dead already!'

Verton stood up and bowed.

'I will not fail you, supreme commander.'

The eight ships left the mother ship and descended vertically towards Australia. Verton had learnt his lesson: don't take this now hostile planet for granted. He was going to be as covert as possible on this mission.

Just west of Rat Island on Australia's western coast, Verton's wing slipped into the still waters of the Indian Ocean. Heading west towards the Cape of South Africa, deep in the depths, Verton felt more secure, his destination the Atlantic. After all it had served him well once before.

## JOHN P. GLEDHILL

\* \* \*

They were west of Cape Town, just coming over the Walvis Ridge, and south of Saint Helena. Now deep in the south Atlantic ocean.

Suddenly Verton's proximity detector lit up. It was not an electronic signature but a contact nevertheless. He signalled the wing to full stop and defensive stance, while he slipped off to investigate.

In his V-shaped assault vessel Verton could have been mistaken for a huge sting ray gliding effortless over the seabed, quite a fantastic sight, and in its own way soothing. Verton was enjoying his time below the waves.

As his ship descended into one of the many troughs, Verton could see a rough shape looming in the distance; he slowed his craft nearly to a standstill and slowly circled the object. The object was a long, round metal tube, full of holes and totally devoid of life, apart from the many fish and other sea creatures that called it home. Verton wondered what it was, or what its purpose had been. He quickly decided that it posed no threat, and with that ordered the wing to rejoin him.

What Verton had just seen was the U-860, a German U-boat which had been sunk in 1944, during the Second World War. It was also one of the many Dropas warning stations, used for tracking undersea activity.

There were hundreds of these sophisticated tracking stations in the seas of our planet, generally in wrecks like the U-860. These tracking stations were all controlled from Sub Sea One and directly under Thourus's command.

Verton and his vessels were now approaching the coast of North America. He updated his section leaders with his plans.

The conditions above the North Atlantic were stormy and inclement. Verton hoped to be able to use this to his advantage. It should allow him to land his ground troops successfully, then he could get his mission to find the resistance and eliminate them underway.

Verton and his craft made land at Loch Arbour, flying low and very slow as they headed west towards Freehold, New Jersey, which was the town that had been picked to decamp the ground troops. Verton was well aware that it had been around here the most resistance had originated. With a bit of luck they would be able to flush them out and teach them a fatal lesson.

The ships were taking no chances this time, hugging the rooftops of the buildings below them and constantly sweeping for electronic signatures around them. Verton slowed his craft to a full stop. There was a perfect spot for the troop transport to land, a large green open space surrounded by trees. He ordered the troop transport to land and disembark the ground troops.

The huge troop transport spun round to line up with the selected landing area and started to descend slowly but surely into the clearing below it. The landing was a textbook exercise, and the doors of the troop transport gently unfolded to let the troops disembark. The decamp was a well-practised exercise and within ten minutes the landing area had been secured.

Verton landed his own craft next to the troop ship and disembarked. The sight of so many Annunaki troopers was impressive, Verton sought out the squad leader to give him his final instructions.

JOHN P. GLEDHILL

\* \* \*

The squad leader was a seasoned Annunaki warrior, well rehearsed in the theory of war, considering that it had been an age since actual combat had taken place with the Dropas – or anyone else for that matter.

The brief was simple: a street-by-street ground search, find the enemy and engage; the assault vessels would supply air support and the enemy would be vanquished; an appropriate area would be selected and secured as a ground base; then more troops could be brought in to secure the rest of North America.

Verton was well pleased with the way things were finally going. Gone were the negative thoughts of defeat, and the confidence, arrogance and complacency had returned. This feeling that he was now experiencing was probably the Achilles' heel of the Annunaki. All of them had it, from the supreme commander to the lowest trooper, an inherent flaw, if you like, also an extremely dangerous one.

Verton contacted Tannacha, to let him know what progress had been made, Tannacha was pleased but reminded Verton of his earlier threat. He acknowledged his commander and thanked him.

Unknown to Verton, Tannacha had repositioned his flagships orbit back over North America and was watching his every move closely.

The ground troops were now filtering out of the secured landing site and spilling onto the streets of Freehold, as they headed slowly in a northerly direction towards East Freehold. As the ground troops fanned out, they took on a diamond formation, one on point, one on either flank, and one bringing up the rear. Slowly and methodically they worked their way through the streets between Freehold and East Freehold, along Dutch Lane Road and the surrounding area.

Verton was hovering in his assault craft along with the rest of his formation, eagerly anticipating the commencement of hostilities. The seven craft were criss-crossing the area just in front of the ground troops, looking for any sign of activity. Nothing was stirring and Verton was starting to get nervous. Is there anybody out there, he thought to himself?

Suddenly and from apparently nowhere, a single ESG assault craft flashed past Verton's front view window heading towards Washington DC. Verton barked a command to the rest of his wing and they engaged in a high-speed pursuit with Verton taking point. He was committed to getting a kill, and pursued with a vengeance, pulse weapons spitting out death and destruction in front of him.

The ESG craft was elusive and carried out some hair-raisingly low manoeuvres, still just keeping out of the line of fire from Verton and the rest of his wing. Nonetheless, it surely could only be a matter of time before Verton's superior numbers and fire power would overcome him.

Unknown to Verton, however, now over the heart of Washington DC the ESG troopers on the ground had let loose a volley of their Ariel mines. The skies over Washington were thick with them, and only the Dropas pilot knew about them.

All the ESG ships had been fitted with a clever positive field emitter, so when coming into proximity with a small but deadly positively charged mine, the two positive charges would repel, and the mine would be swept harmlessly out of the craft's way. This also had the added advantage that no two mines could crash together and explode, not to mention the constant fluid effect of the mines repelling each other and constantly moving like ripples on a pond.

Verton's wing didn't stand a chance as they ploughed into the minefield blind, vessel after vessel crashing into the deadly hockey-puck-sized mines. Tannacha would not have to punish Verton for his latest blunder. All seven Annunaki pilots and ships were lost. Verton's arrogance had cost the Annunaki war machine dearly, yet again.

As soon as the Annunaki assault ships started to take off in pursuit of the ESG craft, the sniping began. Most of the Android troopers had been posing as dead bodies. They were perfect for this, no life signs, and suppressed electronic signatures, lifeless to Annunaki scanners.

Pulse weapons-fire was everywhere, Annunaki troopers were dropping like stones. The surprise element had once again been lethal. It was a massacre. Even though the ESG Android troopers were outnumbered ten to one, they produced a hail of deadly accurate fire that cut through the formations of Annunaki like a scythe through hay. Then the two Dropas pods in East Freehold joined in. It was like taking a sledgehammer to a nut. The Annunaki ground troops didn't stand a chance.

On board the *Nephilimis*, with a snarl, Tannacha gave the order.

'Widespread pattern, fire!'

The banks of pulse weapons on board the flagship spat into life. Huge blue teardrop-shaped streaks of death started raining down on the area south of East Freehold. The slaughter of the Annunaki ground troops had now progressed to the vaporisation of everything, both Annunaki and ESG, stopping short of the troop transport still on the ground and extending up to and into East Freehold itself, destroying one of the pods completely and virtually disabling the other. Five square miles of devastation in all.

Two fully complemented troop transports were already on their way to the area laid waste by Tannacha, their escort of fifty assault vessels around them. Verton and his troops had just been bait to draw the enemy out.

Five of the Annunaki ships easily dealt with the remaining pod, levelling it to the ground, while the troop transports landed and disembarked their cargos.

The Annunaki now truly had a foothold on planet Earth.

# 19

On board the Dropas flagship Jumouk had been watching events intently. He turned to Konoco and said:
'We need to take out their cruisers, don't we?'
Konoco nodded, then reflectively shook his head and remarked:
'That's going to take a plan and a half. However, we still do have an advantage. They still don't know we have a moon base, so all their attention is directed at Earth, even more so now there's been resistance. So, it's obvious that our best hope is Blue Star Base and a direct all-out attack with our fleet.'
Jumouk started to pace along the alloy decking of his bridge.
'OK, but isn't that putting all our eggs in one basket?'
Lee had been listening and made his way over to one of the display screens.
'Look at this.'
Jumouk and Konoco joined him at the display screen. It showed a three-dimensional image of Earth, the moon and surrounding space. All six of the Annunaki battle cruisers were shown in their relative positions in orbit above our blue planet, and by now, a constant stream of troopships and support vessels could be seen coming and going between the fleet battle cruisers and all the continents on Earth.

Lee continued:

'Why don't we concentrate on the closest three battle cruisers, and use a two-pronged attack with just half our forces, that way we can keep the rest in reserve?'

Jumouk smiled and patted Lee on the back.

'Go on, Lee, you've got our attention.'

Lee resumed.

'If we come round this side of the moon again, it's going to look like we came from the moon, and there's a good chance they will cotton on and discover our Blue Star Base, but...'

He made a hand gesture on the three-dimensional moon, indicating the long way round the moon.

'If we come around the long way it looks like we just arrived in Earth space, and we keep the advantage of our Blue Star Moon Base not being discovered.'

Jumouk looked very pleased.

'And the second part of the attack?' queried Konoco.

Lee smiled

'That's the easy bit, but also the clever bit. We launch seventy-five TAG assault craft from Sub Sea One, but we don't launch until we've engaged the three cruisers. That way the Annunaki will be in so much confusion dealing with our attack from space, with a little bit of luck they wont see the TAG assault craft till it's too late.'

Jumouk and Konoco looked at each other.

'Lee, you're brilliant!'

Jumouk smiled and nodded in agreement with Konoco.

Jumouk clapped his hands together.

'Everyone agreed, then?'

All three nodded in unison.

'OK let's talk numbers then and get this organised.'

# 20

Terry had just been brought up to date by Konoco on the latest plans. Everything had been going well on earth, and the pods were standing up to ground attack on all continents. The only problem was, once they were discovered and exposed, they were extremely vulnerable to attack from the cruisers in space.

Earth Central itself had still not been discovered by the Annunaki, and Terry was instructing assault craft to harass and confuse the enemy by appearing from nowhere, attacking them and then disappearing into thin air. This strategy was working extremely well and had the Annunaki commanders in total disarray.

Sub Sea One was also using tactics similar to Terry's, but had the advantage of all the world's oceans to use as cover. They would then pop up seemingly out of nowhere again on whichever continent that suited, carry out their objectives and then disappear back under the waves.

Earth was certainly holding its own against the attacking Annunaki even though they now had a foothold on every continent on Earth.

The Annunaki had made good headway north of Freehold and had established a series of well-defended base camps, along with a base of operations. Every continent on Earth now had a substantial Annunaki presence; all the commanders had received their specific orders directly from Tannacha. The Annunaki plan was going well, at least this was the case from Tannacha's point of view.

Their assault craft were patrolling the skies of Earth regularly, and providing air cover for the now regular troop and equipment movements across the planet. The only annoying thing was the regular appearance of ESG assault vessels which was taking its toll on their air superiority. They appeared to come from nowhere and disappear into thin air, in-between times doing as much damage as they possibly could.

Every now and again a duo of Dropas pods would be discovered and a fierce fire-fight would ensue, air cover would be brought in and, if all else failed, a cruiser would be repositioned in Earth's orbit to deal a fatal blow from its deadly array of pulse weapons.

Terry knew that the proposed attack on the Annunaki cruisers would, if everything went to plan, significantly change the balance of power in the ESGs' favour. It was now just a matter of patience. After all, the element of surprise had worked extremely well for the ESG up till this point. All that he could do just now was follow the plan to harass and confuse the enemy as much as possible until the odds were evened up.

Thourus was just departing Sub Sea One with a wing of seven assault craft, leaving Balac, his right-hand Android in charge. He was heading for Europe, specifically London, where the Annunaki had a base of operations for Europe. He had a choice of keeping to an underwater route or taking a risk and flying low and fast over continental North America. He chose the latter.

The seven craft burst out of the waters of San Francisco

Bay and headed east at high velocity. Rooftops were just a blur and terrain was like a fast-flowing river beneath them In just four minutes they were flashing over the main Annunaki base of operations at Freehold, heading towards the North Atlantic. The weapons fire coming from the Annunaki base didn't stand a chance of hitting their target, and within seconds they were over the North Atlantic and diving beneath the choppy, dark, surface waves. The object of the game now was stealth and surprise. Accordingly, all the craft had now slowed down as they skimmed the bottom of the ocean.

Thourus had a fantastic view: it was a different world down here, full of life and activity, so many diverse species.

They were now in mid-Atlantic and just passing the wreck of the *Volturno*, a Dutch cargo vessel, which had exploded and sunk back in 1913 with the loss of all hands. Thourus had been watching it as they passed by, when a sudden movement caught his eye, unrecognisable at first, just a huge shape in the distance, eerie in appearance, and more than a bit disturbing.

Thourus thought he had seen everything beneath the waves, but his database was struggling to identify this looming object, he was even having difficulty ascertaining its speed or direction.

He ordered the TAG craft to a full stop, then checked his proximity detector for any electronic signatures. All it displayed were the six TAG craft around him. When he looked back up, there was nothing.

As suddenly as it had been spotted the ghostly apparition had now disappeared. Not a trace was to be found, apart from the gentle wafting of displaced water under the bellies of the TAG craft.

Being an Android, Thourus didn't have feelings as such, but still he felt something was wrong, very wrong indeed. He quizzed the other pilots in his wing, but none had seen or detected anything. The small group of TAG craft resumed their mission, slipping through the water just above the sea bed and at a comparatively slow speed.

On arrival in the English Channel no more incidents or unusual sightings had occurred. The good old English Channel, thought Thourus, predictable, but interesting in its own way, thanks exclusively to the amount of shipping wreckage on the sea floor. They had just passed the wreck of the *Toward*, sunk by a mine in 1915, and were rounding Dover and heading for the Thames.

Gently slipping up the Thames, the seven TAG craft didn't cause so much as a ripple on the surface of the river. There was a high tide and the TAG craft were now travelling in single file, the idea being to get as far up the river as possible without breaking cover.

The Annunaki had become over-confident and had set up their European Base at Heathrow Airport. While you could see the advantage of the sprawling areas of runways, it did leave them open to a surprise attack if someone could sneak up close enough to them.

This is precisely what Thourus intended to do.

Kew Bridge was the point of no return. Thourus and the TAG craft left the Thames behind and carried on at rooftop height, slowly at first so as not to attract attention to fast-moving craft, then just over Cranford they went into full attack mode. Hurtling into the air space over the airport, each of them picked targets of opportunity, shuttles, troop transports, assault craft and anything on the ground that moved.

Pulse weapons fire filled the air, both TAG and Annunaki. Already Annunaki assault craft that had been patrolling the skies of Europe were on their way.

Thourus was looking for the main command centre, and suddenly spotted it. They had had the cheek to set it up in terminal 1. Thourus didn't hesitate and strafed the Terminal with pulse fire. The building burst into flames and collapsed in on itself. Thourus thought to himself, no one could have survived that, but still continued with criss-cross fire from his pulse weapons.

So far two of the TAG vessels had been wiped out and one had asked permission to try to limp back to Sub Sea One.

The damage on the ground was immense. All kinds of ships had been destroyed where they stood – fifty or sixty at least – it was difficult to tell in the carnage. Buildings had been laid to waste, equipment and dead Annunaki troopers were everywhere. The main operations centre was totally destroyed. All in all the mission had been a total success.

Thourus gave the order to retreat back to Sub Sea One with all haste and the TAG wing complied. Escape routes were always well planned in advance of an operation. All involved subterfuge so as not to give away the position of Sub Sea One. On this occasion the wing would split up and head in opposite directions.

Thourus opened up his drive to maximum. Soon he was over Paris, heading south-east towards the Gulf of Aden with ten Annunaki assault vessels hard on his heels. Thourus had made sure they were well prepared for evasive tactics and had issued a hundred airborne mines and instructions on how and where to use them to each of the TAG craft, and pilots, before leaving Sub Sea One.

Now he was going to see his plan in action, as he approached the clear blue seas of the Gulf of Aden. Five hundred feet before he hit the water he released his mines in an umbrella shape behind him.

Still travelling at maximum speed he crashed through the surface water just south of West Sheba Ridge, banked hard left and grounded his craft powerless at the bottom of the Alula-Fartak Trench.

The Annunaki pilots had spotted the mines being released in front of them and had done their best to avoid them, scattering their craft in all directions. One of the Annunaki assault craft was powerless to do anything as he ploughed into the edge of the mines, setting most of them off in unison with each other. His craft disappeared in the inferno and never reappeared.

The rest of Annunaki ships fared rather better. Only two were badly damaged and limped off to seek repairs. The rest re-formed and sped off in the last-seen direction of the TAG craft.

Thourus sat at the bottom of the Trench for a further ten minutes, with the power off and motionless. In the deepest part of the Trench he was virtually invisible.

The Annunaki vessels were now long gone. Thourus powered up his craft and swung south, heading towards the general direction of the Falkland Islands and ready to round Cape Horn and head up the coast of South America, then on to Sub Sea One. As the TAG craft sped along the bottom of the South Atlantic Ocean, Thourus couldn't help wondering how many of his TAG vessels would return to base. He was well aware, in all probability, he would be the last to return as his escape route had been the longest.

Putting the thought behind him, he returned to watching

the spectacular underwater landscape. As all kinds of marine life were flashing past his front viewing window, he could tell what part of the world he was in just by looking at the marine life, and knew all the wrecks on his well-travelled underwater trails.

He had made a particular point of finding out the history behind these underwater attractions, indeed it was his own idea to use the better positioned wrecks as listening stations.

This had also given him the perfect excuse to explore some of them, a job he found extremely interesting.

He was rapidly approaching Sub Sea One, built deep within the Taney Seamounts, a collection of five undersea volcanoes, 4,500 thousand metres below the waves, just to the west of San Francisco Bay. Thourus slid his assault craft gently onto the landing pad and then, after disembarking, hurried to the main control room where Balac was waiting to debrief him.

The mission had been a total success, even better than had been hoped for. Jumouk had personally called to congratulate Thourus on a job well done.

All the TAG ships and crews apart from the two that had been destroyed had returned safely, albeit some of the craft had been damaged, none though beyond repair.

All in all a real bloody nose for the Annunaki!

# 21

On the bridge of his flagship Tannacha was seething at the latest news. How could the ESG have pulled off a raid like this with such shattering success? He had lost at least fifty-five vessels of all shapes and sizes, and his European base of operations was in disarray. The most worrying thing, though, was the ease that the ESG were showing in the ability to appear and disappear at will.

As Tannacha pondered that thought, suddenly all hell broke loose. Alarms were sounding all over the bridge, panicked movement was everywhere as a fleet of two ESG battle cruisers and fifty assault craft had just appeared from nowhere and were launching an attack on the three Annunaki battle cruisers stationed on the other side of planet Earth.

Lee was commanding one of the of the ESG battle cruisers. The other was under the command of a highly skilled Dropas called Wesell. He had immediately engaged two of the three Annunaki cruisers to great effect. The initial banks of pulse weapon fire had taken them both completely by surprise. This was playing on the Annunaki weak points of complacency and arrogance.

Both Annunaki cruisers suffered extensive damage to their weapons systems and their drive engines, leaving one of them a virtual sitting duck for the twenty-five ESG assault vessels escorting Wesell. The other Annunaki cruiser banked sharply and started evasive action, which involved the spontaneous release of the assault craft in its complement – what was left after more than half of them had been assigned to Earth the previous day. The remaining fifteen Annunaki assault vessels decamped from the cruiser to take on Wesell and his escorts.

Lee had not been quite as fortunate. As he had manoeuvred to target the bridge on the third Annunaki cruiser, he had been spotted and had run into a hailstorm of pulse weapons fire. The escorting ESG assault ships flanking his cruiser were being destroyed and the Annunaki cruiser had now released its full complement of fifty assault vessels, all of which were now bearing down on Lee and what was left of his twenty-five escort vessels.

Back on Earth, in San Francisco Bay, Thourus and his attack force of seventy-five assault craft burst though the still waters and rocketed vertically at maximum thrust on a direct course for the third Annunaki cruiser that was giving Lee such a hard time.

The TAG assault craft caught the Annunaki cruiser completely by surprise, unleashing a terrifying tsunami of concentrated pulse fire to the Earth-side flank of the massive ship. In this instance size didn't matter: the whole cruiser erupted in front of them with debris cascading in every direction.

Thourus now began to concentrate on the Annunaki assault vessels that were mauling Lee's cruiser and escorts. Again the element of surprise was on his side. His TAG assault wings swept in like angels of death on the stunned Annunaki assault craft left reeling from seeing the loss of their cruiser. Lee broke off from his initial course in an effort to evade the Annunaki assault ships and let the TAG pilots have their hour of glory.

The experienced TAG pilots were in their element, and with the Annunaki vessels in disarray, the pickings were easy. Most of the Annunaki craft were now making a break for it, heading in all directions only to be chased down by a TAG craft and atomised.

However, two of the Annunaki ships that had managed to make a break towards the dark side of moon were making good their escape, skimming the lunar surface and, using craters for cover, they remained undetected.

The rest of the surviving Annunaki assault ships made for the other side of Earth and the relative safety of the three battle cruisers there. In all only twenty-one of the sixty-five craft made it, along with the badly damaged cruiser.

Wesell had turned his cruiser to give chase to the Annunaki ship that had made a break for it. He could see that Lee had got himself out of the fix he was in and was busy licking his wounds.

Suddenly the proximity detector on Wesell's bridge snapped into life advising of an impending collision. It was the Annunaki cruiser he had left to be finished off by the assault escorts. Somehow it had raised enough power to lurch itself at Wesell's cruiser and was now on a collision course in a frantic attempt to even the score.

Wesell screamed commands to his bridge crew, but to no avail. The Annunaki ship was on them. The two ships bonded together and fell in an almighty death-throe. Together they lit up space as implosion followed explosion, a sight that transfixed everyone in view, and one, if you were lucky, you would only see once in a lifetime.

\* \* \*

Lee couldn't believe his eyes as he stood watching the spectacle which had so swiftly gone from a frenzied fight to a slow-motion dance, and now seemed to be going on forever.

Then suddenly there was nothing. Where five huge cruisers and numerous assault vessels had been, there was just empty space. A deathly quiet was returning, the fog of battle subsided, and a huge price had been paid by both sides.

Twenty-two assault vessels had been lost in the battle, along with Wesell's cruiser. Lee and the surviving twenty-eight assault craft were slowly heading around the far side of the moon towards the dark side and the Blue Star Base. It should have been a glorious return, but the loss of a cruiser had been a bitter pill to swallow.

As Lee's cruiser came to rest under the mag shield above the base, ACM Androids were already scurrying over the hull of the huge ship like ants on an anthill. There were a lot of repairs to be done, Lee's ship had certainly taken a pounding.

All the craft were now safe under the cloak of invisibility above the base; Jumouk was debriefing Lee and could almost physically feel his pain. Lee blamed himself for the loss of so many ESG ships; he also felt responsible for the loss of the cruiser. If only he had gone in like Wesell, all guns blazing.

Jumouk interrupted his train of thought.

'Lee, what ifs and maybes won't change what happened. At the end of the day the overall result was a good one for us. At least now we are on a more comparable footing, but I have the feeling our luck might just be running out.'

Lee looked quizzically at him.

'How do you mean, Jumouk?'

'Well,' continued Jumouk, 'if I was commanding the Annunaki forces, I think by now I would suspect the moon was not all it appeared to be.'

Jumouk was right.

Even as they spoke Tannacha was receiving word from the two Annunaki craft lurking in the craters on the dark side of the moon. Apparently the ESG fleet had just disappeared on the dark side of the moon, as if by magic. Tannacha didn't take long to put two and two together.

'Shit! They have got a shield of some sort.'

This outburst was more typical of Tannacha.

'Call all my commanders and have them meet me in my war room.'

# 22

The word had gone out and all Tannacha's leading commanders were on their way to the war room on board the *Nephilimis*. In all there were six commanders left, the rest having perished in differing ways, mainly at the hands of the ESG.

Tannacha had ordered the *Serpitus*, the damaged Annunaki cruiser, to land at Perth Airport, Western Australia, a main Annunaki base, and have the necessary repairs carried out. He preferred to use airports as bases, as they served well and were almost purpose-built for the Annunaki craft, from the smaller shuttles to the massive battle cruisers and everything in between.

As the huge cruiser landed it dwarfed the Perth International Tower and placed it in the cruiser's shadow. Salis, second in command aboard the *Serpitus*, was anxiously giving final commands as the cruiser came to rest. Normally it would have been Nalater the commander giving instruction to the helm, but he was now on board the *Nephilimis* in a meeting with Tannacha and the other commanders.

As soon as the cruiser had come to rest, a small army of Annunaki maintenance technicians set to work. It was going to be a big job. The *Serpitus* had suffered a lot of damage, and most of the main systems had been affected.

## BATTLE FOR THE EARTH

\* \* \*

The security surrounding the base was extremely tight after the devastating attack at Heathrow. There was a minimum of ten Annunaki assault ships patrolling the air space around the base at any given time. Ground troops had been strategically place around the base to thwart any ground or air intrusions. Salis was confident in the security protecting his cruiser, but still had his own crew on high alert, just in case.

Bailey's Crossroads, Fairfax County. Terry had been watching the increased activity in space and around Earth. Earth Central had also done its fair share of Annunaki harassment, mainly in North America, and although the Dropas pods at Bailey's Crossroads had been discovered and eventually taken out by the Annunaki, the base at Earth Central was still safe and Terry had only lost seven of his ESG assault vessels out of the fifty he started with.

Terry had watched and probed the Annunaki as they had moved their base to Dulles International Airport in line with the rest of the continents and Tannacha's orders. Security had again been tight, and Terry had up until now only limited success. However, after consultations with Jumouk a new strategy had been devised.

Any future attacks on North America would now come from Sub Sea One, and Earth Central would now command attacks on Earth's other four continents. The logic behind this was simple: to keep the risk of Earth Central's discovery to a minimum.

Terry now had his eye on the cruiser that had just landed

in Western Australia. It would certainly be a feather in his cap if he could eradicate that threat.

The good thing about Earth Central's position at Bailey's Crossroads was when the ESG assault ships screamed out of the magnetic shield. They were only visible for a few second before disappearing into the depths of the North Atlantic ocean and on to their targets.

Up to now Terry had used this to his full advantage with lightning strikes at soft Annunaki targets. Hitting Perth Airport, Western Australia was going to be considerably more of a challenge for a lot of different reasons. Terry would need to ponder this long and hard if he was to come up with a plan that had any chance of success.

The sun was just starting to break over the eastern horizon. A brand new day at Bailey's Crossroads.

Suddenly three wings of ESG assault craft appeared from nowhere, leaving Bailey's Crossroads and heading east at high velocity. They broke the surface of the North Atlantic at Tom's Canyon, dived to a thousand feet below the calm seas and headed south in the general direction of Bermuda.

The eighteen craft spread out in a large V formation, with Terry taking the lead and his right-hand man Grant Ashdown at the rear covering their six. Grant had been in the air force with Terry, and had been a natural choice for Terry's second in command when Terry was made commander of Earth Central by Lee.

The ESG craft settled into a well-disciplined plan of action. Everyone had a job to do and they all knew the plan inside out, from the route there to the method of attack and everybody's escape route.

Grant was bringing up the rear of the wing and watching his wing comrades veer left and right, up and down, hugging the underwater landscape like fleas on a dog. To their right-hand side lay the wreck of the *Nola* which sank in December 1863 after grounding on a reef just northeast of Bermuda. All that was left now was a couple of steam boilers and two paddle-wheel frames strewn on their sides.

Old wrecks were often used as handy landmarks by the ESG. It was so easy when configuring routes quickly, and the wrecks were easy for everyone to remember. There was also the security aspect. Intercepted coordinates could give a game plan away to the Annunaki, whereas a name here and there was a lot more difficult to follow.

Grant knew the next wreck of significance would be the *Mary Celestia* – not to be confused with the *Mary Celeste*. The *Mary Celestia* had sunk in 1864. A paddle steamer and a Confederate gun runner, she came to grief south-east of Bermuda on a reef, allegedly through the captain's misjudgement.

This wreck was important because the wing would swing left here heading south-east towards the next wreck of importance, the *Comet*, which was sunk in May 1861 after colliding with a schooner during a fierce storm.

As the wing glided on its way, Grant wondered why Terry had been so ready to take up this particular method of navigating the world's oceans. Then he remembered. It was down to some Android. What was its name again? Thourus. That was it. An Android that likes shipwrecks. How does that work? Does it have feelings or curiosity?

The wing had now swung south-east and was heading for the *Comet*. Grant hadn't really seen or had any real contact with the Androids or at any rate those Androids that flew spaceships. He had dealings with the Androids defending the pods round Earth Central but they just seemed ordinary – not special in any kind of fantastic way. What made the TAG different?

Still, Terry knew what he was doing and this way of navigating was working really well, easy to use, and with no interceptions as yet.

All of a sudden Grant had a feeling, a bad feeling. The hairs on the back of his neck stood up on end, and it reminded him of the early days of the Iraqi war where he had served as a young pilot and learned to trust his instinct. The feeling was almost paranoid, like someone was watching him or had got the upper hand on him.

He immediately checked his instruments and ran a scan, looking out his view windows into the depths around him. Neither the scan or the visual sweep was showing anything out of the ordinary. All the same, something still didn't feel right.

Suddenly, like a flash of inspiration it hit him. The current! It felt more like a wake – like the rise and fall of mountainous swells a rowing boat experiences as a large ship passes slowly by.

'Terry, Terry, did you feel that?'

'Feel what?' Terry responded.

'That wash or whatever it was.'

'You're imagining things, Grant. It can happen down here. Trust me, I know.'

'No, seriously. It was a huge wake, I'm sure it came from behind me, but there's nothing on the proximity detectors, and I definitely can't see any sign of anything.'

'It's probably just been caused by seabed movement. Don't worry about it, Grant, the proximity screens are clear and we are good to go, buddy.'

Still uneasy, Grant nevertheless accepted the explanation from Terry and acknowledged his last transmission.

However, right up until they reached the *Comet* he had one eye on the proximity detector and one eye on his rear-view screen.

As the *Comet* flashed passed on the left-hand side of the wing, Terry implemented a slight change in course, heading towards the next wreck, the U-860. This lay south-east of St Helens, and Terry knew that about one-third of the journey was now behind them.

As they left the U-860 behind them and headed towards the next wreck, the *Custodian*, which had run aground in the South Atlantic Ocean south-west of Bouvet Island in 1982, they would then turn east and past the French Southern and Antarctic Lands, midway to the next wreck which lay off Western Australia. This was the *Carlisle Castle*, which ran aground on Coventry Reef, south-east of Perth back in 1899. At this point they would rest up before the attack on the cruiser which was in for repairs at Perth Airport.

As Grant came to rest on the sea bed at the rear of the wing he felt relieved. Ever since the episode with the mysterious wash he'd had a bad feeling that something was going to go disastrously wrong. But, no, they'd made it to the *Carlisle Castle* OK. He just couldn't actually see it from where he was positioned, right at the back.

Still, not to worry, the action would be starting soon and he could get to do some proper flying. Although it was a novelty, Grant still preferred flying to cruising the sea bed, so the planned attack would be right up his street. Although he understood the reasons for stealth, he still preferred good, old-fashioned, head-to-head combat and the adrenalin rush that came with it.

Terry checked with everybody and made sure they all

new the plan inside out and, just as important, the escape routes and evasive actions. After confirming everyone was up to speed and wishing everyone good luck he barked the command:

'Go! Go! Go!'

# 23

Tannacha was in his war room with his six commanders. The seven of them were perusing a large 3D console at the end of the large war-room table. The exact position of Blue Star Base had been plotted onto the lunar surface, and the topic of discussion was the best way of obliterating it.

Tannacha had now suffered enough humiliation at the hand of the ESG and was poised to give the order for the total destruction of mankind and any surviving Dropas. Revenge and attrition were now the order of the day, but first of all was the destruction of this annoying base on the moon.

Nalater was the first commander to come up with a plan.

'It's quite simple, supreme commander. We do what they did.'

'How do you mean?' demanded Tannacha.

'Subterfuge, commander. We send one cruiser directly at them. They won't want to disclose their position as it approaches. Meanwhile two cruisers slip round the far side of the moon and take them completely by surprise.'

'Excellent, Nalater! At last a commander with some knowledge of tactics! I'm impressed. Once the details are worked out, come and see me on the bridge.'

With that Tannacha left his subordinates in the war room to sort out the details and returned to the bridge.

With quiet confidence Nalater approached Tannacha at the main viewing window on the bridge and made his presence known to his commander with a low barking cough.

'Everything is prepared supreme commander and we just await your permission to begin.'

'Good, I have decided to put you in charge of *Nephilimis*, Nalater, and you also have control of the fleet, answering only to me. Do you think you're up to the job?'

Nalater looked confused, but decided a positive response was called for without questioning his supreme commander's motives.

'Yes, supreme commander. I'm honoured and I won't let you down.'

Tannacha's face contorted into what could almost be mistaken for a smile.

'Then get on with it and keep me informed. I'll be in my quarters. Oh, and assign a new commander to the *Serpitus* immediately, I want that battle cruiser to hunt down any Dropas or Earthling resistance on the planet surface and destroy them without exception, understand? The only living things on Earth are to be Annunaki warriors.'

'Consider it done, supreme commander.'

From the moment Nalater began issuing his orders to the three battle cruisers, the fate of the moon base, Blue Star, was sealed.

Nalater had a new confident air about him. There was steel in his voice and his already formidable presence had become even more intimidating.

He had assessed the three commanders available to him for the purpose of commanding the battle cruiser *Serpitus* in its new role of hunt and destroy. His mind was now made up. It would be Gargius, a commander of some experience but, what was more to the point, totally ruthless and unforgiving. Just the man for the job, thought Nalater. If he can't hunt down the rest of the scum on Earth and make sure they will be extinct as a species, then no one can.

The command was given for Gargius to take a shuttle and meet up with the *Serpitus* at Perth Airport to start his new mission: the extinction of mankind and any remaining Dropas.

Gargius was absolutely delighted with his new command. After all, his battle cruiser had been one of the first casualties on entering this god-forsaken solar system when they had run straight into a meteor shower. Unfortunately his cruiser had been completely destroyed and he himself had only just escaped death by abandoning his own warriors and saving himself. In Annunaki culture the captain never goes down willingly with the ship. He then had to endure the embarrassment of being an encumbrance to another commander aboard their battle cruiser. But now he had a cruiser of his own again.

'A new mission.' Gargius was running Nalater's words over and over in his head. What were the exact words again? The only living things on Earth are to be Annunaki warriors, and he was to hunt down any Dropas or Earthling resistance on the planet surface and destroy them without exception. That was it.

That's it, thought Gargius. That's why there's no population. They're not on the surface of the planet, they're under it! It was now as plain as the grimace on his face. The Dropas specialities were technology and mining. Where else could they keep the population of a planet but underground? Why had nobody else come to this conclusion sooner? It was obvious the Dropas had been instrumental in this and by all accounts had made an excellent job of creating an environment of subterfuge.

Gargius now knew what he had to do. The only questions that remained were: how and where?

# 24

Marie and Ravel were intent on watching the approach of a single Annunaki battle cruiser, Blue Star Base was on full alert, and in silent mode. The cruiser looked as if it was just on a fishing mission, but they couldn't be sure. It was around 500,000 miles out on the long-range sensor console and on a course directly towards them but, strangely, moving very slowly.

Jumouk and Lee were on board the *Katchinas*. Konoco was on the ESG battle cruiser *Iron Duke*, all within the ESG fleet above Blue Star Base, and under the mag shield. Everyone was on full alert, and every commander was watching the slow approach of the Annunaki battle cruiser; Jumouk felt uneasy and raised the question everyone was thinking.

'Why is it travelling so slowly, Lee?'

'Maybe it's damaged,' Lee speculated.

'Where has it come from?'

Jumouk and Lee had spoken more or less in the same instant. Neither had an answer and neither would allow his eyes to stray from the console. It was almost mesmerising, watching the craft ambling along like some kind of huge albatross in space. This was exactly the result Nalater had hoped for. He had carefully instructed the commander of the battle cruiser to act out of character, hoping this would distract the moon base from the real intention of his cruiser's approach. That way the other battle cruisers could sneak slowly round the other side of the moon, effectively blindsiding the moon base.

When Nalater had given the orders to the cruisers, the decoy cruiser was to head directly towards the sun during the next solar flare. Solar flares always affected proximity detectors and scanning technology. Keeping the Earth between itself and the moon, spin round the sun, then hyper-space to the far side of Jupiter and rapidly approach the Earth's moon, slowing down when it was around 500,000 miles out.

Jumouk didn't like what he was seeing. He had a very bad feeling about it. Something just didn't add up. For the first time in what seemed an eternity Jumouk slowly raised his eyes from the console and looked at the three-dimensional representation of space around the Earth and moon. This was situated directly in the middle of the table, and was unusually hazy.

'Where are the three Annunaki battle cruisers that were in Earth's orbit?'

Lee spun round. The cruisers were no longer in Earth's orbit. Frantically he began scanning, short range, long range and Earth itself.

Damn these solar flares, he thought to himself! They affect everything.

The scanners were having a lot of difficulty identifying what was going on. They had picked up the Annunaki battle cruiser that was being repaired in Western Australia, but there was still no sign of the other battle cruisers. Jumouk looked at Lee, they were both thinking the same thing. The moon base's cover had been blown.

Lee snarled the command.

'Battle stations! All cruisers break cover now, and launch all assault craft.'

Too late! The *Katchinas* rocked under the volley of pulse fire from the two Annunaki battle cruisers bearing down on the stricken Blue Star Base. What was worse the third decoy Annunaki battle cruiser had now joined the fray.

The three ESG battle cruisers bolted in different directions, spewing out assault ships as they fled in confusion. All three cruisers had now taken substantial damage but were not being pursued by the Annunaki, who were now intent on pummelling the moon base and its surrounding defences.

The mag shield had now collapsed around the moon base and the true nature of the damage being inflicted could be seen by all. In fairness to the moon base and its surrounding defences, they were putting up a ferocious defence and indeed inflicting significant damage on all three of the attacking battle cruisers. Assault vessels, both Annunaki and ESG, had engaged each other in a mass of brutal, individual dog fights scattering above and over the lunar surface and base.

Ravel was in the Blue Star Base control room, trying desperately to co-ordinate the moon base defence. Things were happening so quickly, communications had gone down and Marie was doing what she could to get them restored.

An ESG assault craft that had been chased down by three Annunaki assault ships skimmed over the clear roof of the control room, making everyone inside duck as a reflex action.

Watching in disbelief, the horrified onlookers saw the vessel hit the lunar surface and literally bounce into one of the defence pods, bringing its fight for survival to an end. The three Annunaki assault ships carried on firing, this time targeting the other defence pod.

The Annunaki vessels were not to get it all their own way, however, as two of the craft disintegrated amongst the rain of pulse fire from the defence pod. The other Annunaki craft peeled off and sped away to hunt down more ESG prey.

The defence pod now came under fire from one of the three Annunaki battle cruisers lurking above it. Even with its energy-absorbing qualities the pod didn't last long before it imploded in on itself.

It was now becoming clear that the moon base was stricken as Ravel struggled with the systems and emergency back-ups. Fortunately for him the automated air-lock systems were still all functioning.

As structure and area after area failed, Ravel was desperately considering the best way to evacuate the base. One of the main problems was there were still no communications, even though Marie had left a while ago to expedite the repairs. All of a sudden there was a deathly hush in the control room. Ravel looked round to see everyone with their heads tilted upwards, He joined them. The sight he saw astounded him. An Annunaki battle cruiser was being savaged almost right above them by two ESG cruisers. The Annunaki cruiser simply crumpled and smashed into the lunar landscape as if in slow motion, the shock wave from the impact rattling through the whole moon base to threaten the very integrity of the polycarbonate glass panels which made up the major part of the roofing on the structure.

Still the show wasn't over. Away in the distance the *Katchinas* was in a fight for its life with another Annunaki battle cruiser. Help came in the form of the two ESG cruisers turning their attention to the Annunaki vessel and enveloping it in a barrage of pulse weapons fire.

Finally the Annunaki battle cruiser succumbed to the weapons fire and started to roll onto its back, dropping as it went, its bow high above its stern in a last dance of death. The resulting explosion seemed to caress the *Katchinas* before she too, as if in sympathy, erupted in a fireball.

All who watched the spectacle in the control room stood aghast at the loss of the *Katchinas*. It was only when the shock wave hit them that it seemed to bring them all back to reality.

After the shudder had passed, a loud sound of rushing air could be heard, and the two airtight doors leading into and out of the control room automatically snapped shut. Ravel looked upwards. The problem was obvious. One of the polycarbonate glass panels making up the roof had splintered, and now disintegrated, venting the precious atmosphere into space. Ravel looked around him frantically. Time was short, they had to plug the hole or die in minutes.

The panel was approximately two foot square and, fortunately, flat.

The table, he thought!

There in the corner under the coffee-making machine was a small, steel, portable table. It was approximately four feet square and would cover the gaping hole perfectly. The pressure in the control room would do its job to keep the table in place. Ravel ran over to the table, scattering the clutter on top including the coffee maker as he went, grabbed it, and ran across to a point directly under the hole in the roof.

The next part of his plan was really hit or miss. With all his might he launched the table upwards towards the hole, relying on the powerful current of air rushing to the hole to carry it to its new home, with luck sealing off the hole. The table hit the hole at a forty-five degree angle, and bounced precariously, finally coming to rest directly over the hole and sealing it off.

Loud applause rang out around the control room. Ravel had been so caught up in what he was doing that he hadn't noticed everyone was watching his every move. To Ravel the whole episode had been instinctive; to everyone else, it had been miraculous.

Ravel felt embarrassed, but nodded in acknowledgement anyway. The best news was that he could hear the hiss of pressurisation in the background. Now at least, he thought, they should all be safe.

The weapons fire that had been battering the moon base now seemed to subside, although alarms were still sounding everywhere. It almost seemed to Ravel that the Annunaki assault vessels were retreating to the one remaining battle cruiser. It could be seen fairly clearly from the control room and, sure enough, one after another Annunaki assault craft were returning and docking with the huge craft.

Ravel took comfort in this as he could see the two ESG battle cruisers coming in ready to hover over Blue Star Moon Base. Then, suddenly, without warning two Annunaki assault craft that had been chasing down an ESG vessel broke their attack on it and released a final flurry of pulse fire onto the moon base before retreating to the waiting *Nephilimis*.

Ravel saw the bright blue streak of the pulse weapons fire heading straight for them. His last thoughts were for the fifty or so souls in the control room whom he had so bravely tried to save, now alas in vain.

At the start of the attack Jumouk ordered his three battle cruisers to engage the Annunaki vessels. For the first time the two foes were more or less on an even standing. Lee led the attack with the *Katchinas*, this time powering in with all pulse weapons blazing, followed by the other two ESG cruisers, *Victory* and *Iron Duke*.

Nalater stood on the bridge of the *Nephilimis*, watching one of the last pods around the moon base disintegrate to a pile of dust on the lunar surface. The main part of the moon base was still intact, but only just.

Without warning the bridge on the *Nephilimis* suddenly and violently arched and flexed, and but for the quick thinking of the Annunaki helmsman, the cascade of pulse fire from the *Katchinas* would have cut the *Nephilimis* in half. As it was she was tumbling at a very precarious angle towards the lunar surface, the helmsman fighting with all of his experience to regain altitude and yaw.

All that Nalater could do was to watch as the lunar surface and the moon base – at least what was left of it – hurtled towards the front viewing window. Slowly but surely the darkness of space started to replace the fearsome view of the moon base and the lunar surface, as the helmsman battled his ship back onto an even keel and out into open space.

Tannacha had now joined Nalater on the bridge and they could both see the other two Annunaki battle cruisers were in serious trouble. Just as he was turning to speak to

Nalater, one of the huge ships shuddered in a death throe under a hail of pulse fire from the two ESG battle cruisers that had been hounding it. The spine of the huge ship fractured in four places and the cruiser crumpled like a discarded tin can being crunched underfoot before disintegrating into the lunar landscape.

The *Katchinas* was now in a life or death struggle with the other Annunaki cruiser. Both colossal ships unleashed a blanketing of death from their vast arrays of pulse weapons. At first sight it looked as if the Annunaki battle cruiser had the upper hand; the *Katchinas* was in a very bad way and was listing very badly to the port side with serious fires on virtually all of her decks.

All of a sudden both ESG cruisers involved in downing the first Annunaki battle cruiser, opened up with a deadly barrage of pulse weapons fire. This was directed onto the Annunaki battle cruiser which was mauling the *Katchinas*. The Annunaki battle cruiser could no longer avoid its fate and exploded in a fireball, unluckily taking the *Katchinas* with her.

Nalater immediately recalled all of the Annunaki assault ships that still hadn't docked and any stragglers from the other cruisers. Once they were all safely aboard, he powered his engines and headed for Western Australia.

# 25

Both ESG cruisers began a search for survivors from the *Katchinas* and the moon base, Blue Star orbital. The surface of the moon was littered with escape pods, mainly from the *Katchinas*.

Jumouk and Lee had already commenced the abandonment of the *Katchinas* well before the Annunaki cruiser had exploded around them. It had been clear to both of them that the unfortunate *Katchinas* was not going to survive this confrontation and they had taken steps to ensure minimum loss of life amongst the crew. Shuttles were sent from both cruisers and the rescue of survivors began with the retrieval of all the life pods showing signs of life.

The moon base was a total scene of devastation; Marie had survived but Ravel had died when the control room was destroyed. There were only a few pockets of survivors where the automated airtight safety doors had created areas of relative safety.

Marie was in the communications room along with thirty other people. She had gone there after communications had failed in the main control room, leaving Ravel to oversee operations there. Although the communications room was airtight for the moment, its structural integrity was in serious doubt, Marie was well aware that at any time one of the many cracks on the polycarbonate glass panels that made up the roof of the structure could fail.

Through the panels of glass that were not damaged Marie had seen the demise of the *Katchinas* and wondered if Jumouk and her good friend Lee had been able to escape safely. It was now looking like the ESG was in serious trouble and their ability to defend Earth was weakening by the day. Tens of thousands had been killed on the moon base alone and the base itself was now virtually destroyed.

Marie was just coming to terms with the hopelessness of the situation, when directly above her a shuttle had come to rest and the pilot was making desperate hand signals at her.

Marie assumed that the pilot wanted her to get ready to open the air lock, although this was not obvious from the mixed-up jumble of hand signals that the pilot was giving.

She went to the control panel next to the airtight door and prepared to open it manually. In the meantime the shuttle cleared the debris, mainly destroyed corridor from the other side of the of the door. This was quite a tricky operation for the pilot as he had to be very careful not to put any further strain on the airtight room for fear of structural failure.

After around twenty minutes of nail-biting tension both for the pilot, and survivors in the airtight room, he was now in the position to back his shuttle carefully up against the airtight door and create a seal for an air lock between his shuttle and the room.

Finally Marie heard the knock on the door signifying that the pilot was ready for them. She wound the small wheel which would manually open the door as fast as she could; at last the door was open wide enough to slip through into the safety of the shuttle. Once everyone was safely on board the shuttle the pilot disconnected the air lock and gently glided away from the structure, heading back towards the two ESG cruisers and safety.

Jumouk, Lee and Konoco were all in the conference room aboard *Iron Duke*, one of the two remaining ESG battle cruisers, when Marie came bursting through the door. She could not contain her delight at hearing both Jumouk and, especially, Lee had been rescued safely from the lunar surface. Konoco had already been on board *Iron Duke* during the furious fighting.

Lee spun round with a big grin and wrapped his arms around Marie. They were obviously more than delighted to see each other. Jumouk smiled then went back to concentrating on the job in hand. The first thing they had to determine was what forces they had left, and the battle-worthy condition of the Annunaki fleet.

Marie and Lee rejoined him at the conference table. They knew this was going to be a tough job. They had two cruisers left, *Victory* and *Iron Duke*, but they were still waiting for a head count on the assault vessels, both in space and back on Earth. Then there were the ground forces. The one thing they all agreed on was that now they had inflicted a lot of damage on the Annunaki fleet, and they had to keep the pressure on.

# 26

As Terry and his three wings of assault craft burst through the waters off Western Australia, the timing couldn't have been worse. More or less right above them the *Nephilimis* was coming into land at Perth Airport.

Terry didn't stand a chance. The *Nephilimis* banks of pulse weapons spat blue death all around them. Nine of the ESG assault craft almost instantaneously disintegrated, one spinning off frantically, trailing smoke and reddish yellow flames and eventually crashing into Garden Island. Taking advantage of the confusion, Annunaki assault ships spilled from the battle cruiser and mauled the ESG craft. Within a few short minutes seventeen ESG craft had been lost and only four Annunaki craft destroyed, with no damage whatsoever to the battle cruiser.

Only Grant had managed to turn tail and get his craft back to the relative sanctuary of the deep ocean. Now he sat on the sea bed in total shock. He had powered his craft down in a place called Perth Canyon, around 9,000 feet below the surface. It had all happened in less than ten minutes, he thought. Seventeen craft. Seventeen! He was having difficulty comprehending what had just happened.

Meanwhile, on board the *Nephilimis*, Nalater was jubilant. His quick thinking on spotting the wings of ESG vessels leaving the ocean was inspirational, and had been well noted by Tannacha. He had certainly delivered a humiliating blow to the ESG. In fact neither of the two commanders realised the full extent of the damage they had done.

Grant had given it twenty minutes on the sea bed and was now traversing the depths of the oceans, making his way back to Earth Central, his heart heavy with recent tragic events.

The journey on the way back was incident free, and Grant docked under the protection of the mag shield at Earth Central. He still had no idea of the recent events on the moon, and was taken by surprise at the sombre atmosphere within the control room. He began to wonder if they knew of the events that had just taken place off Western Australia.

Fiona Green, the senior control room manager, brought Grant up to speed on the catastrophic events that had befallen the Blue Star Base and the *Katchinas*. He was stunned. Worse still, he had to break the news to Fiona, who already had tears rolling down from her misty blue eyes, of what had happened off Western Australia. He composed himself.

'Fiona.'

He had caught her just beginning another sentence.

'Fiona.'

He repeated himself.

'I've got some bad news as well, Terry's ... well ...'

He took his third sharp intake of breath in as many seconds and blurted it out.

'Terry's dead. I don't know what else to say. I am so sorry, Fiona. It was almost like they knew we were coming, we ran straight into one of their battle cruisers.'

Fiona sank back and shook her head, She was having difficulty taking the news in; Terry had been extremely popular. He was always a likeable boss, and a huge source of motivation to everyone that knew him. He had also planned and carried out numerous successful covert strikes against the Annunaki, causing untold damage and confusion. Without doubt Terry's loss was going to be a huge blow to the ESG.

'How many of our eighteen craft survived?'

She straightaway wished she hadn't asked the question.

Grant lowered his gaze

'Just me, I think, I waited a while before I left the area. Didn't see anyone else.'

Fiona turned without a word and moved directly to the communications console to contact Jumouk on board *Iron Duke* to break the tragic news. Lee watched the expression on Jumouk's face change from neutral to sudden anguish. The news came out of the blue and took him completely by surprise.

After a few seconds' pause Jumouk thanked Fiona and said he would contact her in the next two hours with his instructions. His next job would be to break the news to Lee. He knew how close Lee and Terry had been and that Lee would not take the death of his close friend well.

'Lee.'

Jumouk hesitated. Lee guessed what was coming had to be bad news. Jumouk was very rarely hesitant.

'I've just heard from Fiona. I'm sorry, but Terry's dead, my friend.'

Lee looked up from the console he and Marie had been poring over.

'Dead? I don't understand, Jumouk?'

'Apparently he went on the mission to Western

Australia, and they were ambushed. We lost seventeen assault craft including Terry's craft.'

Lee was visibly stunned.

'But I told Terry specifically not to go on any missions himself. He was there to plan and organise, not to fight. Plan and organise, that's all.'

Jumouk shook his head slowly.

'You know Terry was hands on. It was inevitable especially after the success of Thourus's attack on Heathrow.'

Jumouk looked to Marie then back to his friend.

'Lee, I am so sorry but we need to put this behind us. We now have a real problem. We have a lot of planning to do, my friend.'

Konoco looked at Lee and nodded.

Marie put her arm around Lee. She could feel his pain, but Jumouk was right: they had a lot of planning and damage control to do.

# 27

The *Nephilimis* came to rest next to the *Serpitus* at Perth Airport. The *Serpitus* had now been fully repaired and Gargius had taken up his position as commander, making sure Salis knew his place as second in command. Both battle cruisers had a full complement of assault craft: one hundred between the two of them.

The commanders had their orders from Tannacha: find the human civilians and wipe them out. They knew the first place they were going to look, North America somewhere around Washington DC, where the first contacts were made. Gargius and Nalater were sure of this: somewhere there the humans were hiding. The two huge battle cruisers lifted off and headed towards North America at low level together with an escort from within their ranks of twenty assault craft.

Fiona Green was in Earth Central's control room watching the 3D visualisation of Earth. She could see the two Annunaki battle cruisers with their escorts approaching. It didn't take much to figure out where they were heading. No, the more important question was: why?

The resources she had left to protect Earth Central were now very limited after the disaster in Western Australia. In fact there were just twenty-four assault craft left which would be no match for the approaching Annunaki assemblage of ships.

Grant put a comforting hand on Fiona's right shoulder, and asked:
'How are you holding up, Fiona?'
Her reply was not unexpected for a seasoned professional.
'Oh, OK, I guess, Grant, but I could well do without this.'
She pointed to the approaching Annunaki forces. Grant pulled a face.
'What can we do?'
'Not much, I'm afraid, Grant. We've only got twenty-four assault craft left, and no defence pods.'
Grant flinched, mostly because of the guilt he felt, not so much that Western Australia had been his fault, more the guilt of the survivor who had got out alive.

Jumouk and Lee were watching the progress of the battle cruisers on their image of Earth. It had already been decided between the four of them that direct confrontation at this time would not be a wise move. Their forces had been depleted and now stood at two cruisers and around one hundred and forty-four assault craft, split between Earth, sea and space. The only thing they weren't short of was ground troops, although these weren't much use against battle cruisers.
Marie came over and stood beside them.
'Anything we can do without all-out confrontation?'
Lee looked at Jumouk.
Jumouk shook his head.
'We just have to hope they don't discover Earth Central.'

'And if they do?' Marie enquired.

'Then it's head-on, I'm afraid. Fight to the death as they say.'

Konoco had been quietly thinking in the background.

'Why don't we use a decoy to lead them away, at least for the time being?'

'What sort of decoy did you have in mind, Konoco?' asked Jumouk.

'How about we start a fight?'

'What do you mean, Konoco?'

Again it was Marie who asked the question.

'Well, most of the action we've seen up to now has been airborne. Why don't we use our ground troops to take out, say, Heathrow? Bear in mind we've already done quite a lot of damage there. On reflection we could always get Thourus and the TAG to back up the ground troops.'

'Brilliant! If that doesn't distract them nothing will.'

Lee slapped Konoco on the back by way of congratulation.

'Can you set it up for me, Lee?'

Lee turned to face Jumouk.

'Sure thing, sir,' he said. 'My pleasure.'

Heathrow was fairly quite, although security had been stepped up since the TAG attack that had been so successfully orchestrated, Annunaki ground warriors were everywhere and the sky was regularly patrolled by assault vessels.

Most of the movement on the base were shuttle craft going to and fro from the gold reserves held at the Bank of England in London, and capital cities around the rest of the world. Heathrow had been chosen to be a holding station for the gold reserves until they were loaded onto the

Annunaki battle cruisers, which could land at Heathrow and be loaded easily.

Clarence Finnegan was the battalion commander of the ESG land forces that were about to storm Heathrow. He had a mixed bunch of a thousand ESG troopers and five hundred Androids spread all around the perimeter of Heathrow.

The plan was for the Androids to go in first, taking most of the casualties. Then his ESG troopers would back them up, quelling any further resistance from the Annunaki. Thourus and his TAG assault ships would provide air support. Once the airport was secured more reinforcements would be flown in using shuttles, and the two ESG battle cruisers would take up defensive positions above the airport. If by any chance the Annunaki wanted to bring the fight to them, then so be it. They were now at least on a par with the aggressors.

The Androids were given the command to attack, and immediately engaged with the Annunaki guards on the outer perimeter. The fighting was vicious. The opposing foes were a match for each other, their warrior qualities not in question, and bravery second to none.

The Androids did have one major advantage in the fact that they felt no debilitating pain from injuries, they just kept advancing, like an unstoppable freight train. The skies above the airport filled with Annunaki assault ships, targeting the ESG Androids, but still they came, hacking through the Annunaki warriors, building by building. The low-flying Annunaki assault craft were a gift to Thourus and his fifty TAG assault craft. They outnumbered the Annunaki two to one and had the advantage of surprise. The hardest part of the attack was finding any Annunaki assault vessels that hadn't already been targeted.

The ESG Androids had by now confined the Annunaki warriors to Terminals 2 and 3, and the ESG troopers were now securing the perimeters of Heathrow and mopping up any straggling Annunaki warriors.

Thourus had only lost five of his craft in the battle of the airspace above Heathrow. the Annunaki had lost twenty craft and the remaining five craft had disengaged, and disappeared off to the west, presumably to seek shelter with the two Annunaki cruisers that were just arriving at Washington DC.

The fighting at Terminals 2 and 3 was becoming more sporadic, signifying that the ESG Androids had now gained the upper hand over the remaining Annunaki warriors, though the cost had been severe. At least two hundred Androids were totally beyond repair and half of the remainder had minor to severe damage. Still, Heathrow Airport had been retaken which was an achievement in itself. Clarence Finnegan, or Finney as he liked to be known, was delighted with the performance of his troops.

Nalater and the two cruisers were just approaching Washington DC, when news of the attack on Heathrow Airport reached him. His first instinct was to turn the battle cruisers around and head for the mêlée, but the timely arrival of Tannacha on the bridge made him think twice.

Tannacha seemed remarkably composed, Nalater had expected at the very least the brutal slaying of one or two of the subordinates on the bridge. Nalater was starting to get a very bad feeling as to the exact reason for Tannacha's unusual behaviour.

Nalater brought the two huge battle cruisers expertly to rest at Dulles International Airport.

# 28

Heathrow was now Annunaki free, and the two ESG battle cruisers had taken up defensive positions above the airport.

Finney had been running around like a headless chicken, organising things himself in preparation for the imminent arrival of Jumouk, Lee, Konoco and Marie. Lee and Konoco were the first to arrive at Finney's makeshift office in Terminal 3.

The office itself was shabby looking and basic, with none of the high-tech gadgets you might expect. OK, Finney had only about an hour to clear out all the Annunaki trash and tidy up as best he could, but he still felt bad.

He greeted his two visitors with open arms and made them as welcome as he could. Lee asked Finney if he had ever heard of the word 'delegation', and Finney's face turned as red as his hair. Lee laughed.

'Don't look so worried, Finney, I'm only joking. Seriously, good job recapturing Heathrow. I take it everything's secure now?'

'As secure as we can be. Checked it out myself.'

Finney immediately regretted making the last remark when he saw a wry smile appear on Lee's face. Jumouk entered the room and Finney instantly jumped to his feet, Jumouk gestured for Finney to sit back down and pulled up a chair for himself.

'Looks like we've got a bit of a stalemate going on. Those two Annunaki cruisers have parked themselves at Dulles, and don't look like they're going to be moving anytime soon.'

Lee finished off the sentence by relaxing back in his seat. Konoco looked deep in thought.

'What do you think they're up to, Lee?'

The question caught Lee off guard.

'How do you mean, Konoco?'

'Well they must have a plan, don't you think?'

Lee pondered the question for a few seconds.

'Have we? What I mean is, have we got a plan?'

Konoco looked at Jumouk.

'What do you think, Jumouk?'

Jumouk shook his head.

'I think Lee might have a point. We are too evenly matched now, so it's going to be a brave man who takes the initiative, and I for one am rapidly running out of ideas.'

Marie interrupted them, startling them in the process. Everyone had been so deep in thought that no one had noticed her standing at the door.

'Yes, we are evenly matched, but remember – at one point we were outnumbered nearly three to one, so it can't be all bad, can it?'

The positive attitude couldn't have come at a better time, and Marie knew it.

'So, come on, guys, let's get our thinking caps on and do what we do best: solve the unsolvable. What's the real problem here? The Annunaki have set up their main base right on the doorstep of Earth Central, bad luck I know, but there it is!'

'Well, at least they haven't found Earth Central yet, which is a blessing,' Lee added.

Marie grabbed a chair and joined the rest of them round the desk.

'Yes, but I suspect that they think it might be there or at least something like it, and if they start looking for it in earnest, they will find it.'

'What if we withdraw the assault craft back to here?'

Lee looked round the room.

'Well, we can't move Earth Central, can we?'

'That's for sure,' replied Marie.

'Remember the Blue Star Moon Base, it didn't take them that long to twig and discover that! What's more important, look at the resources they threw at it, everything they had, and absolutely no mercy.'

'So, basically what you're saying, Marie, is we can expect the same for Earth Central and the close on a million people down there?'

Lee was shaking his head despondently as he ended his last sentence, but Marie was still upbeat.

'We just won't let them find it, Lee, this is your field of expertise. Get your thinking cap on and don't be so defeatist.'

The room went quiet again. This time it was Finney's turn to break the silence.

'I hope you don't mind me saying, but maybe we're looking at this the wrong way? It sounds to me like the number one priority for the Annunaki now is the extermination of mankind and everything that's not Annunaki.'

'And the point of this observation is?'

Lee wasn't meaning to be curt with Finney, but frustration was starting to take over. He was blaming himself for not having come up with a solution yet, and unwittingly Marie had just made it worse.

Finney blinked nervously but carried on.

'Am I right in assuming that the old Mars underground base that the Dropas had when they were mining for Moissanite is still there?'

This caught Konoco's attention.

'How do you know about that?' he demanded

Finney looked like a public school boy who had just been caught playing truant.

'Well, if the truth be known, one of my old school chums did a bit of tendering work – well quite a lot actually – got to go to Mars and everything, it was for a Dropas company back in late 2018, all hush-hush, you know, the mining was all being wound up at the time, and well, long story short, he told me all about it.'

Konoco looked astounded as did Lee and Marie, Lee butted in.

'I didn't know anything about this.'

He threw a glance at Marie, who said jokingly:

'Don't look at me, I didn't have a clue that was going on.'

Jumouk felt he better take the situation back in hand.

'Please, it was an old mining operation that's closed down now. We just didn't feel at the time it was important to mention it.'

Lee looked sceptical. He thought he had known everything about the Dropas operations. It was Konoco who got them back on track.

'I understand your concerns, Lee, but could we just see where Finney is going with this?'

All eyes turned to an uncomfortable-looking Finney, who hadn't expected the conversation to go this way. After all, he hadn't known the ESG high council were unaware of the mining operation. Now he wished fervently that he had kept quiet about it – after all in the scheme of things he was just a lowly ground-troop battalion commander, unlike the big cheeses sitting around the table with him making decisions that would affect the fate of mankind.

'Well?' snapped Lee.

Finney stood up as if to make a point. The real reason was that his back was giving him gyp and he had only just noticed it.

'The way I see it is – to quote – if Mohamed can't come to the mountain, the mountain must come to Mohamed.'

It was a misquote, the nerves were now beginning to show, also the pain in his back was getting much worse.

'What I mean to say is ...'

Lee interrupted him.

'Brilliant! The man's a genius!'

Lee stood up as well.

'It's simple. We take the entire population from Earth Central and put them up in the mining complex on Mars. Job done'

He emphasised his point by slamming his hand on the desk.

At this moment Marie put her head in her hands and thought: if mankind's fate is in our hands, God help us!

Lee saw the look on Marie's face as she looked up.

'No,' he said, 'I mean it. All we need to do is use three of the Dropas mining craft, set up an underwater base off the eastern seaboard, tunnel through to Earth Central, then evacuate them into the largest Dropas transports – at a push they hold up to two hundred and fifty thousand at time – take the transports underwater over to somewhere off Western Australia. If we cause enough of a diversion with the two Annunaki battle cruisers, we should be able to slip the transports off the planet without being noticed and get them to the underground facility on Mars.'

The room fell silent again. Jumouk looked at Konoco.

'It's possible, isn't it?'

Konoco nodded.

'Thourus has got a movable underwater station. We bring that in, the tunnelling can be done in a matter of hours. Then it's just the time to evacuate Earth Central. Sure it's possible.'

Lee looked to Finney.

'Well done, Finney, you've played a blinder!'

Jumouk stood up and asked Lee if he could sort out the details, Marie and Konoco would help organise the logistics involved.

# 29

Thourus was busy organising the movement of the undersea station. It was a fair size, able to hold easily between seventy to one hundred thousand people at a time. It was completely self-sufficient and comfortable.

Once the anchors holding the station in place had been removed, the flotation tanks were filled to support the base. It could now be towed by two shuttle craft with surprising ease.

The journey from the Labrador Sea, where the station was positioned, to a point off Washington DC was a fairly short one, but certainly not without its difficulties. These were mainly caused by strong currents.

Thourus oversaw the anchoring in the new position personally. Everything went perfectly to plan. The three Dropas mining craft were already halfway to Bailey's Crossing at a depth of two miles underground, and an airtight connection had been made between the three tunnels and the undersea station. Everything was being done with maximum security to prevent the Annunaki getting wind of what was going on.

Konoco and Marie had slipped off Earth in a small shuttle and were on their way to the underground base on Mars, so they could see for themselves the condition of the base.

Marie was perfect for this, after her experience of

running the moon base. Lee in the meantime was trying to come up with a suitable diversion so when the time came the transports could get away safely.

As Marie and Konoco set down in a heavily disguised landing station equipped with its own gravity and atmosphere, far on the other side of Mars, the secret nature of the mining operation was becoming apparent to Marie.

They entered the mine entrance and proceeded to a series of lifts all apparently going in different directions. The scale of the mine must be huge, thought Marie, although she said nothing of her thoughts to Konoco, who was looking more sheepish and uncomfortable by the minute.

Finally she blurted out:

'Where do we start?'

It was an uneasy attempt to break the awkward silence.

'We must check the power source first,' Konoco replied.

He was checking the audio-visual map to the right-hand side of the lifts.

'Good. We take this one.'

Konoco ushered Marie into one of the lifts. For some reason he seemed suddenly a lot more confident. Once out of the lift they entered a huge room filled with electronic gadgetry, weird-looking even by Marie's standards. She thought she had seen it all on Blue Star Moon Base.

Konoco went straight to a console on the left-hand side of the room and began to flick through its three-dimensional imagery. It was more than apparent to Marie that Konoco had been here before, probably lots of times. She wondered what the Dropas had been using this base for. It was obvious that some mining had gone on, but the base was far too big to be just a mine.

Konoco turned to her.

'Well, the power source is fine, and everything should come on line just shortly.'

Marie looked concerned.

'Won't that leave a huge electronic signature, Konoco? It will be like we turned on a light in a dark room, a gift to the Annunaki sensors.'

'Don't worry, Marie. It's totally shielded from detection. The Annunaki wouldn't know we were here even if they were standing right next to us.'

Marie was very impressed, and even more so when systems started coming on line all around her. The thought even occurred to her that it was almost like standing in the engine room of some gigantic space craft.

Back on Earth, Fiona Green was pacing the floor of the control room at Earth Central. Things had gone from bad to worse. Not only were the Annunaki warriors almost knocking at her door, but to top it all she had totally lost communications with Jumouk and Heathrow.

She had technicians crawling all over the communications systems for hours now, but all they kept telling her was that the systems are all working fine. In truth she was starting to fear the worst.

The only good news seemed to be that the Annunaki battle cruisers that had landed at Dulles didn't seem to be searching the area – at least for the time being.

Nalater was in personal contact with all of his patrol commanders as they spread out from Dulles International Airport. Shuttles were landing and taking off at regular intervals. Reinforcements had been brought in from all over Earth in the search for this elusive ESG base. Nalater couldn't prove its existence; he just knew that it was there.

This was, of course, a fairly big gamble for Nalater to take. If things went wrong, the vengeance of Tannacha was notorious, and he would no doubt feel the full force of it.

The patrols of Annunaki warriors had got as far as Mclean, Falls Church, Jefferson and Annandale. The search was carried out door to door, street to street, and involved now more than fifty thousand ground warriors backed up by fifty Annunaki assault craft and assorted sizes of shuttles. If anything was there, Nalater was confident he was going to find it. After all, he knew only too well the consequences if he didn't!

The next towns to be searched would be Bethesda, Arlington, Bailey's Crossroads, Franconia and Groveton, in a search pattern fanning out from Dulles.

Back at Earth Central, Fiona was right to be worried, She wished Terry had been there, he would have known what to do for the best. Grant was a great aerial tactician, but didn't have the same expertise with ground troops. She felt like a rat in a trap.

Jumouk and Lee were on the north mining craft as it penetrated floor two of Earth Central where the command centre was based. The two south craft would penetrate on floor four, the non-combatants' shelter.

Tunnels in a perfect circular shape, and around eight hundred feet in diameter, had been bored out. This was complemented by a solid level floor two hundred feet wide. The mining craft had huge retractable lasers and crushers on the front of them. The lasers cut a path and fed the crushers, which pulverised, and super-compressed anything that passed through them. The compressed material was then converted in the second section of the craft to a substance a thousand times stronger than cement.

This finished substance was called Geronosite, and was used to make the walls and floor of the tunnel, which was all done automatically by the second section. A third compartment dried and sealed the Geronosite instantly, making it rock hard, without the need to be shored up. The fourth compartment was the driving engine behind the process and could drive the tunnelling at an incredible speed. At the end of the day you had a perfect, wide-floored tunnel, ready to use.

What used to take mankind years and years was now done in less than two hours.

The mining craft simply retracted their lasers and crushers and reversed down the tunnel to the awaiting undersea station. A series of shuttles on floor four would use the two tunnels in one circular direction, picking up people from floor four and dropping them off at the undersea station ready to board large transports, thence returning up the other tunnel to collect more people. Round and round the shuttles would go until the job was complete and everybody had been safely evacuated.

Jumouk and Lee disembarked from their shuttle and headed for the control room.

# 30

Marie and Konoco had left the room housing the power source and were on their way to the mining operation control room. With every step that Marie took she was becoming less convinced this base had just been about mining. If it was just about mining, why so hush-hush? Obviously, mining had taken place here, but the sprawling underground base was far too vast to account for any mining operation that could conceivably have taken place. No, she thought to herself, there was definitely an ulterior motive to this base.

As they entered the control room Marie stopped in her tracks in astonishment. This was the largest and most technologically advanced control room she had ever seen. It made the one on the ill-fated moon base look like an ancient relic.

'What's going on, Konoco? And please don't say "mining".'

Konoco had already made his mind up to tell Marie the full story when they had reached the lifts, which probably accounted for his change in mood at the time. He thought to himself – where do I start?

'Marie, this is going to take a bit of explaining.'

Konoco led Marie across the huge control room to an annexe, a pleasant room, well furnished and comfortable. They sat down on a plush couch and Konoco voiced a command to the computer.

'Computer, two green teas, thank you.'

Marie stared about her in disbelief.

Moments later a person, or perhaps even an Android, appeared, carrying a tray with two green teas on it, then proceeded to lay the tray on a small table in front of them.

'Anything else, sir?' the Android enquired politely, its voice was steady and self-assured with a soothing tone.

'No, thank you.' replied Konoco with the greatest of courtesy.

Marie was speechless. She had never seen an Android like this one before; it could almost have been human. Regaining her composure, she had a sip of the green tea, politely returned the cup and saucer to the table and relaxed back into the comfortable couch.

'Well, Konoco, you were about to explain.'

Now that Marie seemed relaxed, Konoco stood up.

'Well, it's not so much that we simply lied to you, but we had really to appraise the situation. You see, we didn't actually build this base; we stumbled across it about ten years ago. Our scientists have been exploring and studying it ever since. It's only just recently we decided that it could safely support life on a sustained basis.'

'You mean you didn't build it?

Konoco shook his head, and the next question was obvious.

'Who built it then?' Marie didn't disappoint with the question.

'We don't know. Our scientists have been arguing about that for the past ten years.'

'You mean there's a base this size and you don't know who built it?'

'Simply put, no.'

'How about when was it built, then?'

Marie couldn't believe what she was hearing, but then a thought struck her. She was going to have to explain all this to Lee when she got back.

'Again, we don't know. The technology is far more advanced than our own. Where do you think the idea for the magnetic light refractor shield came from?'

'Jesus!'

Marie wasn't at all religious but she was now wondering, what in God's name was going on.

'What about the Androids here? Can't they shed some light on this?'

'Again, they are far more advanced than the Androids we're used to. Even Thourus doesn't come close.'

'Why don't you dissect or disassemble one, or, well ... you know what I mean?'

'We can't.'

Marie interrupted.

'Can't?'

'Ethics. Our scientists cannot rule out the possibility that the Androids are sentient beings. Dropas laws don't allow that kind of intervention, if you are not sure. We have questioned them at great length but to no avail. Each one in their own way is, how do you say, keeping mum, when asked pertinent questions.'

'Jesus! They're alive?'

'As I said, I don't know.'

'Could the Androids have built the base?'

'I don't think so, They just seem to run it, almost like caretakers, I suppose.'

'How many of them are there?'

Marie was now starting to get concerned. It was bad enough having to deal with the Annunaki, but this was a totally unknown quantity.

'We don't know. At least four thousand, perhaps, but we still, even in ten years, haven't covered all the base.'

Marie took another sip of her green tea. Her mouth had gone dry, in her case a sure sign of tension.

'How much of the base has been explored?'

'We think around seventy-five per cent, but it's hard to tell, it's just so big.'

'Is it safe to bring up non-combatants, from Earth? After all you don't seem to know that much about the base?'

'Well, we do and we don't, if you see what I mean. Nothing at all harmful has been found, and the Androids are more than happy to make you comfortable. Besides, I don't think we have much choice.'

'Well, I honestly don't know what to say.'

Marie was dumbfounded. Her best bet, she thought, was to speak to Lee. Konoco picked up his green tea which had now cooled down and swallowed it in one gulp. He replaced his cup and saucer on the table. Then, turning to Marie, he gestured to her to follow him.

'Let me show you what we know of the control room.'

They re-entered the control room from the annexe and approached what appeared to be a main console. Konoco pulled up an image and started flicking through it.

'Some of it's self-explanatory. On the whole the systems seem to run themselves, air conditioning, venting, lighting – the day-to-day things. They have a very clever food replication system. We haven't worked out how it works yet, but you can get anything, and as much as you want.'

'What about housing the people, when they come up from Earth?'

'One level of the base is dedicated to living areas, and there are thousands of well-equipped dormitories, which could easily cope with Earth Central's population.'

'What is this place, Konoco? This is going to sound really silly, but you don't think the Martians could have built it, do you?'

'No, not silly, but we did rule that out a long time ago.'

'OK, so we have food, sleeping and recreation – oh, and we've also got waiter and maid service. This place is too good to be true, I thought we had done really well with the shelters on Earth, but this is incredible.'

Konoco closed down the display and turned to her.

'Do you think Lee will be OK with this? I know it's a bit of a shock, but bear in mind it was a shock to us as well, Earth's defence was in hand, and we really just didn't know where to begin explaining this. The plain fact is we still don't have an explanation.'

Marie mulled Konoco's statement over in her head. A bit of a shock, she thought? That's an understatement. Still, it isn't his fault.

'No, Konoco,' she said. 'I'm sure he'll be fine once I've talked to him. Just leave it to me.'

# 31

When Jumouk and Lee entered the control room at Earth Central, Fiona Green couldn't believe her eyes.

'Where did you come from, I mean how did you get here? Don't tell me you walked.'

Lee laughed out loud.

'Not quite, Fiona.'

Lee brought Fiona up to speed on everything that had happened, She was visibly relieved at their arrival, she felt as if an unbearable weight had been lifted from her shoulders, so much so that she was having difficulty taking in what Lee was telling her.

'Mars?'

She stared in disbelief, Lee carried on with the story. By the time he'd finished, Fiona's face was a blank.

'What do you want me to do now, Lee?' she asked.

'The first thing you need to do is organise the evacuation of Earth Central. Use any resources you need, but it must be done as quickly as possible.'

Fiona nodded.

'I'll get on that straightaway, Lee. Trust me, it will be done as quickly as possible.'

With that she scurried off with a new sense of purpose.

Meanwhile Jumouk had been watching the advancing Annunaki warriors on one of the view screens.

'It doesn't look good. I think we're going to have to delay them.'

Lee took a closer look.

'Maybe not. They seem to be fanning their search pattern outwards, they obviously don't have a clue where we are. OK, I agree they're eventually going to stumble on us, but I think we've still got some time in hand.'

Jumouk took on board what Lee had said, and nodded in agreement.

'Do you think we should deploy troops, just in case?'

Lee thought for a few seconds.

'No I don't think so. How about deploying Androids to the perimeter of Bailey's Crossing? That way they can stall the Annunaki warriors if necessary, or we can also use them for a diversion when the time comes. Bear in mind we've still got twenty-four assault craft here as well. They should help in the diversion.'

'Perfect. Can I leave you to organise that, Lee? I'm just going to track down Fiona and see how she's getting on with the evacuation plans.'

'OK, leave it to me, Jumouk, I'm going to need to talk to Grant, though.'

Fiona was doing an excellent job overseeing the evacuation; things were going extremely smoothly, shuttles were picking people up from level four at intervals of around three minutes, the journey to the undersea base was taking around ten minutes and with eight shuttle craft each carrying up to two hundred people, it wasn't going to be long – maybe forty-eight hours – before the base would be completely deserted.

The tunnels could then be severed from the undersea base, and Earth Central and the tunnel complex flooded.

Jumouk was pleased with the progress to date. His only

fear was that the base would be compromised before the evacuation was complete. This thought had also crossed Fiona's mind but she had an idea. She turned to Jumouk.

'Do you think it would be a good idea to seal up the entrances to Earth Central? I mean after the Androids have been deployed and the pilots have got to their assault craft.'

Jumouk nodded in agreement.

'Good idea, Fiona. Just to be on the safe side. After all, we won't be using them again, How do you suggest we go about it?'

'Well, it's just a thought, but remember the barrels of expandable foam that we were going to use for insulation? That stuff is as tough as old boots once it's expanded and it also goes a long way.'

'Go on.'

Jumouk was impressed by the inventiveness of the people around him.

'Well, when the last of the Androids leave they could burst the seals on the barrels and dump them down the lift shafts, that would seal everything up nicely.'

'How many barrels have we got?'

Jumouk was looking a bit sceptical.

'More than enough to seal all five turbo-lift shafts completely.'

Fiona signalled to one of her commanders. She sat with him at a small desk and instructed him on what she wanted to happen. The commander confirmed his orders and took his leave.

Jumouk came over and sat down beside Fiona. Smiling, he said in an enthusiastic tone:

'You know, we might just pull this off, Fiona.'

\* \* \*

Meanwhile Lee had organised the perimeter defences around Bailey's Crossroads, and was talking to commander Jefferson regarding the sealing of the turbo-lift shafts.

Five Androids would be sent to the top of each shaft with enough barrels of expandable foam to fill it up. After all the other levels had been evacuated to level four, the lifts would be disabled at the bottom of each shaft, and the Androids would start their task of sealing the shafts.

When they had finished this successfully, they would then deploy to join the other Androids in the defence of the perimeter, along with the assault craft.

It had now been twenty-four hours since the start of the evacuation and one of the large transports with two hundred and fifty thousand people on board had just arrived off Western Australia. The other two remaining transports were rapidly filling up at the undersea base.

The Androids on perimeter duty were a whisper away from engaging the Annunaki warriors. In all, two thousand Androids were spread out along the Bailey's Crossroads city limits.

The first encounter wasn't particularly spectacular. As the eight-foot tall Annunaki warrior entered the door of the quiet suburban house, he looked intimidating, an air of arrogance and the attitude of invincibility all summed up his confident posture.

He had been in what felt like thousands of similar dwellings and had found nothing. However, this one was different.

Despite the obvious difference in size and stature, as the

Annunaki warrior passed the line of sight of the open door, a Dropas Android flew from the back of the door and latched itself onto the huge Annunaki neck, snapping the unfortunate warrior's spine instantly.

The Annunaki slumped to the floor stone dead, without having made a sound.

The Dropas Androids might only have been five foot in height but they had the strength of twenty men and the speed and lightning responses of a cobra.

The fighting had begun, initially only a few sounds of pulse weapons, then a barrage of weapons fire. The Annunaki had been taken by surprise again. They had for so long been searching without any action, they had become complacent, and sloppy in their approach. The Dropas Androids had gained the upper hand, at least initially.

Nalater was quickly informed of the commencement of the fighting. He knew now that his gamble had paid off. The city limits of Bailey's Crossroads were ablaze with weapons fire, He was sure they were on to something big. Tannacha would be impressed.

He ordered the assault craft into the fray, and brought up reinforcements from the surrounding towns.

The Dropas Androids were putting up a good fight, using urban guerrilla tactics, moving quickly from house to house to make themselves a hard target for the assault craft and surprising Annunaki warriors as they went. Any advance the Annunaki tried to make was quickly halted and then countered, stretching the Annunaki reserves to the limit.

The fighting was particularly intense on Belleview Drive. The shape and lay-out of its houses made it a particular problem for the approaching Annunaki warriors.

The eight or so L-shaped buildings provided perfect cover for each other, and air-defence positions had been established in another line of buildings close by. These were now protected by the L-shaped buildings.

Every time an Annunaki assault ship came near, a hail of pulse fire would erupt from the line of buildings. The Androids had also released air mines above the structures which were now taking their toll on the Annunaki assault craft as well. The Annunaki were advancing, but it was a slow, costly, advance, and Nalater was growing impatient.

Twenty hours had now passed since the start of the fighting and the body count was rising on both sides. The Dropas Androids still had a stronghold in and around Belleview Drive. Five hundred or so were now dug in and putting up a ferocious fight, holding back the ever-increasing number of Annunaki warriors determined to rout them.

As if from nowhere a large blue flash enveloped the half-square mile where the resistance was strongest and laid waste to everything within it. The area was destroyed, not a structure surviving. Annunaki and Androids alike vaporised without distinction.

Tannacha had given the order to vaporise the area and quell any final resistance. There was absolutely no regret for the loss of his own warriors, just the order to Nalater to clear the area.

The two huge Annunaki battle cruisers had travelled from Dulles and come to rest above the stricken neighbourhood. This was the final nail in the coffin for the Dropas Androids. The few that were left were quickly mopped up by the advancing Annunaki warriors.

Just outside the levelled area an Annunaki warrior was

investigating a damaged building. Something didn't seem right about the cellar. There were what looked like heavy metal runners visible on the damaged interior walls.

One of the entrances to Earth Central had finally revealed its position.

Tannacha and Nalater swiftly flew to the site to see for themselves this ground-breaking discovery.

Jumouk, Lee, and Fiona were watching the last shuttle being loaded. It had been a hard slog, but all of the people that had been sheltering inside Earth Central were now safely on transports heading for Western Australia, and the final staff members including themselves were now to return to Heathrow.

As they took their seats on the shuttle, each had their own thoughts. Fiona was just very relieved that the evacuation had gone so well. Lee for his part was now planning the final stages of the distraction. The fact that the cruisers had moved was a good sign – upheaval was always good. Jumouk was thinking about the Mars base and wondering how Konoco and Marie were getting on.

When they arrived at the undersea base, they found Thourus getting ready to move the station and flood Earth Central along with the three tunnels leading to and from it.

Jumouk thanked Thourus for his help in the evacuation, and the shuttle set off back to the ESG base at Heathrow.

Thourus gave the word and Earth Central was no more, flooded out by the mighty Atlantic Ocean.

The undersea base was back on its way to its original position; the three huge transports were at rest off Western Australia; and Thourus was on his way back to Sub Sea One.

JOHN P. GLEDHILL

\*  \*  \*

Nalater couldn't quite figure out what was in the lift shafts, but it was resisting every attempt to drill or dig through it.

It was Tannacha's intervention that saved the day. He ordered both cruisers to use fine pulse beams to bore through the ground above the base. It was long and laborious but eventually did the trick, providing two rough tunnels which came out on level two. Tannacha and Nalater used a type of hovering jet-ski to make the mile-long journey to level two, which was a lot quicker and more comfortable than walking.

When Tannacha and Nalater eventually came out of the tunnel on level two, all became apparent. A map of the base revealed how so many people could disappear at once. Nalater couldn't help but marvel at the ingenuity of it all. Tannacha had a quite different opinion, and also wanted to know where everyone had gone.

All of a sudden there was a terrific rumbling sound and a noticeable increase in air pressure, so great that it knocked the both of them off their feet. As they picked themselves up, the rumbling noise began to turn into more of a thundering sound, with immense air pressure variations. Neither knew quite what was happening, but it was now obvious to both that this was not a healthy place to be.

They had just mounted their jet-skis when the first of thousands of tons of water burst out of the tunnel connected to level two. The race was now on. Bailey's Crossing was only just above sea level, and the tunnels the Annunaki cruisers had just bored would very shortly be filled with part of the Atlantic Ocean.

Each took a separate tunnel with the pounding water rushing behind them as they struggled to keep ahead, and were very much in danger of being over-run as the pressure drove the water up the constricted orifices. They arrived on the surface at more or less the same time, shooting out of the watery tubes like champagne corks out a bottle.

The sight would have been hilarious if the Annunaki had a sense of humour.

# 32

Jumouk was in constant contact with Grant Ashdown at the forsaken Earth Central Base. Grant was now in charge of the twenty-four ESG assault craft still under the protection of the mag shield. He had been watching the unfolding events at the old base and even cracked a smile at the farcical scene played out by Tannacha and Nalater.

Grant was also well aware that the protection provided by the mag shield would be compromised at any second due to the flooding of Earth Central, and the demise of the generators therein.

Grant bit the bullet and told Jumouk to give him three minutes and then have the transports go for Mars.

Tannacha and Nalater were shaking themselves down after their episode in the tunnels, when all hell broke loose. Suddenly ESG assault vessels were everywhere; the Annunaki warriors on the ground along with the unfortunate Annunaki assault ships that had landed to view the base, were being destroyed by pulse fire, and the assault vessels that were in the air weren't faring much better.

Tannacha and Nalater both broke for cover, the nearest shelter being a pile of rubble just across the road from them. As they dug into the rubble to provide some form of protection, Nalater spotted an empty Annunaki assault craft just two hundred feet away from their refuge.

Nalater gestured to Tannacha in the direction of the assault craft and Tannacha nodded in approval, knowing what Nalater had in mind.

Grant was having a field day. It was like shooting ducks in a barrel. A state of confusion reigned within the Annunaki ranks, yet again surprise had played a major role in his success up till now.

On board the *Serpitus* battle cruiser the commander Gargius had already given the order to engage the ESG assault ships, and both cruisers were now moving in with all weapons' banks blazing.

Tannacha and Nalater had seized their chance and bolted for the empty Annunaki assault vessel, as the two cruisers diverted the attention of Grant and his fellow pilots. Around ten minutes had passed, and on the other side of the world three large transports had broken water unnoticed in the confusion, and were safely halfway to Mars.

Grant ordered his squadron to break and head for Sub Sea One. The job was done.

The Annunaki assault vessel that Tannacha and Nalater had just boarded fired its engines and under the control of Nalater bolted directly upwards heading for the safe haven of the *Nephilimis*, cutting through the retreating ESG ships on the way without a single shot being fired.

When the assault craft had landed back on the *Nephilimis*, they both headed back towards the bridge, but just before they got there Tannacha stopped short at his quarters which were on the way, and without a word of explanation left Nalater to carry on alone to the bridge. Nalater couldn't understand Tannacha's strange behaviour. He seemed to spend more time in his quarters these days than anywhere else, the trip down to Earth Central to view it for himself being nowadays a rare event.

Still, there was work to be done, Nalater gave the order to re-group at the base within Dulles International Airport.

Back at the ESG Heathrow base Jumouk and Lee were going over what had just happened, and exactly where that left them, when all of a sudden Finney burst in. He had just been given the worst possible news.

The main Russian base, miles below the streets of Reutov, not too far from Moscow and with more or less the same lay-out as Earth Central, had been discovered by an Annunaki patrol. Even as they were speaking, it had come under heavy attack. The two Annunaki battle cruisers had diverted and were already there, the outer defences and weapons pods had been obliterated and Annunaki warriors were down to the second level, although they hadn't as yet taken the control room.

Lee wrung his hands in despair.

'Is there anything we can do?'

Jumouk shook his head slowly.

'No, my friend, if they have penetrated the base that far I'm afraid they are lost. We must think of the bigger picture.'

'We surely just can't leave them to die. What about dispatching our battle cruisers?'

'Sorry, Lee, this time their fate is sealed. Without losing everything, there is absolutely nothing we can do.'

Lee sank back down and put his head in his hands. This was really the first time the enormity of Earth's dilemma had really sunk in.

Sure the moon base and the *Katchinas* were a loss, but they were a military loss and somehow that was different.

This time there were civilian losses and he was well aware the Annunaki would not be taking prisoners.

The Annunaki assault on the Russian base was savage and involved a lot of hand-to-hand combat, with the ESG putting up a determined defence, but fighting a losing battle the whole time. The Androids were the only match for the Annunaki warriors, in most cases holding out remarkably well against them, but overwhelming numbers were now taking their toll. The control room and level two held out for six hours before the Annunaki finally suppressed all resistance.

Tannacha had again personally come down to study the lay-out and control room of the base in detail. Naturally, anything of importance had been destroyed and the computers' hard drives fried, so that nothing was left to help the Annunaki in any way.

The third level had now also been taken, and Annunaki warriors were inside the fourth level, but experiencing no opposition from the human population sheltering there.

Tannacha wandered around the base at his leisure. Very clever, he thought to himself, the Dropas have a lot to answer for. His train of thought was interrupted by one of his commanders wanting to know what to do with the humans.

This was a quandary for him. He had expected, and prepared for, some kind of intervention from the ESG forces at Heathrow, and to his surprise nothing had been forthcoming. Tannacha waved the commander away while he gave thought to his dilemma, and what to do for the best.

He knew that he now had a distinct advantage over the ESG. All he had to do was to find where the underground bases had been hidden and that would be an end to this troublesome species.

# 33

Konoco and Marie were watching the approaching three transports. No attempt had been made by the Annunaki to intercept them, Marie assumed their departure had not been noticed by the Annunaki and that whatever distraction Lee had organised had worked.

They had no idea at all of the events that had been unfolding on Earth. Even the people on the transports were oblivious to the disaster in Russia, thanks to the radio silence. Marie had instructed the Androids on the Mars base via the computer to escort the arriving guests to appropriate quarters and settle them in.

There seemed to be a chain of command within the Android society. Some appeared to be taking command and issuing orders to others. One Android approached Marie and started to ask relevant questions as to the placement of the refugees, something which Marie was not expecting at all. It was a coherent conversation and the Android was obviously capable of thinking for itself.

This was quite different from Android behaviour on Earth, even Thourus, who was the most advanced Android on Earth. He still relied on logic and orders, while the Androids here appeared to have their own opinions and ideas.

Marie asked the Android if it had a name. It answered 'yes', it was called Pausanias.

The name, for some reason, seemed familiar to Marie but she couldn't quite put her finger on it. Pausanias seemed to have everything under control, making requests to the computer for instructions to be passed on, even naming individual Androids with specific instructions. Marie soon excused herself. She could now quite understand why the Dropas were so undecided about the Androids. She still had a nagging doubt in the back of her head, however. That name, where had she heard it before?

Events were starting to overtake her. The three transports were getting closer now. Konoco was expanding the force field around the landing area. He didn't know how it worked, but with the computers' help he had found out how to make enough room for all three transports to land at once. Given the sheer size of the transports, this was an achievement in itself.

The Mars base was a hive of activity and the transports hadn't even landed yet.

Marie made her way to the top of the lift shafts ready to help greet the people from the transports. Around about two hundred of the Mars-based Androids were waiting to usher people in the right direction when the huge transports landed. They would then be taken to the appropriate lifts and shown to their new quarters, given a hot meal and settled in. The computer would then give a virtual guided tour of the base and its facilities on huge three-dimensional viewing stands, two of which were placed in each dormitory.

This had all been arranged by Pausanias, and his higher-ranking Androids.

As the three transports set down within the force field, Konoco joined Marie in the assembly area in front of the lift shafts.

'It's going well, Marie, don't you think?'
'Thanks to Pausanias, yes,' Marie replied.
'Who?' queried Konoco.
'Pausanias – you know, the Android leader.'
'He has a name?'
'Of course he has a name. Didn't you know?'
'We never asked. As far as we knew they used numbers for identification.'
'For ten years you've just used numbers to identify them?'

At that moment Pausanias joined them.

'Pausanias, why didn't you tell Konoco that you had a name?'

'There was no need. The Dropas were quite happily identifying us with numbers. It seemed to work well for them.'

Marie was astounded. Even back on Earth Thourus had a name, although on reflection, not that many Androids did have names, just the higher-ranking ones.

Again events were starting to overtake her. The first of the new inhabitants were beginning to arrive, Marie smiled and went forward to greet them. After all it had been a hectic three days for everyone.

It was going to be a long haul getting everybody settled in and comfortable, although the facilities were second to none, and a huge improvement on Earth Central.

After the first couple of hours, once she had satisfied herself that everything was going smoothly, Marie returned to the control room with Konoco. The first thing they noticed there was that a whole new array of instrumentation had come online.

Marie asked Konoco tentatively if he knew what they were for. Konoco confirmed Marie's suspicions that he didn't have a clue; they had never been online before, in fact he hadn't even known of their existence.

Marie was just about to ask Pausanias to join them when he appeared at the control panel and started confidently adjusting the screens. Marie joined him. For some reason Pausanias seemed to like Marie and Marie requited the feeling.

'What do these controls do, Pausanias?'

Marie smiled gently as she put the question, not wanting to appear dim-witted.

'These control the internal habitat. I'm adjusting them to suit the arrival of our new guests – oxygen levels, humidity, temperature and the like – we want our new guests to be comfortable, now don't we?'

Marie was beginning to feel at her ease with the easygoing and, at times, almost humorous Pausanias. The Dropas were right she thought, there was a lot more than nuts and bolts to these Androids.

Konoco was at a different control station, one which looked much more complex. He had a puzzled look on his face.

'Pausanias, could you look at this for me?'

Konoco had just rephrased the question, 'What's this?'

That was neat, thought Marie.

Pausanias joined Konoco at the control station. He adjusted a few interactive sliders, rotated his hand above his head and both he and Konoco were suddenly enveloped by a three-dimensional plan of the universe. Konoco was obviously flabbergasted. The Dropas had a wide range of technology but nothing on this scale.

Pausanias selected our galaxy and touched it with his finger. That section expanded until it showed just our home planets and space surrounding them. He then selected Mars and the visual display expanded to show Mars and its surrounding space.

The red planet looked impressive, and Pausanias stood spinning it slowly with his finger till he reached the point he wanted. He then touched that point on the surface of Mars and again it expanded and zoomed right in to the three transports sitting there, with a clarity that would have been hard to believe, unless you had seen it with your own eyes. Marie had now joined them at the control station again, amazed at the sight before her. Konoco was the first to speak.

'Is it just a map, or can you track movement?'

His remark was not meant to be dismissive. He was in fact almost in shock. For ten years the Dropas scientists had been able to access only the most basic elements of the Mars base. Now within minutes it seemed as if a Pandora's box was opening, but someone else was in charge of this hive of technology.

'There are many things we will need to discuss, Konoco. The first is this. It is indeed more than a map, my friend. It is a complete defence structure for the security of the Mars undertaking.'

Pausanias's whole persona had now changed from subservience to become almost authoritarian. Marie and Konoco exchanged glances. Marie felt it would probably be better if she took over the conversation. After all, she felt she had now built up an understanding with Pausanias.

'Do you have weapons here, Pausanias? I mean some kind of pulse weapons for defence?'

Pausanias smiled, a wide smile as if he had anticipated the question and where it would come from. Marie immediately went on the defensive.

'I don't mean to be intrusive, but you have to admit this is all new to us.'

Any thoughts Marie and Konoco had that Pausanias could just be an Android were now quickly dismissed. Then suddenly it came to Marie, the answer to that question lingering at the back of her mind: like a bolt out of the blue, you don't know why, it just suddenly comes back to you.

'Pausanias, you're named after the ancient Greek writer. He was first century or, no ... second century, he wrote books, geography, ancient geography.'

Pausanias looked impressed. Konoco hadn't picked up on the relevance of this.

'The name is over seventeen hundred years old, an ancient name like John and Mary. They survived the test of time thanks to the Bible, but also mainly ease of use. Names like Pausanias never survived past the first or second century.'

Marie paused for thought.

'You built this base, didn't you?'

Pausanias laughed out loud.

'Not by myself.'

Marie and Konoco exchanged glances again.

'You're sentient, aren't you?

'We'll cover that later if you don't mind. First I must show you this.'

Marie noticed he hadn't given an answer to the main question.

He was spinning the representation of Mars again, where little red areas were appearing on the surface of Mars. He zoomed in on one of the areas and a menu appeared. Carefully selecting differing options from the menu, he satisfied himself that the configuration he wanted was set, then pressed one more digit and the red spots turned green.

'What just happened?'

Marie was now becoming concerned about to how she was going to explain all this to Lee and Jumouk.

'That's the defences around Mars activated now. We will be safe from any Annunaki attack or interference.'

Pausanias closed down the representation and headed towards one of the many annexes scattered around the perimeter of the control room. Marie and Konoco followed him.

# 34

Lee was still reeling from the loss of the Russian base. Jumouk seemed to be handling it better, even though there were probable many Dropas losses as well as human. There hadn't been any confirmation of the fate of the occupants of the Russian base, but Lee was in no doubt what he thought would have happened. The Annunaki had no compassion whatsoever, so the chance of anyone surviving would have been extremely slim.

However, it wasn't all bad news. The three transports that had left Earth were now assumed to have landed and decamped safely on Mars under the direction of Konoco and Marie.

Finney had been called out of the room a few moments ago by one of his commanders. He reappeared with two bedraggled figures in tow, one human and one Dropas. Apparently survivors of the ill-fated Russian base, they carried with them an ultimatum from Nalater. The total surrender of all ESG and Android forces within the next twenty-four hours, or the slaughter of the civilian population held within the Russian base. He had even been kind enough to provide the exact numbers of what were now hostages.

This was turning into a nightmare for Lee. If the Annunaki had already killed everyone, there truly would have been nothing he could have done, but this demand changed things in ways for the time being he could only imagine.

Jumouk led Lee into the corner of the room away from prying ears. Again it was Jumouk who came to Lee's rescue.

'You know, Lee, this doesn't really change anything. We can't sacrifice the rest of the world for one base.'

'I know, but we must be able to do something?'

Jumouk shook his head.

'The Annunaki know we won't agree to this. It's just their way of twisting the knife. They're trying to unnerve us.'

Lee turned to Finney and asked him to take the two survivors and get them cleaned up and fed. He was still running things over in his mind in a futile attempt to come up with a plan. In the back of his mind though he knew Jumouk was right.

Fiona had been struggling to hold back her tears. This was all too close to home for her. After all, if it hadn't been for Jumouk, Lee and the daring evacuation at Earth Central, it would have been her fate too.

Lee was watching the Annunaki forces at Reutov, when without warning the battle cruisers and assault craft started moving out.

'Jumouk, come see this.'

'Where are they going?'

Lee was genuinely stumped.

'I don't know, and why are they leaving?'

They were both thinking the same thing. This has to be a trap.

'They look like they're heading back to Dulles, but why? Surely they don't think we would fall for such an obvious trap?'

Jumouk made a quick decision.

'Lee, contact the transports and get them to go directly to Reutov. Fiona, contact Grant at Sub Sea One, and tell him to mobilise Thourus and all of his TAG assault craft, then meet us at Reutov.'

Lee looked at Jumouk with a blank expression.

'They don't expect us to fall for it, that's exactly why we're doing it. Now get the cruisers ready to go.'

Lee sped off in the direction of the two ESG cruisers, leaving Jumouk to give Fiona and Finney their standing orders.

Strangely enough, this wasn't an Annunaki trap. A large group of human resistance fighters had attacked Dulles and, although they were using conventional weapons, they were doing a significant amount of damage.

Tannacha couldn't allow this to happen and had ordered his cruisers and available assault craft back to Dulles. Nalater had wanted to leave one of the cruisers at Reutov but Tannacha overruled this, telling him that the cruisers had to stay together.

Back at Dulles the fighting was mainly hand to hand and extremely ferocious. Around five thousand resistance fighters had captured half of Dulles International Airport.

These resistance fighters had formed when Earth Central had first been put under threat. They had organised within Earth Central, and then been given permission to slip out over a period of time and meet up at Manassas.

They were mainly ex-US forces – marines, air force, army, navy and the like – but there were other disciplines as well. They were organised and well armed with conventional weapons and their commitment was unquestionable.

The leader's name was Mark Howden. He had been a

major in the marines, before being discharged on medical grounds. When the ESG was first formed, Mark had applied, but after training as an assault craft pilot, he had been turned down again on medical grounds. Now, however, he was showing his true worth.

The set-up and organisation of the resistance was his idea and he had done an excellent job bringing together a disciplined and motivated force of around ten thousand resistance fighters in a very short space of time.

This was their first action against the Annunaki and up till now it was all going well. It had been totally unforeseen by Tannacha or Nalater, and surprise had yet again been shown to be the human's best friend.

Tannacha had even considered this was an ESG trap of some sort, which was one of his main reasons for not splitting his cruisers up. For some reason he desperately wanted to defend his base at Dulles. Nalater had put this initially down to personal pride but now he wasn't so sure, Tannacha had seemed to lose all interest in Reutov and the hostages there. His only interest was now the rooting out of the resistance from his precious Dulles.

Mark saw the approaching Annunaki battle cruisers and assault craft and passed the order to thin out back around the perimeter of the airport. This was an effort to make air attack more difficult for the Annunaki.

He knew that now they would not be able to take the airport but at the very least they had given the Annunaki a bloody nose.

Just as the Annunaki cruisers took up position above the airport and the assault vessels stated to strafe the resistance positions a spectacular sight appeared from the north, Mark couldn't believe his eyes.

BATTLE FOR THE EARTH

\* \* \*

Unknown to Mark but common knowledge to air force personnel, armed and prepped F-22-Raptors, about forty of them, had been hidden away just north of a town called Leesburg, around forty-five miles from Dulles. The air force personnel and pilots had split from the main resistance group and headed to Leesburg to retrieve the aircraft and pull off a surprise attack of their own.

Mark watched as the forty F-22-Raptors screamed into the airspace, rockets loosed and cannons blazing.

Technically the Raptors weren't much of a match for the Annunaki assault vessels, but they were certainly taking their toll of the unsuspecting Annunaki pilots. Dog fights had broken out everywhere, and Mark saw this as a perfect chance to withdraw his troops back into the suburbs and then onto their temporary base. He gave the order and the resistance melted into suburbia.

The Raptors kept the Annunaki busy for just over an hour and, although all the aircraft were eventually lost, most of the pilots had bailed out safely and were heading back to the resistance headquarters with the knowledge that four fewer Annunaki assault ships were in the skies.

Back at resistance headquarters in Manassas, Mark was reviewing with his officers what had been achieved. They had certainly made the Annunaki sit up and take notice, then the sight of the Raptors had been a huge boost for morale. Granted that in reality they were now no more than a thorn in the Annunaki side, it still all counted in the fight for survival.

Mark couldn't have been more wrong. He had just

helped to save the lives of seven hundred and fifty thousand people.

The ESG forces had arrived at Reutov. There had only been light resistance from the Annunaki warriors who had been left to guard the base. Once they had been suppressed, the transports had landed and were now filling up quickly. Everyone was well aware that time was critical and the Annunaki cruisers would only be distracted for so long.

Lee found himself inside the Russian base and was amazed how much it looked like Earth Central. Fortunately with five huge turbo-lifts and several smaller lifts the evacuation of the base was going well.

As he walked around inside the base the damage that the Annunaki had caused was plain to see. Destruction was everywhere. Still, six hours ago he had never thought he would have been here and a rescue would be underway. He still had no idea why the Annunaki had all but abandoned the base, especially as it now didn't appear to be a trap.

Jumouk was on board the *Iron Duke* glued to the proximity scanners. He was convinced the Annunaki would spring their trap at any time, but there was nothing. He had witnessed all the activity at Dulles but couldn't make head or tail of it. They just seemed to be chasing each other around.

Of course the Raptors didn't show on the proximity detectors as ESG. They didn't have the technology fitted to them, hence the confusion on Jumouk's part.

Jumouk was just now counting down every second until the transports were full. He had already made the decision to abandon Heathrow and pull most of the ESG resources up to Mars.

# BATTLE FOR THE EARTH

\* \* \*

Tannacha seemed pleased with himself. The return to Dulles was a double-edged sword. He had just easily downed forty aircraft and quelled an attack at his Dulles base. He was also now waiting to see where the ESG would take the survivors from Reutov. This would be his next point of attack where he could smash the ESG and the humans once and for all.

Finally all the transports were full and the Russian base at Reutov was empty. Jumouk gave the order for the three transports and the battle cruiser *Victory* commanded by Lee to head to the Mars base. Meanwhile the TAG craft returned to Sub Sea One via differing circuitous routes to keep the location of the base secret.

Jumouk gathered all the ESG troopers, Androids and ESG assault craft and set off for Heathrow with the battle cruiser *Iron Duke*. He still didn't know why Tannacha hadn't attacked them at the Russian base, but nevertheless counted his blessings that the civilians had been rescued safely.

As the *Iron Duke* came to rest over Heathrow, Fiona and Finney were watching Jumouk's shuttle landing. Both were keen to hear how Russia had gone. They still couldn't believe there had been a stay of execution on the Russian base, leaving enough time to mount a rescue attempt.

Jumouk greeted them, and they retired to the small room that was being used as a land-based headquarters. If Jumouk had been pleased with the rescue he wasn't showing it now. Jumouk brought Fiona and Finney up to speed with what had happened in Russia. Finney then asked the inevitable question.

'Why didn't the Annunaki attack you in Russia or at the very least have a go at us here at Heathrow?'

Jumouk just shook his head.

'I don't have an answer for you, Finney. I expected an attack but it never came. I can only assume the Annunaki supreme commander had his reasons, which unfortunately will probably, before long, become blatantly clear.'

Fiona chipped in.

'At least we got everyone out safely. Where do we go from here?'

'I'm glad you asked that, Fiona. In a word, Mars. We move everything apart from the undersea bases and consolidate at the base on Mars.'

Finney looked increasingly uncomfortable with this; he had never been in space before, let alone on a distant planet.

For her part, Fiona seemed delighted with the prospect of a space adventure and meeting up again with all the people she had known at Earth Central.

# 35

On board the *Victory*, Lee was watching Earth shrink into the vastness of space. He so enjoyed flying. It was one of the great perks of saving humanity, a task which he now considered his main purpose.

Grant had joined the *Victory* after the Russian operation. He was full of excited anticipation about arriving at the Mars base, since he had heard so much speculation about it. Looking out into vastness of space was mesmerising and electrifying at the same time. It was so quiet and Mars looked so far away.

Lee had left the rear observation window and joined Grant, interrupting his moment of quiet reflection, Lee apologised and asked Grant how he was enjoying the flight. The excitement of being on one of these huge battle cruisers never seemed to wear off. It was just awe-inspiring, and the only thing that seemed to spoil it was when you had to get down to the job in hand.

Grant smiled at Lee and said:

'Brilliant! Thanks, Lee. Is there anything you need me to do just now?'

'No thanks, Grant, You just enjoy the flight for the time being.'

Lee moved over to one of the proximity detectors.

'I wonder what they're up to.'

Grant joined him; there was very little movement on Earth especially at Dulles.

'More to the point, Lee, what's so important at Dulles? As any great commander will tell you, knowing what your enemy knows can win wars.'

Lee mulled this over. Grant was right. It would have to be something extremely important for the Annunaki to have virtually abandoned the advantage they had at Reutov. Grant nearly hit the nail on the head, when half jokingly he quipped:

'Maybe they just wanted to see what we'd do?'

Lee reflected on this. It wasn't quite as funny as it seemed.

'Of course! They wanted to see where we took the survivors! They knew we would take advantage and evacuate the base. They left us alone to see where we took the survivors. That would lead them to at least our next base's location.'

'Hadn't we better warn Jumouk and Konoco?'

Lee thought about this.

'No, the damage is done now, and besides I don't think the Annunaki will react straightaway. When Jumouk gets to the Mars base we can discuss it then. There is a silver lining. With luck they will stop looking for any more bases on Earth. After all, they will know if they are going to take on our base on Mars they're going to need all their resources for that.'

'True, I suppose,' said Grant. 'They've only two battle cruisers left. That alone puts them in a difficult position.'

The front observation window was now filling up with the trade-mark red surface of Mars. The battle cruiser was perceptibly slowing down and positioning itself above the surface of the red planet.

Lee could see the transports start to position themselves, ready to land within the force field surrounding the entrance to the Mars base.

He was also keen to see the Mars base. It had seemed to have become a legend, overnight – some kind of mystical retreat from the oncoming Annunaki menace.

As Lee and Grant landed their shuttle next to the transports, Lee was visible at the controls, much to Grant's disappointment.

The figure of Marie was seen approaching them. She would never have missed this opportunity to impress Lee, even though Konoco had offered to meet them himself. Marie had insisted that it would probably be better if she met them, leaving Konoco free to oversee the disembarking of the transports. After all, Konoco was fluent in Russian.

Lee hugged Marie and then introduced Grant. As the three of them made their way to the entrance of the Mars base, Grant couldn't help but be impressed. The atmosphere was pleasant if perhaps slightly warm, but the air was fresh and clean. It was turning into everything he had been promised and they weren't even inside yet.

The trip down in the turbo-lift was full of expectation for both Lee and Grant. As they emerged into the massive corridor system, it was clear to both of them this was a totally different experience from the bases on Earth. In fact, without wanting to criticise the Dropas in any way, the bases on Earth now seemed to them like cave dwellings by comparison.

Marie led them straight to the main control room. When they entered the massive room, the expression on Grant's face said it all. There was activity everywhere, mainly involving the Mars Androids. It was like watching a well-choreographed ballet.

Marie suggested they retire to one of the annexes and get some refreshment.

Marie asked what they would like, and as it had been a long week with very little sleep, they both opted for coffee. Marie instructed the computer, and within a minute an Android appeared. Neither Lee nor Grant had had a proper look at an Android, they were so overwhelmed by the state-of-the art base. Now they could see for themselves how life-like the Androids were.

'Wow!' exclaimed Grant.

Lee looked slightly more thoughtful. He thought to himself: obviously not as well programmed as our Androids on Earth. It's not even carrying a tray and certainly no coffee.

The Android stopped by the table and spoke.

'Good afternoon, Miss Baker. My name is Alexa. The computer didn't specify what type of coffee you required so I took it upon myself to ask personally.'

She began to run through a list of types and specialities of coffee, but Marie interrupted before she could finish.

'Just three lattés please, Alexa.'

Marie looked across to Lee and Grant and they both nodded. Lee couldn't believe what he was seeing. These can't be Androids, can they, he thought? They must be sentient.

Grant looked at Marie and asked the question that was on Lee's mind.

'Are they for real?'

Marie struggled to reply.

'Well ... I believe the Dropas have been studying them

for around ten years, but they have only just recently started to behave like this. So at least till we know more about them, we have to treat them as sentient beings. Does that answer your question, Grant?'

'Well, if that's all you've got, I guess it'll have to, for now anyway,' Grant muttered.

'Please bear in mind there is so much we don't know about this whole base. More or less everything about it is fantastic, and it's way above the Dropas level of technology.'

Again Grant came in with the obvious question.

'Who built it, then?'

'Hmm, we think it was the Androids. Wait a minute. Alexa ... that's a female name. All the Androids seem to have Greek or ancient Greek names, but that's the first time I've noticed a female name.'

Lee and Grant looked at each other. Female Androids or whatever? The thought crossed both their minds at the same time but both quickly dismissed it.

Marie looked out across the control room and saw Pausanias approaching them. This should be interesting, she thought to herself. She stood up and introduced Pausanias to Lee and Grant as politely as she could, then sat back down.

Pausanias pulled up a chair and sat down. Before Lee or Grant could say anything, Pausanias spoke.

'Gentlemen, I know you must have a lot of questions for me, but you've had a hard time on Earth, and I would suggest I have one of my colleagues show you to your quarters so you can refresh yourselves and catch up on a bit of sleep. The base is quite safe and nobody will disturb you, then once you've had a good rest, and feel refreshed I promise to answer all your questions.'

Lee and Grant couldn't help feeling they had just been dismissed by a superior, but they also knew what Pausanias had said made perfect sense. Out of nowhere a colleague of Pausanias appeared and ushered Lee and Grant to their quarters.

The quarters issued to them were by any standard luxurious, and compared to what they had been used to, palatial. After a shower to freshen up, and some fruit from a complimentary bowl, both weary men succumbed to slumber on the comfortable divans provided.

# 36

Heathrow was being wound up and was alive with activity. The *Iron Duke* was slowly filling up with ESG troopers, Androids, all kinds of assault vessels, both large and small, medium-sized and small troop transports – anything at Heathrow that was worth taking was on its way to Mars.

Jumouk had climbed up to the bridge of the *Iron Duke*, leaving Fiona and Finney to oversee the winding-up operation on the ground. This was more up Fiona's street than Finney cared to admit.

Fiona was a wiz at logistics, and an expert in organisation, and thanks directly to her efforts everything was going extremely well. Finney, on the other hand, would have been the first to admit that loading boxes definitely wasn't his thing. Boredom had soon set in. This was giving him far too much time to think – mainly about travelling through space and landing on other planets. As time went on, thinking about it didn't make it any better; if anything it made it worse.

He was now at the stage of trying to think up plausible excuses for him to stay on Earth. After all, he was a battalion commander in the ESG land forces. Within his own mind he stressed the last part of the title, *land forces*, not sea forces not air forces and certainly not space forces. No, he was in the right, even his title said so.

All this of course had nothing to do with the fact that he was petrified of flying.

To pass the time away while he avoided anything to do with the job Fiona had taken on, and, locked in his own thoughts, Finney had been idly scrolling through radio wave bands on the communication equipment. Owing to radio silence restrictions the chances of coming across anything would be slim to non-existent – it was just really an exercise in wasting time.

All of a sudden the air waves sparked into life, albeit faintly. Voices could be heard.

The radio chatter was sporadic and, although it sounded as it came from a military source, it didn't sound like any regiment Finney had ever heard of. He was mesmerised. He didn't have a clue how long he had been listening when Fiona rudely interrupted him.

'Finney, are you going to help at all?'

Finney simply waved his hand at her to be quiet. She obeyed and sat down next to him, Finney looked up at her.

'There's some kind of resistance movement out there. I can hear them.'

'How do you mean, "resistance"?'

'British resistance. OK by the sounds of it not very well organised, but all the same, resistance.'

'Where did they come from, and who are they?'

Her attention now focused on Finney and what he was doing.

'Don't know, I just stumbled across their transmission. They appear to be looking for something or someone.'

Fiona thought for a moment.

'Can you talk to them, and find out where they are?'

'Don't know if that would be a good idea or not. Bear in mind we don't know who they are.'

'Yes I know, but they're obviously not Annunaki, are they? So that has to make them our friends, doesn't it?'

'You mean, the enemy of my enemy is my friend, don't you?'

'Just talk to them, Finney.'

'This is Clarence Finnegan, battalion commander of the ESG land forces. Please respond.'

Silence.

'Repeat, This is Clarence Finnegan, battalion commander of the ESG land forces. Please respond.'

There was a small crackle on the radio.

'Who?' a voice said.

'This is Clarence Finnegan, battalion commander of the ESG land forces. Who am I speaking with?'

Silence.

'I say again, to whom am I speaking?'

Finney threw a glance at Fiona and shrugged his shoulders.

The radio crackled back into life.

'This is the British resistance against the Annunaki oppression on Earth.'

Finney looked at Fiona again. This time she shrugged.

'What's your name?'

'Stevie, I mean Steven Graham, sir.'

'Steven, how many do you number in total?'

'About three thousand in all, sir, give or take.'

'Who's in charge there, Steven?'

'It's a man called Peter Hadley. He runs everything. I think he's ex-army or something. Anyway, he seems to know what he's doing.'

'Where are you just now?

'We're in a place called Beaconsfield – Woodside Road, I think – anyway, not that far from London.'

Finney and Fiona immediately consulted the map of the UK and pinpointed Beaconsfield.

'What are you doing there?'

'We're tracking an Annunaki patrol.'

Fiona looked at Finney.

'You know where they are, don't you?'

Finney knew very well. There was another base underneath Forty Green just a few miles north-west of that position.

'Is your boss about, son?'

Finney's tone had become more authoritative and urgent.

'No, sir, I'm sorry he's with the guys tracking the Annunaki. I'm doing my best to keep up, but with all this equipment it's not easy.'

'You need to listen to me, Steven. Leave the equipment where it is and go and catch up with your boss. Tell him you've talked to me and to expect reinforcements in the next five minutes. How many Annunaki are you tracking?'

Already Finney was making gestures to Fiona and she knew this time exactly what he meant. She left to organise troops and shuttles.

'I think there's about thirty of them.'

'Good, now go find your boss, son.'

Finney opened a line to the bridge on the *Iron Duke* and brought Jumouk up to speed with what had just happened and what he was planning.

Fiona was ready when Finney came out. Three shuttles each with fifty ESG troopers on board were waiting for him. As he climbed into the first shuttle Fiona wished him luck.

The three shuttles took off with a nervous Finney in the lead. The route to Beaconsfield was already planned so as not to be noticed, and the shuttles flew below roof height, north towards the railway passing through Denham Green. When the shuttles reached Denham Green they turned west along the railway tracks towards the M25, travelling only a few feet above the tracks. Crossing over the M25, they headed on towards Gerrards Cross, passing under the road bridge there. The next stop was Beaconsfield.

After passing under the road bridge at Beaconsfield Station, they left the railway tracks at Woodside Close and landed under the cover of thick and extensive woodland there. Disembarking his ESG troopers, Finney sent out scouts into Woodside Road to find Steven and his group of resistance fighters.

It wasn't long before one of Finney's scouts found them, sheltering under cover in houses on the intersection of Hogback Wood Road and Eghams Wood Road, a small suburban area right on the outskirts of Beaconsfield. It was flanked by a thickly wooded area, and was a stone's throw from one of the largest underground bases in the UK.

Dispersing his ESG forces into the woodland that flanked the houses, Finney took up a position to observe the thirty or so Annunaki warriors. As he watched, he couldn't help smiling. The Annunaki warriors had discovered a house with a rectangular swimming pool in its back garden and were indulging in what could only be described as 'horse play'. The irony of this was not lost on Finney. Here was a race of huge, ugly-looking aliens, bent on the destruction of the human race, playing in an outdoor swimming pool.

Finney was soon joined by Peter Hadley the leader of the resistance. Peter was a rugged-looking man with short dark hair and a ragged stubble that couldn't quite pass for a beard. His face was tanned and Finney thought he was probably about thirty-five. The most striking thing about him, however, was his smile, a warm confident smile that would set anyone at ease in an instant. Finney took to him immediately.

After they had finished introducing themselves and spitting out a rough résumé of their military experience, the two men got down to the business of the day: the fastest and quietest way to dispose of the Annunaki warriors. Peter had a force of two hundred resistance fighters with him. Add that to Finney's one hundred and fifty ESG troopers and they had a resource of three hundred and fifty, more than enough to do the job.

The ESG troopers and resistance fighters were now positioned strategically throughout the woods. Now they simply needed the Annunaki warriors to come out and chase them.

These warriors were enjoying cooling themselves in the outdoor pool on a hot day, when suddenly five innocent-looking civilians stumbled out of the woods, and came to a standstill in front of them. The Annunaki and civilians stared at each other for what seemed an eternity, then one of the male civilians let out a scream of terror, turned and fled back into the woods, still screaming like a girl.

The Annunaki officer in charge barked out a single command, roughly translated as 'kill'. The rest of the group of civilians broke up, running for their lives and scattering in different directions, but each still heading back to the wood. All the Annunaki warriors gave chase. After all, this was the best sport they had seen since landing on Earth.

There were around six Annunaki warriors for each fleeing human, and picking them off in small groups like that would be easy for the ESG. Each fleeing human had their own designated kill zone and would lead the

Annunaki warriors into the middle of it, then hit the deck flat. Each kill zone was encircled by thirty ESG troopers who could easily wipe out the Annunaki warriors within the encirclement in a volley of pulse fire.

The plan worked perfectly. Within five minutes all thirty warriors were dead, with no losses to the ESG or resistance. The plan had mostly been Finney's, and after it was over Peter gave him a hearty slap on the back by way of congratulation.

Finney asked Peter if he would come back to Heathrow and meet Fiona and Jumouk. After all, he had a wealth of intelligence regarding Annunaki troop movements in the area, and he was also well briefed about other resistance movements in Britain and around the world. Peter agreed without question, and instructed his lieutenants and men to return to base.

The shuttles followed the same route back as they had taken on the way out. By the time they got back Fiona had joined Jumouk on the bridge of the *Iron Duke*. Disembarking from the shuttles, Peter and Finney headed from the landing bay on the *Iron Duke* towards the bridge, Peter being visibly impressed with the *Iron Duke*.

On the bridge when all the introductions had been made, Jumouk suggested they retire to the conference room for something to eat and drink.

During the pleasant meal and well-earned drinks, the conversation was intensive, covering everything from the day's events to the stylish décor of the *Iron Duke*. After dinner the real talking began.

'So, Peter, why don't you tell us a bit about yourself?'

As usual Jumouk went straight to the point, not aggressively but certainly with a sense of purpose. Finney on the other hand was already coming up with an ingenious plan of his own. He might have just found a way to justify his continued stay on Earth.

Peter began.

'First, I must apologise for starting with a confession. My name isn't Peter Hadley.'

'You're Russian, aren't you?' said Fiona quickly.

'How did you know? I don't have an accent, I was brought up in the English public school system. My mother was English and my father Russian.'

Fiona explained.

'I was a linguist at one point. You use slightly different idioms at times, barely noticeable but still there.'

Peter nodded and continued.

'I was born in Russia and named Sacha Sergov, my father's given name. My mother and I moved to England when I was four, and I went to school here. I moved back to Russia at the age of fifteen when my mother died, and finished my education. When I was thirty I moved back to England, where I took my mother's name. I've been here ever since.'

Jumouk looked bemused.

'What did you do when you left school back in Russia?'

Peter looked evasive at first, then spat it out.

'I went straight into the army.'

This caught Finney's attention.

'Russian army, I presume. What rank were you when you left?'

'Major.'

Finney felt like he had just struck gold.

'What branch of the forces?'

An awkward silence fell over the table. Finney coughed into his hand.

'Special forces.' Peter said briefly.
He looked uncomfortable.
Finney knew he had struck gold.
'Not ...?'
Finney hesitated.
Peter looked him in the eye.
'Spetsnaz.'
Finney's face lit up.
'Wow!'
Fiona looked lost, although she didn't say anything.
Finney explained:
'Russian forces, then special forces, then the elite, of the elite, Spetsnaz, the cream of the cream, old girl. Defiantly give our SAS boys a run for their money.'

Finney was now in real danger of bursting into army officer talk, but Jumouk brought him to a standstill.

'Sacha, your experience could be invaluable to us. We're about to move all our land-based forces off the planet. Only the underground bases and their guards will remain. If you're serious about a land-based resistance movement, I think we can help each other.'

Finney was in a world of his own now, and it wasn't Mars. Now he knew he was staying on Earth.

The conversation between the four of them went on for hours as they exchanged information. When they had finished, Sacha handed Jumouk a piece of paper on which he had written numerous names and contacts. Jumouk had already delayed the move to Mars by a day because the quality of intelligence already being received from Sacha's contacts.

Finney and Jumouk had a long talk and it was decided that Finney should indeed stay on Earth to help organise the resistance into more of a special forces operation.

To do this he would be given all the resources that he needed, including assault ships, shuttles and ESG troopers together with Androids. Finney was delighted with this scenario, as was Sacha. The two of them worked well together and had a lot of respect for each other.

The first thing they were going to have to do was to establish a permanent and secure headquarters. From there they would be able to organise other resistance units both in Britain and worldwide.

The underground in London would be perfect for the job. Big tunnels that could accommodate shuttles and plenty of side areas to set up bases. The added advantage that an early warning system could be set up to warn of Annunaki sneak attacks was just the icing on the cake.

Jumouk thanked Finney for all his help as he left to set up shop with Sacha. Jumouk smiled to himself and reflected on the thought that this would probably not be the last time he would hear of those two.

# 37

Tannacha was in the course of being informed by Nalater that one of the Annunaki patrols close to Heathrow hadn't checked in, when the ESG battle cruiser on the proximity detectors started to move, followed by an assortment of other vessels, escorted by assault vessels.

Tannacha pointed to the scene on the proximity detector and suggested to Nalater that this might be connected with his errant patrol. Nalater nodded in agreement and they both watched as the convoy reached the Earth's upper atmosphere. Nalater was on the point of asking why they weren't chasing the ESG craft, but thought better of it. Tannacha must have his reasons. No point in getting chewed up for no reason: something which had happened too often already for Nalater's liking.

'They're heading for Mars. The other battle cruiser and transports went there as well,' Tannacha growled

As the pair watched the formation travelling through space, they failed to notice the low-level, very faint ground movement of Finney and Sacha.

As the flotilla of ESG craft disappeared behind Mars, Tannacha now knew they were either using Mars or just hiding behind it. They'll keep, he thought. He could now turn back to his pet project, the reason he had rushed back to Dulles when it had come under threat.

Nalater didn't have a clue what Tannacha was up to, but he would have given his right arm to find out. It must be a hell of an important project to warrant all this attention and secrecy, he thought.

The Dulles base was a hive of activity, Nalater wasn't entirely sure about everything that was going on there. His own project was the strengthening of the defences around the base, which was going well. Indeed, the base was now almost impregnable. He didn't know why Tannacha had insisted on such extreme security, but he did surmise that it must be linked to Tannacha's secret project.

Nalater was in the complex of buildings within the Dulles base checking the final adjustments to his new perimeter security when, as if right on cue, the outer perimeter's automated pulse cannons burst into life. Nalater accessed the view screens to see what was going on.

A small party of humans not wearing the usual uniform of the ESG had breached the security of the outer perimeter and triggered the automated cascade of pulse fire which cut them down more or less instantaneously.

Nalater smiled. The results of his endeavours had been excellent. However, it was unusual to see civilians in combat, and he couldn't help feeling he was missing something here. He turned it over in his head for a few moments, then decided he'd better go and take a look.

As he approached the bodies of the humans, he switched off the defence system. The bodies were mutilated but it was clear to see they weren't ESG troopers. They were, however, armed to the teeth. Nalater pondered this for a moment and came to the natural conclusion that they must be some kind of armed civilian resistance. The ESG must be desperate using untrained soldiers, but he convinced himself that this was no threat whatsoever to the security of the Annunaki.

Mark Howden, the resistance leader in the Dulles area, had been observing the destruction of the resistance fighters as they probed the security around Dulles. It was obvious that the security had been stepped up, and was now quite lethal.

He watched Nalater picking over the bodies of the resistance fighters, and wondered who this lone Annunaki was and what he was doing. The thought of capturing the Annunaki did occur to him, but he was now only too well aware of the destructive force of the perimeter defences.

Any such possibility was quickly removed when Nalater returned to the shelter of the inner buildings of the Dulles base, rearming the perimeter defences as he went.

Mark had decided an all-out attack on the base would be suicidal. However, watching the lone Annunaki had given him an idea, a way to harass the Annunaki, in an old World War Two style. He would place two dozen of his best snipers around the outskirts of the base armed with high-powered sniper rifles. These snipers would take out high-value targets of opportunity. This would have to do until a solution to the perimeter defences could be found, he decided.

Nalater had returned to the bridge on board the *Serpitus*. Apart from strengthening the base at Dulles, the Annunaki forces seemed to be doing nothing and Nalater was getting restless. It was almost as if Tannacha was waiting for something to happen, and it wasn't to be long before Nalater found out what.

Mark's snipers were having limited success, taking pot

shots at whatever were thought to be high-ranking Annunaki warriors.

The trouble was they were so difficult to kill, A shot to the body at times would have virtually no effect against the tough Annunaki hide. Even a head shot wasn't guaranteed a kill. All the same it was harassment, which was better than no action at all.

Tannacha had decided at last to let Nalater into one of his secrets.

The pair entered a building right in the centre of the Dulles complex and, as they descended a flight of dark dingy stairs towards large double doors, Nalater thought to himself: this place stinks. For an Annunaki to notice a smell, it would have to be really bad.

Tannacha threw the double doors wide open, revealing a huge, well-lit medical lab; they entered and he closed the doors behind them. Nalater noticed the look on Tannacha's face: it almost shone with pride. He was obviously delighted with himself.

As Nalater scanned the room looking for some clue as to what was going on, Tannacha pointed him in the direction of a piece of medical equipment, shaped like a large coffin. It stood on its end, and was metallic in colour, probably an alloy. It stood around twelve feet in height and was at its widest point about five feet. There were all manner of pipes and wires protruding from it, along with a complete digital console attached to the wall next to it.

Nalater couldn't deny that he was intrigued by Tannacha's project so far. It looked very interesting.

Tannacha flicked a switch at the side of the coffin-shaped object and the front opened slowly outwards revealing what could only be described as a very large human shape which filled the entire space inside the coffin and was dressed in a silver alloy suit.

The face of the being was covered by an expressionless mask in the rough shape of a face and in the same material as the suit. As Nalater studied the suit more closely he could see it was completely covered by a series of very fine black wires almost like hairs.

Tanacha had already moved to a larger room and waved Nalater over.

This room looked more like a production complex. There was a series of shiny tables, about ten in all. They were arranged in what looked like a production line. Each table had a body on it, apparently at a different stage of the production process.

Nalater approached the first of the tables, which had a body resting on it. It was almost recognisable as human. One of Tannacha's scientists was leaning over the head of the obviously sedated human, and introducing what looked like a very small silver scorpion into its ear.

Nalater could now see why Tannacha was so keen to get back to this base when it came under attack. He still didn't know exactly what was going on but at least now he could have a good guess.

The scorpion had now disappeared completely, and even under sedation you could see the anguish on the face of the unfortunate human. All of a sudden its eyes dilated completely and its fists were clenched. Nalater assumed correctly that it was some kind of mind-control device.

The next table was even more interesting. The naked human on this table had pipes, tubes and electrodes sticking out from all over it. Glancing at it casually, you could mistake it for a hardened body builder who had been on steroids for years. This unfortunate obviously didn't need to be sedated and was under the full control of the scientist attending it. The next two tables were more or less the same, but showed different stages of the process.

The fifth table was completely different. Here the scientist was introducing some kind of organic exoskeleton that appeared to bind itself to the body's endoskeleton, forming some type of organic armour. Again this process occupied two tables and seemed to take rather longer than the previous stages.

Nalater was so far as impressed as an Annunaki could be. He had never in his wildest dreams expected anything like this.

What was on the seventh table was barely recognisable as human. It was nearly twice the size of an average man, obviously the result of the specialist growth hormones and steroid combinations. The other thing that added to the bulk was the now fully developed exoskeleton. This monster now dwarfed the Annunaki scientist working on it. Nalater wasn't quite sure what the scientist was doing to the monstrosity, and to be honest he didn't want to know. Tannacha was a ruthless, even barbaric, son of a bitch, but even he had outdone himself with this butchery.

Table eight was not only a table but also incorporated a pit, which was filled with a silver fluid, with an overhead lifting device attached to it, obviously to be used for dipping the monsters. On the table lay one such freshly dipped creature. How does it breathe, thought Nalater? On closer inspection porous areas could be seen at strategic points all round the torso.

The job of table seven was becoming more clear. The creature on it no longer breathed through its mouth, but had twelve gill-like structures around the torso. Increased oxygen intake, thought Nalater. Clever.

Around where the navel would have been were a series of small connectors, again obviously for nourishment and waste. The whole respiratory and digestive processes had been totally changed at the previous work station. What was even more interesting, the silver fluid had set all the way around the body and exoskeleton, turning into a fully armoured yet extremely pliable second skin.

Table nine had four Annunaki scientists around it, who were applying by hand a fine layer of the black hair-like substance all over the torso and appendages of the body, Nalater didn't have a clue what this was. He had never seen anything like it before.

Just as he reached table ten, Tannacha joined him.

Table ten was clearly for quality control. Two of the Annunaki scientists were scrutinising the finished product that lay there. The finishing touch after quality control was the fitting of the grotesque mask.

They returned to the coffin-like structure in the other room, which was now empty and awaiting its next victim.

Nalater assumed it was probably the last stage to the mind-control process, maybe also a nutrition and waste station.

Tannacha had not said a word as Nalater wandered around, feeding his curiosity.

Now he spoke

'Well, what do you think?'

'Impressive, very impressive. I wondered what you had been doing.'

'I've had a change of heart with the humans.'

Nalater looked at him.

'How do you mean?'

'I mean I don't want to kill them any more. Well, at least not all of them.'

Nalater couldn't believe his ears. Tannacha surely hadn't just said that.

'What are you going to do with them, then?'

Tannacha scowled and gestured in the direction of the coffin. He thought to himself: Nalater can be really stupid at times. I just wish he'd think more like me.

Finally the penny dropped and Nalater spluttered:

'You mean you're going to turn six billion people into robots?'

'Not all of them, and not robots. Sybotes. Good name, though isn't it? Sounds like someone's name. Anyway only one in a hundred of them makes it all the way through the process.'

'Let me get this straight. you're going to create sixty million Sybotes?'

'Not that many. Just some of them, after we've colonised Earth. Our very own, totally obedient slave force.'

'Colonise Earth? I thought we just came for the gold, and to kill humans.'

'Change of plan, my friend. You need to keep up with the times.'

Nalater pulled himself up. The shock of it all had made him forget who he was talking to. He was now in danger of having his head removed from his shoulders.

'Excellent plan, commander. I don't know how you do it.'

'It's a gift, Nalater, a gift. Now we need to get things organised.'

'How do you mean, commander?'

'Let's see if the Sybotes work.'

With that, Tannacha moved to the other side of the

room. He threw open the door to reveal at least twenty-five working Sybotes standing to attention in the large dusky cellar.

# 38

On the Mars base everything was going swimmingly. A routine had been established with the civilians and the staff now running the base, including the Androids who were going down particularly well.

Konoco and Marie had watched the *Iron Duke* and the rest of the flotilla leave Heathrow and had returned to the surface of Mars to greet the new arrivals. Watching the shuttles ferrying people down from the *Iron Duke*, Marie felt a sense of pride at being part of all this. The survival of mankind and I'm helping to achieve it! The thought was overwhelming.

Suddenly Konoco moved away. He had spotted Jumouk and began heading in his direction. Because of the lack of communication there was a lot of catching up to do.

When Lee and Grant had woken up, the six of them – Lee, Grant, Konoco, Jumouk, Marie and Fiona – met up in one of the large conference rooms.

Jumouk welcomed everybody, thanked them for coming, and announced that the first thing on the agenda was the redistribution of responsibilities.

Jumouk was to retain overall leadership, with Konoco his second in command.

Lee would stay as head of ESG, and Grant was made officially head of assault craft squadrons. Marie was now in charge of the Mars base, with Fiona second in command. Pausanias was head of the humanoid Androids on the Mars base.

Finney was promoted to second in command of Earth ESG, reporting to Lee, and in charge of liaison with the resistance. Sacha was directly responsible for Earth resistance and coordination. Mark Howden was made second in charge of the Earth resistance. Thourus remained as first in command of the Android TAG, and ACM forces, with Balac as his second in command.

It had taken a long time to sort out, but eventually everybody's responsibilities had been made clear. Jumouk was satisfied that the mechanics of leadership were now properly in place. The next priority was to establish a new battle plan.

The Mars base was proving to be a godsend for humanity. It was now providing shelter for up to one and a half million people. Even with the worst-possible scenario, this was still enough of a gene pool to start humanity again.

The rest of the population on Earth, however, was still constantly in danger of discovery, even though they were in the camouflaged bases. The Annunaki had already shown how determined they could be at worming out the Earth bases. A plan of action was desperately needed to prevent any more of them being discovered.

Jumouk left this job in Lee's hands. After all, he had already shown a great aptitude for making the impossible happen. Finney would be responsible for coordinating the harassment of the Annunaki ground patrols, especially around the bases, to distract search-and-destroy patrols. Grant's main job would now be the defence of Mars with his squadrons of ESG assault ships along with the two battle cruisers, *Iron Duke* and *Victory*. Thourus and Balac would provide air cover for the remaining ESG forces on Earth, coordinating with Finney and the Earth resistance leaders.

Slowly but surely a strategy and structure were coming together; Jumouk was anxious to leave the fighting to others, run the overall strategy, and return to a structured battle plan.

He called an end to the meeting and asked if everybody could report back to Lee as developments progressed. Lee and Jumouk could then make decisions based on the available information, so as to best utilise the forces available to them.

Marie and Fiona were getting down to serious business, having Pausanias explain all the workings of the Mars base. This was going to be a lengthy task, so Marie was going to have to prioritise: defensive and offensive weapons first, then proximity detection, followed by life support and logistics. Fiona could then take over the more routine aspects of administration.

Marie was fascinated by the proximity detectors. They were far superior to the ones on the battle cruisers, being more accurate and having a much longer range. As she watched the Dulles base she could see almost every movement there. Somehow, whoever had built this base had managed to conquer the line-of-sight problem. It didn't matter what you wanted to see, it was there irrespective of the position of Earth or Mars, or for that matter any other planet. It was so clever!

Pausanias now described the defence systems. Apparently they were scattered all around Mars in generous quantities. Even if a fleet of battle cruisers attacked, the defences would be able to cope. Someone had been expecting trouble, Marie thought to herself.

The long-range offensive weapons were excellent as well. Several banks of them were located within the base and the rest around the planet surface, each bank able to track different targets.

All in all, the Mars base was a pretty good and safe place to be just now.

Grant had now organised low-level patrols of ESG assault vessels, which would skim the surface of the planet looking for anything out of the ordinary. There was also a wing of twenty-five assault ships on permanent scramble in case they were needed on Earth or in space.

Lee had broken radio silence and sent scrambled orders to Finney in London. Finney had responded with an update on his ESG forces and the resistance movement on Earth.

Fiona had the most mundane job of all, but one in which her organisational skills came into play, arranging shift patterns for the staff to ensure full cover twenty-four hours a day. Then there were the meals, the accommodation and, not least, entertainment. Boredom was one of the quickest ways to demoralise a successful community. All this was achieved with the willing help of the base Androids, for which Fiona was eternally grateful, as she had very little working knowledge of the systems.

Meanwhile Jumouk and Konoco were poring over numerous scenarios. They wanted to be prepared for anything and everything. All in all they felt that they weren't doing that badly all things considered. There hadn't been any huge loss of human civilian life as yet and the Mars base was pretty secure and providing new surprises by the hour. The Annunaki had for some reason apparently holed up at Dulles and, although there appeared to be a lot of activity, they didn't seem to be going anywhere fast.

Neither had broached the question that was at the back of everyone's mind: where had the Mars base come from and, if it wasn't the Dropas who had built it, then who had?

This was the missing bit of the jigsaw that really troubled Jumouk. If there was someone else out there, who were they, and were they friendly? Or were they just some race from hundreds of thousands of years ago, and were now extinct? No one seemed to be able to answer him, not even the sentient Androids on the base – or, at least, they didn't seem to want to answer him.

Lee buzzed the door of the annexe room next to Jumouk's quarters. Konoco invited him in. The annexe was in the style of all the rooms on the base, pleasantly decorated, functional and relaxing with mood lighting and comfortable furniture.

'Lee, how can I help you?'

Konoco was glad of the interruption; it had been a long day.

'I just thought I'd bring you up to date. I've talked to London and everybody's being brought up to speed by Finney and Sacha. For some reason everything seems quiet down there – well, for the time being anyway.'

'Good, any more thoughts on that task Jumouk set you?'

'Sorry, Konoco, not as yet. This is going to be a tough one.'

Konoco nodded.

'Thanks anyway, Lee. Keep working on it.'

Lee excused himself, and left for the control room.

# 39

Tannacha was giving instructions to one of the scientists who was running his Sybote operation. The orders were simple. Five of the Sybotes would hunt down all the snipers that were causing a problem round the perimeter of the base. They would be armed with pulse weapons and hand-to-hand combat weapons. They would also be fitted with personal communication devices and an advanced form of CCTV, so that Tannacha and Nalater could monitor their progress.

Sitting back comfortably in front of a line of viewers, Tannacha and Nalater commenced their watch.

All five Sybotes were moving swiftly toward the outer perimeter; Nalater disabled his perimeter defences to allow them through and outside into the buildings and rubble.

'So far so good!' exclaimed an excited Tannacha.

The view from the CCTV couldn't have been better; as a small muzzle flash could be seen from the front of Sybote no. 1, the sound of a hollow point bullet could be heard crunching into the Sybote's head. The Sybote didn't so much as falter, moving with tremendous speed and agility, so that within three seconds it was on to the sniper's position.

The preferred method of termination by this Sybote was removal of the sniper's head by hand, in one lightning-fast movement. The torso of the sniper slumped to the ground and the Sybote held his prize aloft for all to see.

This provoked a hail of sniper fire, pinpointing the positions of the other snipers. Moving remorselessly through the hail of fire, one after another the Sybotes terminated their targets. The bullets simply bounced off their armoured exoskeletons. Not one pulse weapon had been used by the Sybotes. All of them seemed to prefer the 'personal' touch. Half an hour had seen all the resistance snipers wiped out and not one Sybote injured.

Tannacha gave the order to recall the Sybotes. He had one last surprise for Nalater.

At the first stage of creating the Sybotes – the introduction of the electronic scorpion for mind control – it was possible to re-educate the humans in this state to be used as spies. With the proper re-education they could pass for normal, infiltrate the resistance, and pass back vital information about positions and plans.

After the resounding success of the Sybotes, Tannacha had now released ten of the spies into the surrounding area.

However, it would not have been Tannacha if there hadn't been a twist in the tail. All ten of the spies had been afflicted with horrendous injuries by the Annunaki, ranging from amputations to serious head wounds. Some of them wouldn't survive until they were found, but that didn't matter so long as the rest that were rescued were credible.

This game plan really was wait and see; the outcome at this stage was completely unknown.

Mark Howden, the resistance commander in Dulles, was just receiving word that his snipers had been slaughtered. No one could be specific as to how it had happened, only that there were no survivors.

This was the second piece of bad news today. Finney

had contacted him to tell him he was now second in command of all Earth's resistance forces, reporting to Sacha in London. His remit was clear: find, organise and unite any resistance groups scattered worldwide. This would involve setting up an efficient communications network that was Annunaki proof.

It was going to be a massive task, and all while he was fighting the biggest force of Annunaki warriors on the planet, right on his doorstep. Fortunately for Mark he had amongst his band of resistance some of the top communications people on the planet. This would now be their job, a task which Mark had every confidence they would make look easy. After all, it was they who had been able to set up communications with London.

But back to the matter in hand. Mark now had to find out what had happened in Dulles with the snipers. He ordered two patrols to go to Dulles International and see if they could piece together what had happened there. The patrols were under strict instruction not to engage the enemy. This was strictly a fact-finding mission.

As the patrols picked there way around the perimeter of Dulles the carnage inflicted on the snipers was all too apparent, and the fact that they had all more or less been killed in the same way was puzzling.

It was at this point the patrols started to come into contact with some distressed, confused and badly injured civilians. Between the two patrols they picked up six in total, all badly injured. Trying to keep them alive until they got back to the base at Manassas would be a job in itself.

When the patrols did return, they had already lost another two of the civilians to their grievous wounds. The remaining four were taken straight to the makeshift infirmary for treatment.

The patrol commanders reported back to Mark. The news wasn't good. The snipers had all been killed the same way by decapitation, and not cleanly: their heads had literally been torn off, in the most sadistic way possible. Then there was the civilians who had been found, and the death of two of them on the way back to base.

Mark was trying to take all of this in when news of another civilian death on the operating table reached him. This only left three.

Mark slammed his fist down on the table in frustration.

'We need to get inside that Annunaki base and find out what's going on in there. I've got a really bad feeling about all this,' he groaned

Mark was in luck. One of his resistance commanders, Bill Graham, had been an architect for a building contractor, who a few years ago had carried out renovations to the sewer tunnels in the labyrinth underneath Dulles International Airport. The main Dulles Potomac interceptor sewer system was readily accessible and led right underneath the airport. This was the way to get in undetected. Mark couldn't believe his luck at finding his own personal guide, someone who had actually worked and drawn up plans of the maze of tunnels. They would enter the tunnels of the sewer system at Fairfax and then travel north-west. Bill Graham had drawn a map of the intended route and adjoining tunnels, and had also planned an alternative route and two escape routes.

The team Mark had put together were specialists in demolitions, ex-special forces, even an ex-CIA agent, with of course himself and Bill, around forty in all. The entry point would be a manhole at the junction of Lee Highway and Main Street.

Once the party had safely entered the sewer tunnel, they headed north then swung west, following the directions on Bill's map. Mark was surprised at the size and scale of the sewer tunnels, although they were very damp, and extremely smelly, with five or six inches of surface water – no, water was the wrong description. It was actually sludge of varying consistency, oozing all over the concrete walkway. Rats were everywhere – at least Mark assumed they were rats – you wouldn't be able to tell from the size of them. They were as big as cats. Mark couldn't help wondering what they ate, then quickly dismissed the thought from his mind.

Bill had warned that the journey would take the group anywhere up to five hours, depending on how well they progressed.

In the sweltering heat underground it was hard going, Mark had insisted that they stop every hour, and drink at least a litre of water to keep them hydrated.

Three hours into the so-far uneventful journey they had stopped for the usual water break, but this time they also ate a high-energy snack of fruit, apples, pears and bananas, followed by a medium-sized bar of chocolate.

After three hours of acclimatisation to the sewers the food was easier to stomach. In pleasanter surroundings it could almost have been a picnic.

Twenty minutes later the party set off again on the next leg of their journey. Bill had worked out that on their last stop for water they would be under a town called Floris, right on the Annunaki perimeter around Dulles. At this point Bill would refer to a more detailed map so Mark could decide where to break surface within the Dulles complex.

Bill and two ex-special forces soldiers were now on point. The sludge that covered the ground they were walking on had become much thicker and denser in consistency, and even the rats seemed larger. The light was poor and it was very difficult to see for any distance.

Bill was checking the identification markings on each of the ladders leading to the manhole covers on the surface. He signalled to Mark to stop for the last water break of the journey, as he figured they were now under Floris. Bill reached into his backpack and finished the last of his water for the outbound journey, and pulled out the detailed map. Mark joined him at the front of the group.

'OK, Bill, are we under Floris now?'

Bill nodded, still studying the map.

'Yes, now we've got three or four options. It just depends where you want to come up at Dulles.'

'I think the best place would be central, somewhere around the main terminal.'

Bill tapped on the sheet of paper.

'This is the tunnel we want, then.'

'How long will it take?'

'Twenty, maybe twenty-five minutes.'

'OK, let's get to it, then.'

Mark waved the group in the direction of the tunnel Bill had pointed out, and they started off down a smaller tunnel, which was quite cramped compared to the tunnels they had been walking down.

They had only travelled for about five minutes when they came to an unforeseen obstacle. Barring their way was a thick metal grill sunk into the concrete walls. It had a small metal gate which was secured by two large metal padlocks. Mark looked at Bill.

'Shit! I forgot about these, airport security. When I was down here last we didn't come out this far. They put them in to stop terrorist attacks.'

'OK, not your fault. Are we going to meet more of them?'

Bill nodded

'Probably.'

'OK, so we need to find a way to get these padlocks off.'

Bill shrugged.

'We'll need to do it quietly. Any loud noise will travel right under the airport, then that's our cover blown.'

Mark put his hand over his mouth and rubbed his chin thoughtfully.

'Acid. I'm sure we've got acid with us. The demolition guys will have some.'

Mark collected a bottle of powerful acid from one of the demolition men and, taking great care, squirted some into the keyholes of the padlocks, then stepped back smartly. Tiny puffs of smoke billowed from the padlocks, and then droplets of the acid began appearing on the bottom of the padlocks. All of a sudden the first padlock sprang open, followed quickly by the second.

'Well done!' said Bill slapping Mark on the back.

'Too easy,' said Mark ruefully.

He very gingerly removed each of the padlocks and threw the gate open.

'After you, William,' he said with a grin.

Even in adversity, mankind's ability to make the best of things is astonishing, thought Bill.

After another five minutes there was another thick grill, again with a gate and padlock, which this time proved no obstacle at all. Twenty minutes later Bill called a halt to the group at a set of ladders thirty feet directly under a manhole cover.

'This is it,' he muttered, excitedly tapping the sheet of paper in his hand.

Mark signalled for everyone to get down on the ground and stay quiet. He began to climb the ladder, gradually inching his way up until he was directly under the manhole cover. Tentatively he raised the cover enough to look out across the surrounding area, Bill couldn't have got it more right. They were next to a large complex which could only have been the main terminal.

Mark waited for a good five minutes. It was dark outside with very little lighting, so visibility was poor. This suited Mark. There would be less chance of them being spotted in the open. All the time Mark was watching there was absolutely no sign of movement, no guards, nothing.

He remembered the brutal and gory demonstration of the effectiveness of the perimeter security. It was clear that the Annunaki were relying mainly on the perimeter security as their main deterrent.

Replacing the manhole cover quietly in its groove, he slowly climbed back down the ladder and rejoined the group, congratulating Bill as he did so. After issuing his orders and splitting the group into four smaller units, the first unit of ten men emerged from the manhole and made their way to the main terminal, followed by two other units. The last ten men were left to secure the tunnel and the manhole above it along with the escape route from the terminal back to it.

Inside the terminal building it was pitch black. The three units split up in different directions and started to look for clues as to what exactly the Annunaki were up to.

All the units were using night-vision goggles, which made navigating through the terminal buildings considerably safer and easier. Mark could see in the distance some of the areas that were obviously occupied by the Annunaki. With lights blazing brightly they were making

Mark's job far easier, and circumventing these areas was simple.

Mark had ordered his other units to give it two hours of reconnaissance, then meet up with him back at the point they had separated. If nothing had been discovered by then, well – it wouldn't be worth discovering.

The units were also equipped with night-vision cameras so that a record of the interiors of the buildings could be kept, highlighting any changes made by the Annunaki and also documenting which buildings the Annunaki were using regularly and what they were being used for.

As Mark's team entered an annexe of the main terminal, they noticed a strong rotting smell. It was the smell of death, of rotting human torsos and limbs, flung everywhere with no regard for dignity or respect, just left to rot. These were the failed Sybote experiments, the 99 per cent of unfortunates who hadn't made it into the Sybote club.

Appalled and disgusted as they were by the sights and smells that greeted them, Mark's team were conscious that they still had a job to do and, in any case, this was obviously an important discovery.

After taking as many pictures as he could, Mark cut off some of the silver coating on one of the bodies. This involved the gruesome business of cutting the flesh to the bone as the material and structure wouldn't separate from the body.

Mark and his men had now got all the intelligence they needed. It was time to return to the meeting point and the other units.

Slowly but surely the unit backtracked to the meeting point to await the arrival of the others. They wondered if they would have had as much success as Mark and his unit. Indeed, when the other units arrived back they all had their own stories to tell, but now wasn't the time. Mark mainly wanted to get back out without being discovered, so that they would be able to use the sewers again, perhaps even for an all-out attack one day.

The three units slowly made their way back, first to the manhole then down the ladder into the relative safety of the sewer. Once everyone was back inside the sewer system of tunnels, Mark and Bill pored over the escape routes Bill had already highlighted, looking for the best one back directly to Manassas Park, as opposed to going to Fairfax.

The route they chose was going to be a gruelling six-hour journey, but if they were going to be using the sewer tunnels on a regular basis, it would be good training. Mark couldn't wait to get back so he could scrutinise the intelligence they had gathered.

The return journey was as disciplined as the outward one. Each hour they would stop for a litre of water to keep themselves hydrated. At the third stop they would have a high-energy meal break and a twenty-minute rest. Bill along with two soldiers was point duty again, documenting every step of the way – all the different passages, grills, every aspect of the sewers – the more information the better.

# 40

The night had been an arduous one. It had actually taken seven hours to get back to the Manassas base, but after four hours' sleep Mark was up and about again, putting all the intelligence gathered the night before into some semblance of order. It was starting to become very clear that the Annunakis were up to something and, whatever it was, it was big and nasty.

The operation had been a great success. They had penetrated deep into the heart of the Annunaki base and got out again without the Annunaki even noticing them. They had begun to chart the system of sewers all around them in such detail, that Mark had decided to make this a full-time job for Bill.

Mark was sitting at a dusty old table in the living room of one of the houses the resistance had commandeered. Trophies and photographs were strewn around the table awaiting investigation.

The Annunaki were obviously trying to turn humans into something. The photographic evidence from that horrendous room bore witness to that. What was the silver-like material and framework under it, and those ugly black hair-like things which almost seemed to be growing on the material?

Then there were the pieces of metal that had been picked up. Mark took a closer look at one. Then he had to take a second look. It was like a tiny scorpion. What the hell is it, he wondered?

He stood up and scanned the room as if looking for something. He went over to a dusty window ledge and picked up an old pair of glasses, dusted them down and returned to the table and the piece of metal. Holding the glasses a few inches away from the object magnified it three times.

'It is, it's a tiny little metal scorpion!'

He was no longer speaking to himself. Bill had joined him at the table and was desperately trying to get a good look at the object.

'Do you see it, Bill?'

Bill's mouth dropped open. Mark was right.

'It's a bloody scorpion!'

'What the hell does it do?'

Mark's question drew a sharp intake of breath from Bill.

'Maybe its some kind of torture device?'

By the hour, Bill was becoming Mark's right-hand man, a confidant almost.

'I don't think so, they wouldn't have left it in the body, would they?'

The object had both of them puzzled.

'What else could it be?'

'I really don't know. Where was it found?'

'Just on the floor of that room, I think.'

'Who found it?'

'I believe it was Jason.'

'Can you do me a favour, Bill. Go get Jason and we'll see exactly where he found it.'

'No problem, Mark. I'll be back shortly.'

Mark was pouring out another strong, hot coffee, the third of the morning, when Bill returned with Jason.

'Want a coffee?'

It was a question aimed at both the arrivals.

Both men nodded and gratefully accepted a cup of the strong, black brew. Jason took a large swig of the coffee, and instantly regretted it as the hot fluid scalded his mouth.

To cover his embarrassment he picked up the object and whistled, half hoping that that would help to cool his mouth.

'It was under the head of one of the bodies when we moved them. Nearly didn't see it, but it glinted in my night vision sights. I thought it might be relevant so I picked it up.'

'So it had been under the head?'

'Yes, not far from the ear, if I remember right.'

'But under the head?'

'Yes, what is it?'

'It's like a small metal scorpion.'

At this point Jason ceased his investigation of the object and dropped it hurriedly back down on the table. He took a nervous step backwards, instinctively rubbing his hands on his trousers.

'Good God, what's that for?'

'We don't know, Jason, we just don't know.'

Mark's answer did nothing to reassure Jason. In fact, they now seemed to have more questions than answers. Then Bill stepped into the breach.

'Why don't we send it all up to the Mars base where they've got the equipment to examine it properly?'

'My sentiments exactly, but we can go one better. There was a more or less complete body in that room, wasn't there?'

Bill thought about it.

'Yes, there was, right in the corner of the room.'

'OK, well tonight we'll go back and get that body. That way they can do a full autopsy.'

Bill looked at Jason. Jason looked less than thrilled by the prospect – that room was the stuff of nightmares. When no one else spoke, Bill took the initiative.

'Right, sir, do you want me to put a team together or are you going to do it?'

'Thanks, anyway, Bill, but I'll do it. Can you put a route together again and get the provisions organised?'

The journey back to the Annunaki base was more or less the same as the night before, although this time Mark had opted to take fifty men, this was because on the journey back they would be carrying a dead weight and he wanted to rotate the bearers of the dead body as often as possible. Jason had picked the short straw. He and a unit of ten men would have to go into the Annunaki base and retrieve the dead body.

The stench in the room at the Annunaki base hadn't got any better. If anything it was worse. However, getting back to the room had been easy.

Jason spotted the dead body still in the same place, in the corner of the large room. Six of the resistance fighters were sent to place the corpse into an extra large body bag. Then, just as they were turning to go back to Jason's position on the other side of the gruesome room, Jason heard a faint noise coming from outside. He signalled for the unit to hit the deck. To a man they obeyed and blended into the other body parts strewn across the floor of the charnel house.

The twin doors to the outer court burst open and two very large human-like shapes appeared in the dimly lit doorway. They appeared to be silver in colour or at least wearing some kind of silver suit, They were carrying something, but Jason couldn't quite make out what it was.

The two silver shapes flexed themselves and hurled whatever they were carrying the full three hundred feet width of the room. It smashed against the back wall, and dropped right down on top of the six men hiding on the floor. The two beings turned on their heels, closed the doors behind them and left as mysteriously as they had arrived.

Jason left it a minute or two to make sure they were clear of the room, then signalled to the men to return to him.

'What did they throw into the room?' Jason asked one of the men.

'Bodies, bloody dead bodies. Three hundred feet without breaking sweat. That's not natural, now is it?'

Jason couldn't help but agree.

The rest of the trip back to the sewer manhole was uneventful and they rejoined Mark and Bill in the sewer with the dead body. It was now taking eight men to carry the dead body because of its size and weight.

The journey back to Manassas was a nightmare and took twelve hours. Fortunately Bill had packed supplies to cover nine hours out, and nine hours back, so at least they didn't run out of food and water.

Back at the Manassas base Jason was recounting his experience in the Room of Death, as it was now known, to an astonished Mark.

'It was incredible, throwing those bodies three hundred feet like that. What are those things?'

'Unfortunately, I think they are what the Annunaki are making out of humans, some kind of super monster. I'm just wondering if that little metal scorpion is some kind of mind-control device.'

'That would make sense.'

'Right, we need to get this stuff up to Mars. Any ideas?'

'Finney's going to need to send a shuttle for it, isn't he?'

Bill's reply failed to take into account the two massive Annunaki battle cruisers hovering in the sky just north of them.

Mark shook his head.

'No, those battle cruisers would have a shuttle for breakfast. We need something foolproof.'

Jason piped up.

'What about meeting a shuttle at the Potomac? It could arrive submerged then leave submerged.'

Mark slapped Jason on the back.

'Nice one, Jason. You and Bill work out the details and contact Finney.'

Bill and Jason set to work. It certainly was going to involve a long hike for someone. Bill started getting a map of the sewers organised. It would make sense for them to go underground, which was now the preferred method of travelling anyway. Jason set about organising a team to transport the gathered intelligence, and arrange a pick-up point on the Potomac river.

# 41

Finney received instructions from Jason. It should by all accounts be an easy job: quick trip to the Potomac river in America, pick some stuff up, then off to Western Australia, then at an opportune moment off to the Mars base, job done. The shuttle was underwater just off the piers at Featherstone Shores awaiting the arrival of the party from the resistance in Manassas. The signal would be an underwater flare.

The pilot and two ESG guards had been waiting around for five hours and still nothing. They were concerned now and were starting to wonder if the mission had been compromised, when into the murky depths a flare descended slowly but surely towards the muddy bottom, its reddish brown glow signalling that everything was OK. The shuttle immediately surfaced at the most southerly pier close to Boaters Cove Place, and the transfer began.

The shuttle pilot did raise an eyebrow at the unusual cargo: a dead body, unusual looking body parts and other miscellaneous items. The three civilians coming on board he didn't know about, since they were a last-minute addition by Mark. These were the civilians that had been found wandering about with various injuries and memory loss. Mark thought that they would be safer and certainly better off on the Mars base once they had been discharged from the makeshift Manassas hospital.

Now safely loaded with its cargo, the shuttle submerged and headed off to Australia.

Bill, Jason, and the four units of resistance fighters returned to their underground sanctuary and began the demanding journey back to the Manassas base.

The little shuttle shot out of the water off Western Australia, and headed at high speed towards the Mars base. The journey itself wouldn't take that long, but the shuttle was very vulnerable until it got closer to the Mars base. The pilot was watching his proximity detectors intently, half expecting to see a swarm of Annunaki assault ships coming at them, but for the time being he was in the clear.

The passengers on board the shuttle had been extraordinarily quiet for the whole trip under the seas, and being in space hadn't changed that. Normally the voyage into space would provoke a vigorous conversation, but these passengers remained passive to the extent of seeming almost robotic.

Marie and Jumouk watched the approaching shuttle on the visual depiction console, while also keeping a close eye on the two Annunaki battle cruisers hovering above Dulles.

Strangely enough, yet again these were doing nothing to intercept the shuttle. This worried Jumouk. It worried him more than if they had taken some form of action.

What were the Annunaki doing at that base? Still, at least the latest intelligence was on the rapidly approaching shuttle. That might shed some light on what they were up to.

After the shuttle had landed, the body and the various other bits of intelligence were taken off to one of the many laboratories on the Mars base. The three civilians were taken away to be debriefed by Lee in one of the conference rooms.

Pausanias, along with the team of ESG doctors and Dropas scientists, was particularly interested in the dead body. It was more or less complete as far as they could see, and had been through all the stages of the Annunaki process. It was established that the cause of death was an aneurism in the brain.

Pausanias thought this had been caused by the metallic implant in the brain. It was obvious that the implant was some kind of mind-control device, and on attaching itself to the brain, or sometime after, caused a swelling in a blood vessel next to it. Over a period of time the wall of the swollen blood vessel failed, causing a major bleed and instant death.

The exoskeleton was identified as a lightweight, extremely durable alloy intended to strengthen and protect the endoskeleton. It was also used to tighten the silver skin around the body like pliable armour. The silver skin turned out to be unidentifiable, but nonetheless virtually indestructible and fire proof.

The black hair-like substances that had sprung up all over the body were checked under a device similar to an electron microscope, and turned out to be inert strings of Nanites. The function of these Nanites was still unclear, and was causing a debate of some heat between the scientists.

By all accounts the monstrous creation was a formidable foe, and the ESG were going to have to come up with a way to quickly and effectively neutralise it.

Lee had begun the debriefing of the three civilians. Although he had just begun, he had quickly become aware that something was not quite right. All three were all almost totally unresponsive and vacant. None had any memory of who they were or what had happened to them. Lee was starting to become suspicious. These weren't simple cases of amnesia, there was a lot more to it than that.

As a precaution he instructed the medical team to carry out MRI scans on the three. The results left no doubt: all three had small metal implants in their brains.

Lee ordered the three to be restrained and put in one of the holding cells until he had reported back to Jumouk and a proper course of action been devised.

Lee and Jumouk were sitting in one of the small annexes off the main control room, sipping green tea and looking remarkably relaxed. Marie was watching them covertly. She had now heard most of the details about the super monster and was wondering how Lee and Jumouk could look so relaxed about it.

Poring over the ever-increasing pile of data and facts in front of them, they had both come to the obvious conclusion, The Annunaki agenda had changed. All the facts now pointed to the same thing. The Annunaki were looking for total domination and colonisation of the Earth, perhaps using these super monsters to achieve their goal of enslaving mankind as mindless zombie slaves, and making the Dropas extinct.

It seemed to them, however, there was just one flaw in that scenario. The Annunaki forces had been seriously depleted and Jumouk and Lee doubted whether there would be enough of them to carry this plan out effectively. Between the ESG, Dropas, Androids and resistance fighters the Annunaki were fighting hard to hold their own, if not actually fighting a losing battle.

Another two cups of green tea arrived.

'Lee, what are you going to do about the three civilians from Dulles?'

'Hmm, we're going to have to operate. They're brain dead just now anyway; I know it's going to be dangerous but I don't see that we have a choice.'

'Probably not. In any case, we don't know what they are programmed to do, or what their mission is.'

At that Jumouk shook his head.

'I meant to say, what did Mark say when you told him about them?'

'He couldn't have been more apologetic. He's been in contact with Finney and Sacha and we're all doing checks with metal detectors both on Earth and on Mars just in case.'

'Will metal detectors pick up the implants?'

'Yes, we've already checked that. They show up just fine.'

'OK, Lee. Where do we go from here?'

After another sip of green tea, and with a furrowed brow, Lee continued.

'Well, I suggest we let the resistance do their worst. After all they've done a good job up till now. OK, it's only a limited response, but it's still keeping the Annunaki occupied.'

'What about these super monsters?'

Lee eased back in his chair.

'I'll talk to Mark and see if he can organise something to destroy the production line.'

Almost as an afterthought Jumouk added:

'Any ideas on how to kill them? After all, we don't know how many they've got already, and I think it might have been them that killed Mark's snipers.'

Lee nodded.

'Probably.'

'OK, Lee, I'll leave that one with you. Thanks for your input and please let me know how the implant removals go. Bye for now.'

With that Jumouk took his leave, and left Lee to finish his tea.

The removal of the implants didn't go well. Two of the patients died on the operating table, and the third one only just survived, and was now in a coma. The only weak spot that Lee could find on the super monsters was the implant which made them vulnerable to aneurisms.

Pausanias highlighted this when he pointed out the bullet-like mark on the dead body from Dulles. The mark was faint. It was at the front of the skull to the right of the left temple and where the forehead would normally be. The skull hadn't been badly damaged, but Pausanias considered that the impact of a high-velocity bullet might have dislodged the implant enough to cause the aneurism.

This was of course the Sybote that took the sniper bullet to the head before carrying on to kill the snipers. At some point after the slaughter it had suffered the aneurism, died instantaneously, and was thrown into the room of death at the Dulles base.

Pausanias and Lee were right, they had found a weak spot in the Sybotes.

* * *

Tannacha now had a total of forty Sybotes and was keen to put them to good use, Nalater had to admit he was impressed by the Sybote technology. They were mindless killing machines, perfect in almost every way.

The psychological effect alone was outstanding. Imagine ten of these monstrous things coming at you. You would have to be the most courageous of warriors not to think twice about standing your ground.

Tannacha also had ten spies who had now been trained with a version of their past lives and what had happened to them. This he hoped would make them more plausible civilians, unlike the previous ones who had been notable failures.

Four units of Sybotes, ten in each unit, were despatched by Tannacha on search-and-destroy missions around the Dulles base. Their remit was to patrol for ten hours and then return to base. If they came into contact with anything not Annunaki, it was to be obliterated. After the Sybotes had returned, Tannacha would then release his spies to be 'rescued' by the resistance.

Mark received reports back from his look-outs around Dulles that the Sybotes were on the move. He was getting detailed information on the size of each unit, the total numbers and directions in which they were heading.

He had been busy over the past few days. He had detailed plans of all the places where the ordnance had been hidden around the general Washington area. This included two hundred F-22 Raptors, all armed, fuelled and ready to go. As a bonus six Black Hawk helicopters were also included.

Mark had more than enough pilots for these fighters and helicopters and had already assigned crews and ground crews to them. The crews had all been despatched with their specific orders around twelve hours earlier, and by now should be on the various makeshift airstrips awaiting further instructions from Mark.

Five demolition teams and twenty units totalling two hundred men had been sent out to West Springfield to retrieve demolition material and weapons from beneath West Springfield High School.

Mark had the idea of ambush on his mind, and if he was going to do it, he might as well do it right. The demolition charges would be laid in Chantilly, just south of Dulles. The southern area of Chantilly would be one large bomb. From the Dulles Expo and Conference Centre to the Wingate by Wyndham Hotel, the whole area would be totally destroyed.

The idea was quite simple. One that had been tried many times before in mankind's violent history. Get the enemy to chase you, leading them into a trap, and then massacre them with superior fire power.

'Do you think it'll work?' Bill sounded a bit sceptical.

'I think so, those robot things may be combat friendly, but none of them have law degrees. I think they'll take the bait.'

'What about the Raptors?'

'They should get enough cover from the explosion for a rapid approach. They'll all target the same building with rockets and bombs. That should take care of the robot production line.'

By the next day everything was in place, the demolition teams had done their jobs and ground troops were positioned as ordered. Mark signalled the beginning of the operation.

# BATTLE FOR THE EARTH

\* \* \*

A small group of five resistance fighters was spotted by the patrolling Sybotes. Immediately the Sybotes engaged Mark's men, and a fire-fight ensued. The pulse weapons fire was simply absorbed by the Sybotes' body armour. The bullets did have some effect but still didn't slow down the Sybotes by much.

The group of fighters was now retreating towards Chantilly when a Black Hawk suddenly appeared, spewing a hail of fire into the Sybotes' line of advance. This slowed the Sybotes down noticeably but still didn't stop them altogether.

The Black Hawk then hovered overhead, dropping ladders and collecting the five resistance fighters. It then flew south at tree-top height.

The Sybotes were on the point of giving up pursuit when another five resistance fighters appeared and resumed the fire-fight. By now three units of Sybotes were involved in what was now a fast-moving chase.

The resistance fighters were now on Westmore Street exactly in the area they wanted. Thirty Sybotes were bearing down hard on the resistance fighters' position, when once again a Black Hawk helicopter appeared from nowhere, guns blazing as it again picked up the five resistance fighters, then sped off at tree-top height southwards.

Next the commander of the demolition teams gave the order and the whole area erupted in a cataclysm of fire, rubble and smoke.

As the smoke plumed upwards, fifty F-22 Raptors screamed through the dense billowing mass heading for one building on the Dulles base. Rocket fire was first, followed by four small-diameter bombs from each Raptor. The devastation on the ground was unimaginable and the area of the Sybote production facility had become one gigantic crater, with many smaller craters scattered around the surrounding area where the bombs had missed their targets.

Annunaki assault vessels were now spewing out of the battle cruisers, intent on exacting immediate revenge on the Raptors.

The Raptors had had to cut and run, but were being hounded relentlessly by the Annunaki craft. Raptor after Raptor succumbed to the superior weapons and speed of the assault vessels. It was now more of a duck shoot for the Annunaki pilots.

Out of the initial fifty F-22 Raptors only six made it successfully back to their base and under camouflage. It had been a heavy price to pay for the mission but, for all that, the mission had been a complete success, and the production of the grotesque robots had been halted, at least for the time being.

Tannacha was counting the cost of the latest resistance attack.

The resistance really were becoming a thorn in his side, exactly as Jumouk had planned. His production facility for manufacturing the Sybotes had been completely destroyed and, what was worse, all his raw materials and reserve supplies had gone up along with it.

On the other hand, fortunately none of his assault craft had been damaged, and he had lost count of how many Raptors had been downed. To him this had been a victory with very little cost to the Annunaki war machine.

Still, he was going to miss his Sybotes. The unit which hadn't been involved in the skirmish returned to the Dulles base, which meant he still had ten Sybotes: not quite the army he had intended but better than nothing.

In any case, he could still start again. The template for the Sybotes obviously worked; he would just need to get more raw materials.

Mark and Bill were studying the battle reports. The cost of the operation had been high, but the results decisive. Thirty of the grotesque creatures killed and their production halted. However, they also realised that one of the main areas in which they were falling down was in the air, where they were no match for the Annunaki assault craft.

Mark accordingly invited ten of his top pilots to come over and discuss any improvements to tactics, or even hardware. They had to give the planes and their pilots a better fighting chance. This really was a problem area. It would be easier to turn a tank into a racing car. One suggestion stood out from the rest, however: rigging the planes so they could carry airborne mines. At least that way they might be able to down Annunaki craft following them, provided they could gain the element of surprise.

The decision was made to arm the planes with mines in future.

Meanwhile, Bill had been getting on with his documentation of the system of sewers. Initially the suggestion had been to blow up the Dulles base from the sewers, but this plan had been rejected because it would have drawn attention to the sewers, and their favoured safe way of travel would have been jeopardised.

Resistance workers were now travelling regularly around

the sewer tunnels and, indeed, were using some of the smaller tunnels to store weapons and explosives retrieved from their hiding places on the surface.

This was working out so well that Finney and Sacha had adopted the idea in London.

Bill had even come up with a strategy for mining the tunnels so if they were ever compromised they could seal tunnels behind them, thus improving their chances of escape.

Tannacha had ordered the building of a new, permanent factory to produce Sybotes. The original experiment of using them as ground troops had been a resounding success. Besides, he reasoned, the way he had been getting through his Annunaki warriors, he would soon be running out of infantry. Scouts were sent out to scan the surrounding areas for suitable sites.

The other thing he needed was human beings. Unless he could find another human base, accessing this resource was going to be more problematic.

Then Nalater came up with an innovative idea of where to build the factory. Underneath Dulles, construction had been started on an underground railway with its station, called the Silver Line. This would make an excellent facility, deep enough to be safe, and large enough to accommodate the mass production of Sybotes.

Tannacha ordered the building and customisation of the partially constructed station to begin immediately, leaving the scouts free to concentrate on finding human bases for raw materials.

# 42

Marie was exploring more of the Mars base. Up till now she had only scratched the surface, and she had a strong suspicion that Pausanias was still stonewalling over certain aspects of the base. The central question of who had built it had never been answered, as time after time people had asked but been unable to get a straight answer from Pausanias, or any of his personnel.

Marie still only had access to a limited amount of the Mars base's systems. She had repeatedly asked for more access, but Pausanias had always found a reason why the systems wouldn't let her access, passwords he didn't know, secured files and the like.

Hiding her frustration, Marie had persisted, scrolling through animated three-dimensional files, still looking for any clues as to who had built the base or why.

There was a brief reference in one file to the Island of Atlas, but further investigation of the systems were password protected.

Pausanias interrupted Marie's deliberations to point out a blip on the proximity detectors. A small shuttle had just entered hyper-space after leaving the Dulles base on Earth. Marie moved across to the proximity imagery depiction.

'Can we tell where it's going, Pausanias?'

'No, Marie, once in hyper-space there is no way of telling. However, I could probably hazard a guess.'

'Nibiru.' Marie spoke the word at the same time as Pausanias.

'Well, this can't be good.'

Pausanias nodded and began to search through a database.

'With Nibiru's present position, it will be forty-eight hours before the shuttle arrives.'

Suddenly an audible alarm sounded on the proximity console. The two Annunaki battle cruisers were on the move.

'Where are they going?'

You could hear the distress in Marie's voice as she was joined by Lee.

'They're heading east. London, maybe.'

The two cruisers had accelerated, still heading east.

'Doesn't look like London. Europe then, somewhere?'

Still accelerating, the cruisers darted over Germany, over the Black Sea, then the Caspian Sea, and finally into Chinese air space, where they slowed down as they approached Beijing.

'Beijing, they're heading for Beijing,' spluttered Lee.

'They're heading for the underground base beneath the Forbidden City.'

Sure enough, they watched as the two battle cruisers came to a halt directly above the Forbidden City and unleashed scores of assault vessels to join the battle which had now broken out below them. The fighting was vicious. The ESG underground base was probably the largest on Earth and extremely well defended. However, the all-out bombardment from the battle cruisers above the base was relentless and devastating.

Jumouk had now joined Lee and Marie at the console. All three looked on in horror. The Annunaki had discovered the largest underground base on Earth and were in the process of decimating it.

'We need to send our battle cruisers in, Jumouk, We can't leave this to fate.'

It did sound rather as Lee's Chinese roots were favouring his fellow countrymen, however Jumouk was aware that he had only two battle cruisers left and if he lost those he would have handed Earth on a plate to the Annunaki.

'You know we can't, Lee, and you know only too well why.'

Mark had just been informed of the departure of the two Annunaki battle cruisers from Dulles, and wasn't going to let the grass grow under his feet. He immediately ordered an all-out attack on the Annunaki Dulles base.

Leading three thousand resistance fighters, Mark stormed the Dulles base. The defences struggled to hold out, but the sheer weight of numbers of Mark's resistance fighters was overwhelming. Mark was paying a heavy price, though. The defences Nalater had put round the perimeter of the base were savaging the assaulting resistance fighters.

Then, out of nowhere fifty TAG assault craft appeared, slashing through the ground defences like scythes through wheat and decimating the Annunaki assault ships that had been left to provide air cover. Balac led the assault from the air and the Annunaki forces that had been left to protect the base were overwhelmed both on the ground and in the air.

Jumouk had decided that, while direct intervention in China would not be viable, an attack on the Dulles base would provide a distraction and might cause a split in the Annunaki forces.

Dulles was in turmoil. The Annunaki were putting up savage resistance, but were slowly being cut down. However, the Sybotes had now been let out and were proving their worth. Fearless and ruthless they were tearing through resistance fighters as if they were cardboard cut-outs.

The purpose of the black hair-like Nanites had now become all too evident. They multiplied grotesquely and formed a kind of impregnable, lightweight chain mail over the silver body armour.

Nothing seemed to be able to stop them. Bullets and pulse weapons simply bounced off them. For mass killing they had changed their modus operandi from tearing heads off to using two machete-like blades in hand-to hand-combat, slicing through the resistance fighters at will, and causing atrocious injuries before inevitable death.

This was having a devastating effect on the morale of the resistance fighters. There were only ten of these creatures, but they were slaughtering everything they came close to.

The Dulles base was definitely being overrun, but the human cost was spiralling out of control.

Mark was agonising over what to do to stop the Sybotes, when one of them suddenly erupted in a ball of white boiling flame, Bill put the SMAW shoulder-launched rocket launcher back into the relaxed position. The thermobaric rocket from the SMAW had incinerated the Sybote from the inside out, sucking in oxygen from the air around it to fuel the intense heat within it, leaving little besides bits of the armoured suit smouldering on the ground.

It was not the ideal weapon because of the collateral damage it could cause, but it certainly seemed to do its job.

Mark waved a thumbs-up to Bill, and the battle raged on, now slightly more in favour of the resistance.

When he heard of the attack on the Dulles base, Tannacha flew into a rage. Leaving Gargius with the *Serpitus* to finish the job at Beijing, this time he broke his own rule of not separating his battle cruisers. Loading a full complement of assault ships and Annunaki warriors, he left Beijing and rocketed back towards Dulles. Jumouk's diversion had paid off. Now the *Serpitus* was on its own at Beijing, and Jumouk was going to take full advantage.

The two ESG battle cruisers had been waiting on full battle stations alert and were ready to go. Lee and Konoco were on their respective bridges on the *Victory* and *Iron Duke*, Along with Jumouk they blasted out of the weak atmosphere of Mars and headed straight for Beijing. As they entered Earth's atmosphere above China the targeting systems were already locked onto the *Serpitus*.

Gargius had spotted the approaching ESG battle cruisers and had begun to disengage from the attack on Beijing to concentrate on confronting the two cruisers. As the first volleys of weapons fire landed, the *Serpitus* lurched violently sideways with explosions ripping through her port hull. The bridge lifted skyward as if the massive craft was stalling, giving Gargius a perfect view of his executioners bearing down on him. The final weapons fire from the two ESG cruisers ripped through the bridge area of the stricken *Serpitus*, sealing its fate, as the huge craft split in two, showering the combatants below with white-hot debris.

In its last death-throes the *Serpitus* had managed to get a well-aimed, or lucky, barrage of pulse weapons fire directly on to the *Victory*, badly damaging it and leaving the pilots on the bridge struggling to keep the battle cruiser under control.

The destruction of the *Serpitus* had been a huge success but had left the *Victory* badly damaged.

Konoco had taken up position over Beijing, but Lee was clearly struggling to keep the *Victory* stable in flight. If he didn't do something soon he would be in danger of losing the battle cruiser altogether. Jumouk came to a decision. He ordered Lee to take the stricken cruiser to Sub Sea One.

Entering the Yellow Sea, Lee submerged down to five hundred feet, desperately checking for any hull breaches that hadn't been automatically sealed. Fortunately there were none and Lee set off on his hazardous journey to Sub Sea One and the Android corps of maintenance for repairs.

As Tannacha arrived back in the Dulles base airspace he was presented with an unwelcome spectacle. The Annunaki force that had been left behind had all but been routed by the overwhelming numbers of the resistance fighters and TAG assault craft.

The arrival of the *Nephilimis* and its reinforcements quickly swung the balance of power back into the hands of the Annunaki and it wasn't long before the resistance fighters had to retreat back into the cover of the surrounding towns and the sewer tunnels.

Once Balac was sure he had done everything he could to cover the retreating resistance forces, he and his TAG assault vessels disappeared into the North Atlantic, shaking off any pursuing Annunaki assault craft as they returned to Sub Sea One via predetermined escape routes.

Meanwhile Tannacha brought the *Nephilimis* to rest over the Dulles base once more, and ordered his ground forces to get the base into some kind of order before he and Nalater came down to survey the damage.

Nalater was the first to receive the devastating news about the *Serpitus* and Beijing, and knew it was his responsibility to break the news to Tannacha.

For a while now Nalater had been of the opinion that this mission was no longer sustainable, and that they should take as much gold, minerals and crystals as they could, and return home. He had obviously not expressed this opinion to Tannacha for fear of his leader's reaction, but as things went from bad to worse the temptation to cut and run was growing stronger.

The Annunaki forces were now down to one battle cruiser, around forty-five assault craft, two large transports, and a number of shuttles of varying sizes. The ground troops consisted of around seventy thousand warriors, scattered around the world, and ten thousand now at the Dulles base. This wasn't a conquering army any more: now it wasn't even an expeditionary force. No, he thought. Now is the time to confront Tannacha.

His thoughts were interrupted by Tannacha storming up onto the bridge.

'I know!' he snarled, sneering at Nalater.

It was almost as if Tannacha knew what he had been thinking.

'I want all our warriors and troops worldwide back at Dulles by the end of the day. Now do it.'

Nalater said nothing of what he had been thinking. He set off at once to carry out Tannacha's order.

# 43

Marie was watching the visual depiction consoles, and just bringing Nibiru into sight, when sure enough a small shuttle appeared on approach to the planet. Marie had to take a second look.

Within the asteroid belt surrounding Nibiru was a second Annunaki fleet, and the shuttle wasn't heading for the planet. It was now on course for the lead battle cruiser.

Pausanias joined Marie at the console and began expertly adjusting the visual controls. Marie counted the cruisers. After she reached eight she gave up and sat down despondently.

Pausanias took over the count. The final result was heartbreaking after everything they had been through. Now we should have had the advantage, she thought. Two cruisers to one. Well, that's the way it should have worked out. Eleven battle cruisers, five large troop transports and numerous support craft. It was a crushing blow for everyone, and probably a death sentence or worse.

Marie contacted Jumouk and Konoco.

'I've got some terrible news, Jumouk,' Marie stammered. 'The visual display consoles on Mars have picked up a large fleet around Nibiru.'

Jumouk sighed audibly.

'How many, Marie?'

Marie began to cry softly.

'Eleven battle cruisers, five large transports and some other assorted craft.'

Jumouk stared at Konoco. There was desperation written all over his normally expressionless face.

'Marie, go and get yourself a strong, sweet cup of tea, I'll be back to you shortly.

'Konoco, contact Lee and bring him up to date. Find out what condition his cruiser is in.'

Jumouk contacted Mars again, this time talking to Grant.

'Grant, I need the transports here at Beijing. You will need to organise an escort for them. They're too vulnerable to be on their own.'

Grant acknowledged the message and set to work.

Lee was stunned when he heard the news about the Annunaki fleet. His battle cruiser was nearly repaired now. The Android maintenance crews had done an amazing job and had worked non-stop.

Konoco had anticipated Jumouk's thinking and had already started to organise the evacuation of the Beijing base.

On board the now-repaired *Victory* Lee joined the *Iron Duke* over Beijing to provide air cover for the rapidly filling transports. Meanwhile, Jumouk had got back to Marie and explained the new plan of action.

Marie and Pausanias were now busy preparing for the arrival of the refugees from Beijing. Marie didn't know how many people the Mars base could accommodate, but Pausanias didn't seem to have any problem with the size of the new intake, which was reassuring from Marie's point of view. She no longer cared who had built the base; she was just happy that it was there and that Pausanias clearly knew what he was doing. Between Earth and Mars there was now so much going on that nobody had the time to worry about the new threat from Nibiru. They could just move the human cargo as quickly and safely as possible.

The whole operation seemed to be going extremely smoothly with absolutely no interference from the Annunaki presence at Dulles.

As each transport filled up, it left for the Mars base escorted by twenty-five assault craft and Lee in the *Victory*. On its arrival at the Mars base the transport unloaded its human cargo under the watchful eyes of Marie, Pausanias, and the hundreds of Mars inhabitants involved in settling the new intake into their new way of life.

The normal reaction of the new arrivals at the Mars base was one of disbelief at the size and comfort of the underground facility, especially in light of the widespread rumours that the base was a dingy old mine or, worse, mine tunnel.

At times Marie would leave Pausanias to get on with it as she paid a visit to the control room and the visual depiction consoles to check the position of the second Annunaki battle group. So far so good, she thought. At least it hasn't moved yet.

This was the only console that could detect a fleet so far away, and technically it was far more advanced than anything on board the cruisers. Marie didn't have a clue how it worked, but the pressure being what it was, she was simply glad that it did.

It had been a long hard shift but finally the last transport was filling up.

Jumouk was keen to get back to the Mars base for many reasons, the main one being the need to re-group and consolidate the defence of the base. He also wanted to see the massed forces of the new Annunaki battle group for himself. It wasn't that he didn't believe Marie, it was just one of those times you had to see it for yourself.

With the last huge transport filled and the underground base at Beijing abandoned, the battle cruisers and the rest of the craft made their way towards the Mars base.

As the battle cruisers took up their defensive positions above the Mars base, Jumouk and Konoco were already aboard a shuttle, landing in an area around the base protected by the force field. They made their way quickly down to the main control room to join Marie.

'Has there been any further movement of the Annunaki fleet, Marie?'

Jumouk was obviously very concerned as he watched the visual depictions in front of him.

Marie shook her head.

'No, there's been absolutely no movement at all – well, apart that is from the shuttle that docked with the lead battle cruiser.'

'It's two days' flight in hyper-drive, isn't it?'

Marie nodded

'I take it the shuttle was there to bring the new battle group up to date. I need to know what the defensive capabilities of this base are, Marie.'

Marie shook her head again.

'You're going to have to talk to Pausanias. He's the only one who can help with that. I still don't even know how big the base is. Maybe he'll be more forthcoming with you, anyway.'

Lee joined them and Marie welcomed him with a big warm smile.

'What have I missed?'

'Nothing much, Lee, except Jumouk's going to have to

talk to Pausanias to put together a plan for the defence of the base.'

Lee looked around.

'Just on that subject, where is Pausanias?'

'I think he's still settling the new arrivals in.'

This was not in fact true.

Pausanias was actually on a completely different level of the Mars base, a part of it which only the original Mars occupants had been in. Neither Dropas nor humans knew of the existence of this level.

This was the part that controlled all the weapons and defences around the surface and within the base of the red planet. Pausanias was busy now, expertly configuring the defence patterns that would defend the base against any Annunaki aggression. He had personally sat down with the two Mars operators monitoring the controls and reconfigured the systems himself. The response to any attack would be swift and decisive, and would show no mercy.

Satisfied that he had taken all the measures he needed to, he left his operators to oversee the system and returned to the main control room.

'Is that everyone settled in?'

Marie was the first to ask.

'It will take them a few days to settle in, Marie, but everyone's been allocated sleeping and living areas, and my people are assisting with any needs the new arrivals might have.'

Lee thought to himself. *My people*. That's an unusual thing for an Android to say. Everything about Pausanias seemed to be puzzling. He was certainly an enigma.

Pausanias was busy reassuring Jumouk about the defence system of the Mars base. This involved a lengthy and detailed explanation of how the automated defences worked. Finally, Jumouk seemed happy that everything that could be done had been done to protect the civilians sheltering on the Mars base.

# 44

Tannacha and Nalater had personally overseen the clearing up of the Dulles base after the encroachment by the Earth's resistance fighters. The attacked had caused a lot of damage and many casualties. The resistance had shown that they were a force to be reckoned with. In fact, a worldwide network of resistance was now in place and growing stronger by the day. Although Dulles was still the hub, the leadership was based in London.

All the Annunaki forces worldwide had now been recalled to the Dulles base, making it a formidable fortress.

Tannacha was back on his favourite project, the Sybotes. But now he had a definite plan. As usual he just hadn't told anybody what he had planned to do with them – apart, that is, world conquest and slavery.

Another shuttle had been despatched to Nibiru, and Tannacha was looking well pleased with himself again. He had come up with the perfect solution.

While the Annunaki warriors were bad and bad enough, and the Sybotes were even scarier and worse, he had come up with something even better. What about an Annunaki warrior as a Sybote? A mere thousand of these creatures would clear a swathe through Earth, killing and turning humans into Sybote slaves, with no problem at all.

The DNA and other samples needed for this were now on their way back to Nibiru where they would be processed and developed with the help or, perhaps, through the misfortune of the second-class Annunaki workers.

Marie was the first to notice a massive Annunaki craft sitting further back in the debris field around Nibiru, as if it was isolated from the rest of the battle group. It had, she observed, regular visits from a number of shuttles and other craft which docked and took off from there. She was mesmerised as she watched the number of craft coming and going, and wondered what was going on. Jumouk interrupted her reverie.
'What is it, Marie?'
'I don't know, but it's three times the size of a cruiser, and there's a lot of activity going on now.'
Shuttles and other types of vessels were docking and taking off every ten minutes, and Marie was becoming increasingly concerned. They had already come across the human Sybotes and knew that the Annunaki were capable of anything.

On board the massive ship the Annunaki warriors were having a very difficult time controlling the new breed of Sybotes. They were very different from the human form of Sybote: stronger, far more aggressive and less responsive to the influence of the mind-controlling device.
The creatures had to be put in different cells to stop bloody fighting breaking out between them, and this was taking its toll on the Annunaki warriors guarding them. It was also doing nothing to build confidence that they were going to be an asset when they reached Earth.
Morale itself within the Annunaki ranks was reaching an all-time low. They had all heard the stories about Earth

from the shuttle pilots, about its 'ghost' forces appearing out of nowhere, the savage fighting that had gone on, the resistance movement, the massive defeat suffered by the expeditionary force and the problems that they had faced, as battle cruiser after battle cruiser had been destroyed.

Tannacha's reputation for total disregard of his Annunaki warriors' lives had also not been lost on the succeeding generation of warriors.

A solution had to be found before the rabid Annunaki Sybotes could be released into the wild on Earth, otherwise they might prove to be more of a liability than an asset for the Annunaki. None of Tannacha's preparatory research had anticipated this problem, and the Annunaki scientists on board the huge transport were having a terrible time trying to find a solution. It was like a sailors' shore party gone awfully wrong.

Nevertheless, Tannacha had demanded that the Sybotes were to be sent, so that's what would happen. After all, he was the supreme commander.

The final shuttles were arriving on board the *Gerona*, the immense transport craft that would ferry these new Annunaki Sybotes to their destination at Dulles on Earth, and into Tannacha's hands.

Tannacha was making preparations for the arrival of his new battle group, This had been his plan all along. The trouble was, again he hadn't told anyone in his first fleet about it.

He had called Nalater into his conference room and brought him up to date with his plans. Nalater was impressed yet again. At least Tannacha still had the ability to surprise him, time after time. Maybe that's what distinguished him as leader.

# BATTLE FOR THE EARTH

* * *

The scientists on board the *Gerona* had eventually found a quick fix for the Annunaki Sybote's discipline problem. A second mind-control device placed on the opposite side of the brain seemed to calm the creatures down and make them more controllable.

The rest of the fleet was ready to go and waiting for the *Gerona* to be filled with its quota of Sybotes. The rest of the cargo had been loaded. This comprised mainly various ground assault craft, almost tank-like but without tracks, preferring to hover four feet above the ground and bristling with pulse weapons. There were shuttles, small, medium and large, and purpose-built, pre-fabricated buildings.

Around five hundred Sybotes had now been loaded and modified, and more were arriving every hour. The process of modifying the Sybotes had now been transferred to the research facility on Nibiru to speed up the process.

Eventually the prescribed target of one thousand Annunaki Sybotes was achieved and the fleet was now ready to take flight.

Tannacha and Nalater had not been idle at the Dulles base, and the town of Chantilly was in the firing line again. Nalater had been ordered to clear space to the south of the Dulles base and he finished the job that the resistance had started by levelling Chantilly to the ground. A five-square-mile area over Chantilly was flattened until no more than a three-inch-high mound of earth was left.

The conversion of the underground station deep under the Dulles base had been finished and fully kitted out with state-of-the-art equipment to produce human Sybotes by the dozens. The defences around the base were impenetrable for ground attack and daunting for an air attack. Annunaki assault craft were on permanent patrol in the airspace above the base, and were on scramble alert from the *Nephilimis* hovering above the base.

Tannacha was now ready to greet his new fleet and take on the Earth again.

# 45

The battle group started to move out of the asteroid field that surrounded Nibiru and slowly grouped into the designated formation, with the battle cruisers flanking the support ships and transports in a massive V shape.

This battle group was even more impressive than the one that Tannacha had led in what now felt like a lifetime ago. It thundered forward like a huge manta ray, carving its way through space, led by two small, ten-man shuttles, that were able to lead them through the hazards of space on exciting hyper-drive.

All of a sudden the fleet was enveloped, and in the blink of an eye were gone into hyper-space, and on their way to Earth – for better or worse.

On board the lead cruiser, Sutan, the commander of the new battle group, was holding a meeting in one of the sumptuous conference rooms on board his flagship *Orpious*. All ten of his battle cruiser commanders were represented, but because they were all in hyper-space, the meeting wasn't held in person. Holographic representations of each of the commanders were seated around Sutan's large conference table.

They were discussing the reports Tannacha had sent back on the first shuttle from Earth, in particular concerning the two cruisers around the other side of Mars.

Nobody knew that there was a base on Mars. They simply thought the ESG were hiding out there.

The other thing that was on the agenda was the question of the resistance fighters, although this was not seen as a particular threat to a battle group and army this size, especially with the new threat of the Annunaki Sybotes.

Sutan was looking forward to getting to Earth and meeting up with his elder brother, Tannacha. He relished the challenge of fighting these elusive Earth people and skinning them alive. It was just unfortunate in his eyes that there were only two ESG cruisers left. Still, they would have to do for now.

Sutan was something of a perfectionist and liked well-structured plans. Keeping his commanders informed and in the loop was important to him, unlike his brother's more maverick approach to war.

He had not been wasting his time while he was waiting for the battle group to set off. He had put together a plan of action for the battle group on its arrival on Earth. This of course would be at the discretion of Tannacha and not open to debate.

Still, Sutan thought it a good plan.

On arrival at Earth, Sutan would despatch five cruisers to hunt down the ESG cruisers and the transports with them. That would be the end of them. Meanwhile, the Annunaki Sybotes would hunt down the resistance and take care of them, bit by bit, if necessary. This strategy would be repeated all over the globe.

Tannacha could then concentrate on making his human Sybotes and getting ready for the colonisation of Earth.

Sutan had put this plan to his commanders for approval. One and all, they agreed it was an excellent plan. The meeting was brought to a close and Sutan returned to his bridge to check the progress of the battle group.

Marie gasped, and called out for Jumouk.

'They're not in the asteroid belt any more. They must have just gone off into hyper-space.'

Jumouk began scrolling through the visual display screens.

'That's them on their way then. Probably gives us two days. Pausanias has assured me that the defences on the Mars base are up to the job.'

'Doesn't that really depend on what they throw at us? Bear in mind that will give them twelve battle cruisers.'

Jumouk nodded in agreement.

'Well, I'm sorry, Marie. We just can't anticipate the outcome of this one.'

Lee had now joined them.

'I'm afraid Jumouk's right, Marie. The ball really is in their court this time.'

'Still, all's not lost yet. We've got this amazing base. We'll just need to see what Pausanias can pull out the hat.'

'Marie, will you warn Finney what to expect, and tell him to pass it on to Mark? To be honest I think Mark might be at the sharp end first.'

'No problem, Jumouk, consider it done.'

With that Marie headed off in the direction of the communications console.

Jumouk shook his head at Lee.

'It doesn't look good, Lee. Is there really nothing we can do?'

'I think we're just going to have to see how it goes, I can't think of anything we can do to stop the Annunaki battle group now.'

'I'm afraid the war on Earth might now be lost, but we must do everything we can to protect the civilians on this base. There is a possibility that if they get Earth they might leave us alone.'

'I believe that might be wishful thinking, Jumouk. Don't forget how unforgiving they are.'

Marie rejoined them. She wasn't told about the last part of their conversation.

'That's Finney up to date. Mind you, he's not too happy. There's nothing going on in London since the Annunakis pulled out. Personally speaking, I think he's bored.'

'Next time you speak to him, tell him to make the most of the peace and quiet I don't think its going to stay that way for long.'

Jumouk spotted the ever-elusive Pausanias and made his excuses to Lee and Marie.

'I just need to have another word with Pausanias. Will you both excuse me for now?'

With that he took his leave and ushered Pausanias into one of the annexes leading off the main control room.

'Pausanias, I need to know the full capabilities of this base. The Annunaki battle group that was at Nibiru will be here in around two days, and I still have very little knowledge of this base.'

Pausanias rubbed his chin thoughtfully.

'Jumouk, I am sorry but you are going to have to be patient with me when I say we have nothing to fear here.'

'I hear what you're saying, but how can you be so sure we won't have a problem, when they will have twelve battle cruisers to our two?'

'As I say, Jumouk, you're going to have to trust me for the time being. But do not worry, my friend. All will become clear in good time.'

Jumouk shook his head firmly.

'There is obviously something you're not telling me, and I don't understand why you're not keeping me in the loop.'

Pausanias smiled. He had to give Jumouk ten out of ten for persistence.

'Very well, my friend, let me show you something that will help ease your mind.'

He gestured for Jumouk to follow him.

As they entered the turbo-lift, Pausanias punched a code into the control panel and a whole new panel appeared next to the original one. He selected a level and section Jumouk was unaware existed. When the turbo-lift came to a standstill they entered a long, well-lit corridor. Pausanias paused and ran his finger tip over a strip of foil on the wall. A small four-seater floating craft appeared to rise from the floor in front of them. Pausanias gestured for Jumouk to take a seat in the craft.

Pausanias then selected some digits from the control panel, and the craft shot off on what seemed to be a pre-determined course, coming to a stop after three minutes at a pair of large twin doors. They dismounted and Pausanias again ran his finger tip lightly over a strip of foil on the wall. The doors slid open and the two entered a large room filled with consoles and three-dimensional imagery.

The doors closed behind them and Pausanias went directly to a large depiction of what looked like Mars. As the by-now thoroughly mystified Jumouk joined him, Pausanias began to explain:

'This is the heart of our defences. As you can see on this depiction of Mars, we have pulse weapons stations all around the planet intensifying around the entrance to the base. These are defensive positions.'

Jumouk was impressed. The defences did appear to be well positioned and formidable.

'We also have offensive positions which target any incoming craft with pinpoint accuracy at a range of up to ten thousand miles. These are not just pulse weapons, they are beam technology. The beam is less than a human hair in width and is invisible to the naked eye. It travels at the speed of light and – before you ask – no, it isn't a laser beam.'

Jumouk looked dumbfounded.

'How powerful is it?'

'The beam is inert antimatter and only becomes active at critical mass. If you imagine standing at the top of a set of ladders with a cup full of syrup: if you dribble the syrup from the cup in a fine stream, a puddle forms when it hits the floor. The beam works on the same principle: it puddles and builds up on the target's atoms reaching critical mass after a few fractions of a second.'

'And the result?'

'Devastating. It would tear a battle cruiser apart in a second.'

Jumouk wandered round the depiction of Mars, nodding his head approvingly.

'You seem to have it all well thought out, Pausanias. I have to say I don't think the defences could be any better.'

'Thank you, Jumouk. I assume I have put your mind is at ease now.'

Jumouk had moved away from the Mars depiction and was wandering around some of the other consoles that were dotted around the room, acknowledging the operators as he passed them.

'These other consoles, do they also play a part in the defence strategy?'

'Yes, the system is fully automated. Once a threat has been identified, the system takes over and determines the best ways of dealing with it. When the threat has been dealt with, the system then returns to a monitoring mode.'

'How can it tell what is a threat and what is not a threat?'

'The system is monitored by two operators at all times. It identifies activity, then simply asks if that activity is a threat. If weapons fire is detected, the system reacts automatically.'

As Jumouk strolled round the room he seemed pretty well satisfied.

'Shall we return to the main control room now, Jumouk?'

Jumouk didn't really want to go back to the control room; he would much rather have stayed on to explore this level of the base, which he had never seen before. But under the circumstances he felt that he had probably had his fair share of revelations for the day. Besides, now that Pausanias was being a little more cooperative, he didn't want to push his luck and alienate him.

'Yes, that would be fine, and thank you again for the guided tour.'

Back in the control room Marie asked Jumouk if he wanted to go for a tea or coffee in one of the annexes. It was pretty obvious what her intention was. She wanted to know what Jumouk had seen, but didn't like to ask outright.

Sitting at the coffee table and sipping a hot latté, Marie brought the conversation delicately around to the subject of where Jumouk and Pausanias had been.

'Did Pausanias manage to set your mind at rest, then?'

'Yes, he certainly did, Marie. I think I can confidently say this base seems extremely secure, no matter what happens.'

Marie took another sip of her coffee.

'I had a look at the defence console in the control room, but it's not exactly self-explanatory. I know Pausanias ran through a brief explanation of it with me, but as far as I could make out it's mainly automatic.'

Jumouk nodded.

'It is. In fact, the whole system is fully automated and as a back-up measure has two of Pausanias's people monitoring it at all times.'

Marie was reluctant to ask outright exactly where they had gone, but she did feel she was being put off a bit.

Jumouk wanted to speak to Lee soon to reassure him that at least the Mars base and its occupants were safe.

Fiona meanwhile had her work cut out, organising the settlement of the new arrivals at the Mars base. This was a tough challenge, but she did have the help of Pausanias's staff, and was amazed at how well organised they were, and how many people this base seemed able to support.

The food replication machines in the numerous dining areas were excellent. They could produce anything, and what was more, it tasted like the real thing! Everybody was more or less settled in and seemed contented. Pausanias's staff were helping out with any problems, even down to medical requirements. There were two fully equipped hospitals, fully staffed by trained nurses and doctors, even if they were Pausanias's people. It was almost as if the human population had been expected.

Fiona joined Marie at the coffee table, after Jumouk had left to track down Lee.

'How is the settling-in going, Fiona?'

'Great. Pausanias's people have been worth their weight in gold. You would almost have thought they had planned for this somehow.'

'To be honest, Fiona, right now I would believe anything. This place is just unbelievable!'

Fiona ordered a green tea from one of the Android waitresses. She had quite taken to green tea thanks to Lee's penchant for it.

'What's going to happen to all the people left on Earth?'

'I really don't know, Fiona. What I do know is we've got our work cut out for us up here.'

Lee joined them at the table, Jumouk had already brought him up to date regarding the security of the Mars base.

'Hi, Fiona. Long time no see. Is that you finished getting everyone settled in?'

'More or less, thank you, Lee. Initially, anyway. It's going to take time for everyone to get used to this base. Did you know they've got six digital cinemas here?'

'I hear there's two hospitals as well. Has anyone seen anything of Grant?'

Marie and Fiona looked at each other, then shook their heads in unison.

Grant was indeed busy, doing what he liked best. As the Mars terrain flashed fifty feet below him, his assault craft weaved and bobbed between the craters and mounds on the surface of the planet. If it hadn't been for the situation and the predicament they were in, this could have been idyllic. He felt like Buck Rogers.

At least five craft were circumnavigating the planet's

surface at any one time. With the Annunaki battle group on the move nothing was getting left to chance, and Grant couldn't help but put himself in the front line.

He was just passing over Simud Valles just slightly northwest of where the Mars Pathfinder had landed back in July 1997, when his communicator snapped into life.

'Grant, come in, Grant.'

It was Lee.

'Grant, can you hear me, over?'

'Yes, sir. What can I do for you, over?'

'Grant, can you return to base ASAP, over?'

'Sure thing, sir. See you in ten. Anything wrong, over?'

Grant had already changed course.

'No, we just need to speak to you. Thanks, Grant. Over and out.'

Grant was beginning to feel a bit like a schoolboy who had just been caught playing truant.

The Mars base was located under the shadow of Olympus Mons, the largest volcano in our solar system. The main entrance to the base was below and sheltered by a place called the blocks in the Olympus Mons. Although technically not on Olympus Mons, they were pretty close, and made excellent cover for the entrance to the base. The surrounding areas had suffered from sand displacement over the years with craft landing and taking off in the lower Mars gravity, but it was still an ideal location.

Grant brought his assault craft into land within the protective force field surrounding the entrance to the base, and headed to the turbo-lifts concealed within the blocks.

Jumouk and Lee were waiting for him in a large conference room. Like everything on the Mars base the room was very practical, but tastefully decorated, with the emphasis on comfort. Grant entered and took a seat facing Jumouk and Lee. Lee began:

'Thanks for coming so quickly, Grant. Time seems to be of the essence nowadays. Jumouk has raised an issue regarding the people left on Earth. It looks like we're not going to be able to intervene when the Annunaki start to find the Dropas bases, and the defences round the bases are only going to hold for so long.'

Grant looked shocked.

'You can't mean we're just going to leave them to fight on their own?'

'Grant, the Annunaki have twelve battle cruisers, and we have two. We now have around two and a half million people on this base. We have to prioritise. It's no longer feasible to pit our forces against theirs.'

'But there's billions in bases all over Earth. Are you saying we just leave them?'

'No, if we can organise the resistance forces effectively, then they stand a chance.'

Then Jumouk added:

'Finney and Sacha are organising a worldwide resistance movement and I have to say they've been doing a pretty good job up to now. They have been a real pain in the arse for the Annunakis. Although we lost the manufacturing facility on the moon base and obviously the ones on Earth's surface, we still have some capability with the undersea manufacturing facilities. We're not quite dead in the water yet.'

'You mean we can still make cruisers and assault craft?'

'Perhaps, but that's going to be down to Thourus and his Androids.'

Grant was beginning to see where this was leading.

'You mean we hold a guerrilla war until we have produced enough ships to strike back.'

'Exactly. Unfortunately, I think this means a lot of civilian casualties.'

'What about this base here?'

'Pausanias has shown me the defences on this base, and I think we will be quite safe here.'

'OK, so what's my role in all this?'

Jumouk looked at Lee as if he wanted him to take the lead. Lee spoke.

'We think there might just be time to evacuate another base before the arrival of the second Annunaki battle group. Pausanias assures us there is still plenty of room on this base to accommodate more non-combatants.'

Grant sat back in his seat.

'What we want you to do, Grant, along with Fiona, is to take the big transports and escorts to evacuate the base back to here. Jumouk and I will try to distract the Annunaki forces on Earth with our cruisers, with luck giving you a clear run at it.'

'You had me at "what we want you to do". OK, I'm in.'

Lee smiled.

'Thanks, Grant. But you do know it could go seriously wrong?'

'Yes, I know, sir, but we've got to try. Every life saved now is a bonus.'

'Good man, Grant! Can you bring Fiona up to date and get organised as quickly as possible? There really is no time to lose.'

The plan was simple.

The *Victory*, under Lee's command, would buzz the Annunaki base at Dulles with fifty of Thourus's TAG assault craft. Then they would head off to the far side of the moon. With luck this would be enough to distract the

Annunaki for long enough to allow the three large transports to sneak into Queensland, Australia and the Brisbane base. On their return the additional fifty assault craft would be incorporated into the Mars base defences. This would provide room in Sub Sea One for the planned production of more assault vessels by the maintenance Androids.

Grant escorted the transports together with the ten assault ships swiftly into Queensland airspace and on to Brisbane. The main entrance to the base was under the Gabba sports stadium off Main Street.

The first of the huge transports hovered over the stadium, with the shuttles ferrying people from the ground to the transport as speedily as was possible, while the other two transporters waited their turn, hovering patiently nearby. There was no sign of any Annunaki activity so Grant assumed the diversion plan had worked well. Meanwhile the assault ships were patrolling the skies above the Gabba stadium and the transports continued to hover in the airspace around it.

Fiona was already in the Brisbane base organising the evacuation. She was now quite well versed at this, with her previous experience at the other bases.

A steady flow of slightly bewildered people were now appearing and embarking from the shuttles onto the first transport. The evacuation of yet another base had begun. The reason Australia had been chosen was for the diversity of the species – just in case the worst did come to the worst.

This meant that humans from five continents were now going to be on the Mars base.

Lee had met up with the fifty TAG assault vessels and they were heading towards the Annunaki base at Dulles. He felt sure the Annunaki must have been monitoring their approach but, surprisingly, they hadn't so far made any move to intercept him. He wasn't sure if the Annunaki had spotted the transports heading for Australia and were going to attack them and leave him alone, but as far as he was concerned, this was not an option.

Lee increased the cruiser's speed and began to loose off speculative volleys of pulse fire. If they hadn't seen him coming, they couldn't miss him now. True to form a mass of blips appeared on the proximity detectors heading straight for them. The battle that ensued was massive, and brutal, with both sides fairly evenly matched.

Jumouk had wanted to avoid confrontation if at all possible, but the initial absence of Annunaki interest had forced Lee's hand. Now both sides were in a fight for survival, and neither was gaining the upper hand.

Assault ships were being downed at an unprecedented rate with blazing weapons fire from both cruisers and from the defences at the Dulles base. The firefight had now being going for fifteen minutes, and Lee was becoming concerned about the losses he was taking.

Now with the diversionary job done, Lee decided that discretion was the better part of valour and ordered his forces to retreat to the far side of the Moon. The battle cruiser *Victory* opened its engines right up and hurtled vertically towards the Moon, leaving the assault vessels to disengage and follow its lead.

Fortunately for Lee the Annunaki hadn't given chase and had regrouped over their own base. Out of the full fleet that started out from Nibiru, only eighty assault ships and one cruiser had survived.

## BATTLE FOR THE EARTH

\* \* \*

Lee and his cruiser along with the TAG craft had assembled on the far side of the moon. The losses were substantial. Out of fifty TAG vessels only twenty-two had survived the encounter, and Lee's cruiser had also taken a hefty beating.

As they sat on the lunar surface, maintenance Androids from on board the *Victory* were already working on the vessels that had suffered damage, including Lee's cruiser. Five TAG assault craft were in orbit around the moon and watching out for any Annunaki retaliation, or movement from the Dulles base.

Jumouk had been monitoring the proceedings on Earth. Apart from the obvious losses, everything was going to plan and the operation was by all accounts ahead of schedule. The race was on, however, because of the second Annunaki battle group, and the uncertainty about when it would arrive in space over Earth.

He was only too well aware that, if they arrived before the evacuation could be completed, disaster would follow. He made the decision that each of the transports when full would leave immediately for Mars and not wait to travel in a convoy. This was extremely risky but necessary now: he had to limit vulnerability on Earth.

As usual Fiona had done a brilliant job. The first transport with its human cargo was now on its way back to Mars, and the second was nearly full.

Then all hell broke loose.

Annunaki assault ships were suddenly everywhere. Pulse weapons fire smashed into the empty transport hovering round the Brisbane base, knocking it off its axis.

ESG assault vessels were engaging the Annunaki assault vessels but were heavily outnumbered.

Lee and the TAG assault craft he had with him were already on route to the Brisbane base to help out and Thourus had now sent the last of his reserves from Sub Sea One.

In all, sixty ESG and TAG assault ships were involved in the fray along with the *Victory*. They were up against a force of seventy Annunaki assault craft that had come seemingly from nowhere.

This was all Nalater's doing. He had come up with the idea of sneaking his craft out of Dulles and travelling underwater to Queensland to appear suddenly to attack the transports at the Brisbane base. The plan had been stolen from the ESG and had worked well, taking everyone by surprise. And now to make matters worse, the *Nephilimis* had just turned up and joined the fight.

The battle for the skies over the Brisbane base was intense, and so far undecided.

The first major casualty was the empty transport that had been hovering waiting to take on refugees from the Brisbane base. It had been savaged by at least ten of the Annunaki assault craft and had finally succumbed, smashing into the Woollongabba Telstra Exchange, a tall, telephone office building, around two hundred and seventy feet high, bringing them both crashing to the ground in an inferno of fire mixed with rubble.

Meanwhile the two huge cruisers were inflicting enormous damage on each other. Lee ordered the three-quarters-full transport that had been loading, to abandon the Brisbane base and head for Mars with all haste.

The engines on the transport had fired before getting the chance to close the main hold doors, throwing a succession of unfortunates out of the craft as it climbed desperately to reach escape velocity. The base itself was in turmoil as the Annunaki assault craft swooped savagely, time after time, on the defenceless humans caught out on the open playing field.

With the transport now on full power and on its way back to Mars, Lee ordered his ships to disengage and beat a hasty retreat to the Mars base. The Brisbane base was now past saving.

This time, however, Nalater was not giving up and gave chase. He was hot on the heels of the now disorganised, raggle-taggle bunch of ESG craft and the battle cruiser. Lee was getting the pounding of his life and Nalater knew it. He could smell Lee's blood.

The bridge on the *Victory* was a mess and now starting to vent atmosphere. There were breaches in the hull all over the cruiser and she would not be able to withstand much more punishment.

Jumouk ordered the *Iron Duke* and thirty fresh ESG assault craft from the Mars base to go to the aid of the stricken *Victory*. As the battle cruiser *Iron Duke* and its assault vessels flashed past the incoming transport, the sight sickened them. Most of the TAG assault ships had been destroyed or damaged, while the *Victory* was crippled, and losing power rapidly. The *Nephilimis* and its accompanying assault craft were savaging her at will like sharks attacking a whale in its death-throes.

The *Iron Duke* powered in with all weapons' banks spitting out blue streaks of death, scattering the Annunaki assault craft that had not succumbed to the hail of weapons fire in all directions.

Tannacha quickly took command on the bridge of the

*Nephilimis*, countermanding Nalater's instructions and ordering the immediate withdrawal of all Annunaki ships back to the Dulles base.

The *Iron Duke* took up a defensive position between the Annunaki vessels and the *Victory* like a mother protecting her child, while the ESG assault craft looked more like a pack of snarling attack dogs chasing an unwanted visitor from their home.

The *Victory* was now dead in space. The maintenance Androids were doing their best, but even they had their limits. It was starting to look as if the *Victory* had fought her last fight.

However, the *Iron Duke* wasn't going to give up so easily, and three powerful tractor beams latched onto the *Victory*, pulling her into the big cruiser's protective embrace. Then the entourage slowly began the journey back to Mars.

It was a long hazardous journey and the *Victory* almost didn't make it. The main problem was hull integrity and pressurisation leaks, but somehow the maintenance Androids managed to hold her together.

As the two cruisers came to land on the surface of Mars, Jumouk extended the force field around the two ships and vented breathable atmosphere into the bubble of safety.

The transport had landed safely and was now unloading her shell-shocked occupants to the safety of the Mars base. Maintenance Androids were crawling over all the damaged ships, and the wounded were being transported to the hospital facilities within the base by Pausanias's medical people.

Jumouk could now sit down and reflect on what had happened.

All in all it could have been worse. At least they had managed to save two-thirds of the Brisbane base and the

*Victory* hadn't been lost. Still, it was a major setback, especially with all those assault ships being lost, although everybody was now back in the safety of the base and the damaged vessels could be repaired.

Marie watched the Brisbane base for signs of movement. It almost looked as if the Annunaki had now lost interest and were all back at Dulles. She had no doubt that the Annunaki would have suffered badly as well but, still, just to leave the base like that was very strange.

Grant was exhausted. It had been a very long twenty-four hours and he had lost a lot of friends in the battle. His fleet of assault vessels had been badly mauled, with most of them damaged to some degree or other.

# 46

Marie had been right. Back at the Dulles base Tannacha was counting the cost of the last sortie. His battle cruiser was badly damaged and under repair by the Annunaki technicians, who were in all reality nowhere near a match for the ECM Androids. Tannacha only had fourteen assault craft left that were serviceable, the rest being either lost or badly damaged.

If the ESG mounted an attack on the Dulles base just now, the base would certainly be lost and the Annunaki presence on Earth would be terminated. This was the main reason Tannacha had overridden Nalater's orders and retreated from the battle.

It should be said, however, that even with the great losses suffered by both sides, both sides had gained something and the stalemate had been broken, even if it was, for the time being, advantage to the ESG.

Tannacha was scrutinising the proximity detectors on board the *Nephilimis* looking for what was left of the ESG fleet. He assumed that yet again they had sought refuge around the other side of Mars. To him it was imperative that any movement from the ESG fleet should now be detected as early as possible to safeguard the Dulles base.

He had desperately wanted to exploit the human resources at the now undefended Brisbane base for his Sybote army, but now could no longer afford to split his forces. The other problem that he was painfully aware of was the resistance forces around the Dulles base, and indeed world wide. They had been growing in number and strength almost daily, carrying out hit-and-run attacks on any stray Annunaki forces they came across. It seemed they now had the confidence that formerly had been lacking.

Nalater was furious at the behaviour of his superior. From the moment he had to deal directly with Tannacha, he had lost total faith in the leadership of this so-called 'supreme commander'.

The catastrophic loss of troops, ordnance and vessels was unacceptable even by Annunaki standards, but he knew that to say this openly would mean an instant death sentence, such was the stranglehold Tannacha had over his army. Nalater would need a lot of luck and a foolproof plan if he was going to succeed in overthrowing his leader, and he would need to move quickly with the second battle group due to arrive at any moment.

Nalater approached Tannacha on the bridge.

'Supreme commander, would you like me to lead a small force back to Australia and capture some humans for your Sybote experiments in readiness for the arrival of the second battle group?'

Tannacha thought long and hard about this generous offer from Nalater. He did want to impress the new battle group, and his Sybotes were sure to do that. The problem was he had none left, the last ten having been destroyed in the previous battle.

Self-interest decided it for him.

'Very well. Take four assault ships with two large transports and as many warriors as you think you need. I want at least a thousand humans. That should get me at least ten Sybotes.'

Nalater bowed and thanked his leader for the opportunity to serve him. But leaving the bridge he knew the final parts of his scheme were coming together.

The small group of Annunaki vessels travelled directly to Australia. This time there were no ESG ships showing anywhere on the proximity detectors.

Nalater was feeling quite pleased with himself. At last he would have a real opportunity to get rid of Tannacha without implicating himself. The natural progression of Annunaki thinking would then make him supreme commander.

The small Annunaki force set down in the Gabba stadium and the Annunaki warriors disembarked, three of the assault craft circling above like vultures over a fresh kill.

Two hundred Annunaki warriors were now bearing down on the entrances to the base, when a volley of machine gun fire caught them off guard. Six of the warriors fell immediately and two stumbled forward as if struggling to hold their balance. The rest broke ranks and took cover in the seated area around the stadium.

The assault craft didn't hesitate in pinpointing where the weapons fire was coming from, and proceeded to destroy the surrounding area. The weapons fire from the Australian resistance fell silent and the Annunaki warriors carried on with their task.

By now the Brisbane base had all but been emptied of the people left behind, but as in the case of all disasters you get some that leave and some that stay behind. Such was the case here and after some more sporadic resistance about three hundred humans were rounded up. This was nowhere near enough, however, and Nalater knew Tannacha would not be satisfied. He ordered his warriors out of the stadium and on to Wellington Road. They passed along the road and into the suburban areas to the east of the stadium, hunting for humans.

The resistance was intensifying now, as if the humans could guess their fate if captured. Street-to-street fighting was now the norm, with the certainty that the assault ships would bring a swift end to each skirmish.

The death toll was rising, but the Brisbane people were bravely leaving their mark on the Annunaki warriors. It took six hours of intense street fighting for Nalater to achieve the required headcount of one thousand captives, and at least seventy-five of his warriors wouldn't be going back to the Dulles base.

The captives were herded unceremoniously onto the transports by their Annunaki masters. The brutality of the warriors knew no limits, whether it was men or women. Children would be killed on sight as they were considered of no use to Tannacha's project. Nalater now had a plan to stick to.

Eventually the transports were ready to leave, and flying slowly at roof-top height they commenced their journey back to Dulles.

Unknown to Tannacha, Nalater had instructed that the equipment for the first part of Tannacha's Sybote process to be loaded on board the transports. Nalater was personally going to oversee the fitting and programming of the scorpion-like mind-control devices. This was an essential part of his plan, and he needed to get it right, which is why he was in no great hurry to get back to Dulles.

The conditions on board the transports were unspeakable.

It was only too apparent that the Annunaki had no respect for the human species.

Nalater had altered the programming of the scorpion mind-control devices only very slightly: just one spoken word of command by Nalater to be recognised by the Sybotes when he was ready.

Sixty of the humans had now been fitted with the mind-control devices. This was one of the more dangerous phases of the process and already four hundred and fifty humans had perished. Even with the expectation of a very high death rate during this initial part of the process, this was a huge loss of human material. It was probably due to the speed with which Nalater was processing them. He was demanding that one hundred of the humans be converted by the time they reached Dulles.

The dead bodies were simply tossed out of the transport as it flew along consistently at one hundred metres above the still and blue Pacific ocean, heading slowly and relentlessly for Dulles.

Nalater now had his hundred implanted humans. The remaining one hundred and twenty humans who were still half alive were unceremoniously dumped from the transport into the depths of the Pacific.

As the fifty-four survivors of the three-hundred-foot fall into the ocean struggled to keep themselves afloat, things didn't look good for them. The certain knowledge was that tiredness would bring a slow death by drowning, and cold would inevitably bring on hypothermia, with the same predictable result.

In an effort to stay afloat more easily and to retain as much body heat as possible they split into three tightly knit groups huddled together.

The natural leader of this unfortunate group was a tall, weather-beaten Australian just pushing thirty. He was called Burnum, an Aborigine name his grandfather had been allowed to chose meaning 'Great Warrior'. Burnum had shortened this name at a very early age to Bee, a much more practical name for a white schoolboy living in suburban Brisbane.

Bee had organised the groups of survivors and was trying to keep up morale, when the surface of the water suddenly parted to reveal a medium-sized shuttle which settled next to the stunned group of survivors, and opened up. The shell-shocked survivors were ushered one by one into the safety of the shuttle. Once the last of the dishevelled group had been picked up, the shuttle slipped back under the surface and sped off towards Sub Sea One.

Thourus had come along personally from Sub Sea One to supervise this rescue mission. Back in the relative safety of the undersea base the group was debriefed by Thourus in an effort to obtain any useful intelligence.

Time after time the story was the same: the interrupted rescue attempt; the panicky retreat, not knowing whether to flee or stay at the stricken Brisbane base; being hunted down by the Annunaki warriors; but most of all – the death and destruction.

The debrief with Bee was slightly different: he had seen something quite significant.

Bee had been fighting with the resistance, trying to hold back the advancing Annunaki warriors. AK-47s were the weapons of choice and Bee was well trained in the use of his weapon.

The tactics used by the resistance were simple, and had been used before: a firefight would be started and be fought savagely. The resistance would then withdraw leaving five fighters in hiding. The Annunaki warriors would advance in pursuit of the resistance fighters, passing the hidden group and leaving themselves vulnerable to attack from the rear as well as from the front. This strategy had served the resistance well and had helped to balance the odds against the superior Annunaki numbers.

Bee had concealed himself under the floorboards of a suburban house and was able to see the streets around him through the air ventilation bricks surrounding the bottom of the house. The streets were full of advancing Annunaki warriors, blasting away with their pulse weapons.

Abruptly a noise above him alerted him to a presence in the house. Three Annunaki warriors were in the living room above him. Through a crack in the floor he could see they were struggling with what looked like a hemp sack and the sack was putting up one hell of a fight.

Bee moved closer to the struggle looking for a gap in the floor where he could get a closer look. After finding an ideal position to observe he settled down to work out what was going on. All too soon it became apparent that inside the bag was a child, a young boy of around ten years, and the Annunaki were eating him alive, tearing savagely at the boy's live body and gorging themselves on his flesh.

The Annunaki ate humans alive! This put a whole new slant on survival.

Blinded with rage Bee opened up with his AK-47, bullets tearing through the floor up into the Annunaki warriors at nearly point-blank range, ripping into the torsos of the evil creatures. The hail of death also brought a merciful release for the screaming child. Bee emptied his clip, inserted another one and carried on blasting bullets through the disintegrating floor .

The next thing he remembered was waking up with a

seven-inch deep gash across his forehead in the squalor on board the transport among a throng of petrified civilians. Although there had been rumours regarding Annunaki feeding habits, he now knew for certain the Annunaki would eat live humans.

Thourus knew he had to get news of this to Jumouk. Bee would have to be sent to the Mars base with all haste.

# 47

Balac was keeping a watchful eye on his nervous passenger as they broke water just off Queensland. Bee was clearly in shock following his experience of being thrown out of a shuttle into the sea.

The TAG assault craft sped upwards towards the outer atmosphere at a fantastic speed, and without warning suddenly they were in space.

Bee couldn't believe how many times in the past twelve hours he should have died. He had lost count.

Whether through the relaxing experience of space travel or the sheer physical and emotional exhaustion of the past twelve hours, Bee drifted off into a fitful slumber. As the assault craft gently touched down on the red planet surface, he reacted instinctively and abruptly came to.

'Are we there yet?'

'Yes, we are, sir.' Balac was polite and to the point.

Fiona was waiting to greet them. Bee was amazed at the size and complexity of the Mars base, so luxurious compared to the Earth bases.

First of all he was taken to one of the base hospitals to have his head wound properly attended too. The hospital amazed him too, equipped as it was with technology he had never seen before, with staff obviously of the highest calibre. Within ten minutes you would not have guessed that he had been injured at all. They also provided him with a shower and a fresh set of clothes.

Fiona escorted him to the main control room, where Jumouk was waiting in one of the annexes. As Bee recounted his horror story, Fiona had to leave to be physically sick. It came as no surprise to Jumouk.

Bee had a large steaming mug of coffee in front of him. This was to wash down the two burger rolls he had just devoured. In the heat and panic of everything that had happened, he had clean forgotten about food. He couldn't remember the last time he had eaten anything.

The food was good; in fact, the food was excellent, he thought, gulping down another mouthful of strong sweet coffee.

Jumouk had been waiting for him to finish his meal.

'Bee, you must not repeat to anyone what you have just told me. If this gets out, I dread to think what it would do to morale.'

'I understand, I still can't believe it myself.'

Fiona now rejoined them.

'How are you feeling, Bee?'

'I'm fine thanks, Fiona. Just tired.'

'I'm not surprised. If it's OK with you, Jumouk, I'll take Bee to his quarters and get him settled in.'

Jumouk thanked Bee, and they left.

Lee joined Jumouk at the coffee table.

'I've just heard from Finney. He and Sacha have left London and are on their way to meet up with Mark at Manassas. They're planning another attack on Dulles.'

'Do you know what kind of attack?'

'Not really. They're being very hush-hush about it.'

'Did you hear what Bee had been telling us about the Annunaki?'

'Yes, unfortunately the rumours are all around the base.'
'That's regrettable. I don't know how this is going to affect morale.'
Lee nodded.
'To be honest there's not much we can do about it now the cat's out of the bag.'
Jumouk stood up.
'See if you can find out what Finney and Mark are up to. We could do with some good news.'
'OK, sir, leave it with me. I'll do my best.'

Mark Howden and Bill Graham were at the entrance to the sewer complex awaiting the arrival of Finney and Sacha.

The shuttle surfaced and dropped Finney and Sacha on to the small jetty. Making their way towards the entrance to the sewers, they could just make out the eerie shadows of the welcoming party.

With the introductions over, Bill took point and the small group made their way up through the complex labyrinth of tunnels, towards Manassas.

'Tell me, Mark. Do you have many pilots?'

Finney's question was almost nonchalant.

'Yes, we've got all sorts. Why? What you got in mind, Finney?'

Finney glanced round at Sacha and smiled.

'It's really Sacha's idea, and it's so bloody simple, it's obvious.'

'OK, now you've got me interested.'

Mark was well aware of Sacha's capabilities and training. He had quickly become one of those urban myths that grow up in uncertain times, a knight in shining armour, invincible and unstoppable.

'All right, we're going to need ten Hercules transports

with pilots, and enough phosphorous, high explosive and sulphur to fill them all.'

Mark whistled, a long high-pitched whistle.

'Not so easy, I'm afraid, Finney.'

Finney looked mystified.

'How so?'

'The planes, for a kick-off.'

Sacha interrupted.

'I think I can help you there.'

Finney and Mark looked at each other.

'How, exactly?'

It was Finney who asked the question.

'I know where twenty Hercules transports are constantly held on standby.'

'Where?'

'George Bush International Airport, Houston, Texas, my friends. All fuelled and ready to go from a secret underground complex.'

'I was going to ask how you knew that, but I don't need to bother, do I?'

Finney winked at Mark.

'He's the real deal, isn't he?'

Mark shook his head in disbelief.

'Shocking! So much for national security.'

Finney put his arm around Mark and said more seriously:

'Mark, you know that they have started making those Sybote things again, don't you?'

'I suspected as much. They seem to like them.'

'I was talking to Lee. He's confirmed that at least a hundred have been transported in some form or shape from Australia. They're probably arriving at Dulles even as we speak. They may even be there already.'

Mark stopped for a second.

'They're a pain in the arse and even harder to kill.'

'I know. I saw the reports. That's why we've got to stop them. If they ever succeeded in mass-producing these monsters, we really would be finished.'

Back at the Manassas base, Mark, Finney and Sacha sat down to work out the details.

'OK, what have you got in mind?'

Sacha stood up and started to pace around the table.

'We need to get rid of these Sybote things once and for all. It's difficult enough to fight the Annunaki themselves, but if they produce an army of these things, then it's game over.'

Mark and Finney nodded in agreement.

'The plan is for ten Hercules planes. We load them with ten full aviation fuel tankers from the airport, we strap tons of high explosive, phosphorus and sulphur to the tankers, then we fly over Dulles and drop the tankers right on top of the bastards. We get massive explosions, burning phosphorus that will melt anything it comes in contact with, and best of all sulphur dioxide creating strong sulphuric acid to eat and burn away anything that's left.'

'Brilliant! Improvised daisy cutters! Finney, where did you get this guy?'

Mark was thoroughly impressed with the ingenuity of the plan. The so-called 'daisy cutter' bombs were second only to nuclear devices for causing utter devastation.

'Now let's get to it, gentlemen, before any more of the bastards show up,' said Finney.

This last comment was a reference to the expected arrival of the second Annunaki battle group.

# 48

Tannacha was impressed with Nalater's efforts; he had brought him one hundred pre-programmed humans. This was going to save a lot of time processing them into Sybotes. With luck he would have most of them finished by the time the new battle group arrived.

The Sybote production facility was already in the process of creating more human Sybotes out of the new batch that had arrived from Australia. Tannacha wondered if the high council back on Nibiru had made any headway with his idea about Annunaki Sybotes. Anyway, he would probably find out when the new fleet arrived.

Nalater was overseeing the production of the Sybotes personally. He was fascinated by the process of turning a human being into an unthinking killing machine. The process was going well: five Sybotes had already been completed at the cost of just ten human lives.

Tannacha had returned to the bridge of his flagship to await the imminent arrival of the second battle group. He was just practising his welcoming oration to impress the new commanders when Nalater's shuttle docked with the five new Sybotes on board.

Nalater and his Sybotes made straight for the bridge where Nalater immediately gave the order and the Sybotes set to work.

Tannacha and his personal guard of four elite Annunaki

warriors put up a good fight but were no match for Nalater's new assassination squad. The bridge quickly turned into a killing ground, with dead Annunaki warriors strewn everywhere, including the limbless and headless torso of the once-feared Tannacha.

Nalater now took control of all the Annunaki forces on Earth. He brought in key Annunaki warriors who he knew were loyal to him to take charge of the *Nephilimis*, and to proclaim him the Supreme Commander of all Annunaki forces.

His victory was to be short lived, however.

In all the commotion and excitement no one had been monitoring the proximity detectors, and the arrival of the resistance squadron of ten Hercules transports above Dulles had gone quite undetected.

The unusual and somewhat odd-looking daisy bombs had been triggered to explode at five hundred feet above the base. This was to maximise the impact. As aviation fuel, high explosives, phosphorus and sulphur mingled together to create a series of massive explosions, the destruction was total.

There were ten huge explosions in all. Between them they razed the whole base to the ground, leaving not a single structure standing in an eight-square-mile area, with virtually nothing left alive.

In most cases the Annunaki warriors were killed instantly, but some unlucky ones died in screaming agony as the phosphorus burnt though their flesh and into their bones and skeletal structure. The strong sulphuric acid caused by the fusion of molecules of sulphur and $O_2$ during the explosions filtered through every gap in the rubble, eating any surviving flesh or bone, alive or dead.

The Dulles base and production facility had been destroyed totally in one diabolically clever raid.

The *Nephilimis* fared no better than the base. Explosions tore through her outer hull, and white-hot phosphorus burnt through her insides like a blast furnace melting steel.

There were no survivors. What was left of the *Nephilimis* crashed into the ruins of what had once been the Dulles base.

From the Hercules transports the spectacle below was one that signified total victory.

If the Annunaki had ever thought that Earth would just roll over and die, this would be a permanent reminder to them of mankind's determination to survive, even against all the odds.

Finney was elated. Sacha, by contrast, looked thoughtful. He was, after all, a realist. This had been a great success, but there was a new battle group on the way and he knew that this might not be handicapped by such shoddy and inept leadership.

Sacha was right. At the same time as the Hercules transports were landing back at Houston, the second Annunaki battle group appeared from hyper-space orbiting over Earth. With the help of the two small lead shuttles they had successfully navigated the hazardous debris field further out in space, proving from the outset that this commander was to be no one's fool.

The flagship of this second battle group, the *Orpious*, settled into a high orbit above Earth and North America. Sutan, the commander of battle group, had been surprised not to have received any word from his brother, Tannacha.

Leaving most of his fleet in geosynchronous orbit above

Dulles, Sutan took his flagship and two other cruisers down to the Dulles base to investigate.

The sight that greeted them was beyond anything they could have imagined. Total devastation was visible everywhere. Nothing could have survived within the area of the base or indeed in the wreckage which was only just recognisable as the *Nephilimis*.

In a black rage Sutan immediately signalled the battle cruisers back into orbit, with orders to target and pulverise all the capital cities throughout Earth as a taste of the retribution to come. Wasting no time, the battle cruisers broke orbit and shot off to rain death and destruction down on city after city from their massive banks of pulse weapons. New York, London, Paris, Minsk, Tripoli, Pretoria, Edinburgh, Dublin were obliterated, as the Annunaki cruisers moved from continent to continent, mercilessly intent upon wiping out all trace of mankind's presence on planet Earth.

Sutan and his two escort cruisers began the task of finding any ESG ships or cruisers still left operational, although even with proximity detectors this was going to be like looking for a needle in a haystack.

With no initial success Sutan ordered all assault vessels to disembark from the battle cruisers and start searching on Earth, around the moon and on Mars. Hundreds upon hundreds of Annunaki assault craft were now out on search-and-destroy missions, each one of them itching for a fight.

Part of Earth's resistance was know to be in the Dulles area, and Sutan gave the order to unleash the Annunaki Sybotes, one thousand strong, to spread out from the old Dulles base and destroy the resistance once and for all.

The huge transport ship *Gerona* came gently down to rest on the flattened Dulles base. The Annunaki Sybotes that disembarked from the ship were indeed fearsome monsters, and virtually uncontrollable. With the fitting of the second mind-control device they had at least stopped killing one other, but it was still a case of letting the mad dogs out, rabid ones at that.

Sutan himself had very little time for these monstrosities and even less faith in them. They had been Tannacha's idea and had been taken up by the Annunaki high council as an experiment.

Sutan's own perspective on things was much less fanciful and certainly much simpler: just flatten the planet, kill all its inhabitants, apart from what was needed for a future food source, and rebuild it to suit Annunaki requirements.

This is the way things would be. Earth would be ready for colonisation within a month, and vengeance would be taken for the destruction of the first invasion fleet.

# 49

Jumouk watched the arrival of the second Annunaki battle group in despair. He had known it was on its way, and how big it was. Here was the irrefutable fact, in the flesh, and it was already demonstrating a quite different battle strategy.

Dulles had been a huge success, but the timing had been unfortunate with the arrival of the second battle group right on the heels of the destruction of the first fleet. Now these battle cruisers were systematically destroying every capital city on Earth with ruthless and breathtaking precision.

Marie interrupted his reverie. She pointed to the assault craft that were bearing down on Mars.

'We've got company, Jumouk.'

Two wings of Annunaki assault craft, fourteen vessels in all, were rapidly approaching Mars.

'When will the defences kick in?'

She was puzzled as to why the defences had not started to destroy the enemy craft.

'I don't know, Marie. They should have activated by now.'

Jumouk too was now beginning to be concerned. Perhaps the Mars base wasn't as safe as they had been led to believe. He could tell from the look on Marie's face that she was thinking the same thing.

BATTLE FOR THE EARTH

\* \* \*

The Annunaki assault craft were now skimming the surface of Mars. Worse still, three Annunaki battle cruisers were also on their way, heading directly towards the base.

The Annunaki assault vessels had split up and were searching the surface of the red planet methodically. Flying at high speed and fifty feet from the surface, the craft flashed over the planet surface looking for signs of ESG activity. The moon base had already been explored and ruled out as an active base, Sutan having guessed that if there were any other hidden bases the most likely planet would be Mars.

The three massive battle cruisers which included Sutan's own flagship had taken up orbit on the far side of Mars, in constant contact with the assault craft scrutinising the planet's surface.

Sutan was watching the proximity detectors on board his flagship closely, but there was absolutely no sign of any activity on the planet below apart from his own assault craft.

Jumouk could do nothing but watch and pray, Lee had now joined them and was expressing his concerns as well.

'What the hell's going on, Jumouk?'

'I honestly don't know, Lee. The defences don't appear to be working. Do you know where Pausanias is?'

'Sorry Jumouk, not got a clue. I thought he would have been here with you.'

'I've not seen him since the second fleet arrived. Marie, have you seen him at all?'

Marie shook her head.

'No, like you say, since the second fleet arrived there's been no sign of him.'

Lee's eyes lit up.

'I bet I know where he is. He'll be in that other defence control room, but I can't remember how to get to it.'

Marie began scrolling through the schematics of the base.

'I don't see it on any of the schematics.'

'No, it's a devil of a place to get to, I don't think the level that it's on is even shown, at least not on anything we've got access to.'

'I don't know why the battle cruisers haven't opened fire yet.'

'Hold on. Didn't Pausanias say he had deployed some kind of cloaking device?'

Lee nodded.

'That's right, they can't see us. That's why they're not firing at us.'

Jumouk summed it up.

'And that's why we're not firing at them. Pausanias doesn't want to give our position away.'

'Can we find someone to take us to that control room?'

Marie left to find somebody. Within a few moments she had returned with one of Pausanias's colleagues who said he would take them there.

Sure enough, when they arrived at the control room they found Pausanias monitoring the Annunaki craft on the three-dimensional displays. Pausanias had already grounded and camouflaged the ESG vessels that had been patrolling the red planet's surface when the second battle group had arrived out of hyper-space, so no electronic signatures would be found on Mars.

By the look of it the Annunaki were coming to the end of their search. The battle cruisers were already on their way back to Earth and the assault vessels were just finishing their final sweeps of the planet.

Pausanias apologised for not being with Jumouk when the Annunaki fleet had arrived but, as he explained, he had to monitor the situation in case anything had gone wrong. He had fully anticipated the search of Mars and had taken all the necessary steps to keep the base hidden, but if something were to go wrong he needed to be able to access the blistering array of weapons from this control room.

The last of the Annunaki craft had left, none the wiser about the Mars base, thanks to Pausanias's foresight. Earth was now the centre of attention, and the Annunaki battle cruisers were still levelling the capital cities at a frightening rate.

'Will the people in the bases closest to the capital cities be able survive that kind of weapons fire?'

Marie's question was the one that was on all their minds, and nobody had an answer.

The topography of Earth was changing as they spoke, and nobody could do anything about it.

The colonisation of Earth by the Annunaki had begun.

# 50

Sutan was still nonplussed by the absence of any resistance from the ESG. Where were their battle cruisers, if indeed they had any left? After repeated scans of Earth and the surrounding space absolutely nothing had been detected.

Looking on the bright side, the Annunaki Sybotes had unearthed a cell of resistance just south of Dulles and they were now in the process of eradicating it from the Manassas area.

Nevertheless, Sutan was still spoiling for a fight. He hadn't come all this way with a complete battle group in tow just to sit around idly. Virtually all the capital cities had now been razed to the ground and one by one his battle cruisers were rejoining him above Dulles.

It had to be said it was a breathtaking sight.

The resistance fighters at Manassas had taken to the sewer systems in a bid to escape the Annunaki Sybotes. Above ground it had been a massacre.

The mindless killing machines had shown no mercy. They felt no fear or pain. If wounded, they would do anything to continue killing.

At least the tunnels in the sewers gave the resistance a fighting chance.

When Bill Graham, the architect, had mined the tunnels, everyone had been given maps of the lay-out in the sewer system. Now the work Bill had put in was paying dividends and saving lives.

The main aim of the fleeing resistance was to get to the outlets on the Potomac River. Shuttles had been hidden strategically at points just off the river for precisely this kind of emergency. The resistance fighters now only numbered hundreds. They had paid a heavy price for the destruction of the first invasion fleet and its Annunaki warriors, with the subsequent onslaught of the Annunaki Sybotes.

This was a running battle, not only of strength but of wits. At last, however, they were starting to make inroads into the numbers of the Sybotes chasing them. The shock wave created within the smaller space was wreaking havoc even with the heavy armour the Annunaki Sybotes had built into them. Also, as each explosion tore a tunnel apart, collapsing it completely, the Sybotes had to find another way around, which slowed them down considerably. It was a hard-fought battle, but it was beginning to look as if some of the resistance would be able to make good their escape.

Ironically, the resistance leaders were still at George Bush International Airport and, having received no news of recent events, were still celebrating the complete success of the mission involving the Hercules transports and their daisy cutters. That really had been the high point for the resistance, and they were sure that even Lee and Jumouk must have been impressed.

Four shuttles lifted to roof-top height, then, diving into the dark waters of the Potomac, formed themselves into a diamond shape and headed towards the Atlantic Ocean.

In all two hundred and forty resistance fighters survived.

The losses on the part of the Annunaki Sybotes were substantial and unexpected. Six hundred were lost in total. The main reason for this was the total loss of reckoning; they really had been turned into cannon fodder especially in the sewers.

To a man the resistance fighters were aware that they must get to Mark before he returned to Manassas, still unaware that the second battle group had arrived.

They would surface in the Gulf of Mexico then head inland at low level to Houston and on to George Bush International Airport, hoping to rendezvous with Mark and Finney. They could then bring them up to date with the latest events.

Mark, Finney and Sacha were just about to board their shuttle when the four resistance shuttles were spotted coming in low and fast.

'God! They're in a hurry, aren't they?' exclaimed Finney.

The first shuttle landed and Bill the architect emerged.

'Mark, I need to speak to you now.'

'What's all the rush, Bill?'

'It's the Manassas base. It's been overrun.'

'I don't understand, Bill. We took out the Annunaki threat there with the daisy cutters.'

'It's the second Annunaki battle group. It's here, now, and they're bastards. We only just got out with our lives.'

'Don't tell me this is everyone, the only survivors?'

'I'm sorry, Mark it was a massacre. They had these monstrous Annunaki Sybotes.'

Finney was aghast.

'How many people did you lose in all?' he asked nervously.

'Thousands, bloody thousands.'

Mark clenched his fist and looked away from Bill.

'Shit! I can't believe this. When did the fleet arrive?'

'More or less right after you wiped out the remnants of the first fleet.'

'Christ! I just can't believe it. What have we got to do to get rid of these bastards?'

Bill looked shattered. They hadn't stopped since leaving Manassas.

'Bill, I know you're probably knackered, but could you organise the guys that came with you? If you take them to that building over there you can get some hot coffee with rum in it. I think there's also some hot chicken soup and bread. Get your fill then all of you get some sleep.'

'You know we can't go back to Manassas? The whole bloody Annunaki battle group is at Dulles. It's swarming with bloody great cruisers, and after the running battle we had, the sewer systems are a mess.'

'I know, Bill. Go get sorted and leave it with me.'

Bill was right of course and Mark didn't have the answers yet.

Mark, Finney and Sacha sat down together with three mugs of straight rum.

'Well, what do we do now?'

Mark's question was to the point, but unwelcome nonetheless. They had already been through so much under the worst circumstances. How long could they keep pulling rabbits from the hat? Sacha replied wearily:

'I don't know Mark, I really don't. How many are in this battle group?'

'From what I understand, maybe a dozen battle cruisers and probably six hundred assault ships, and of course the supporting vessels. Not got a clue how many warriors or Sybotes.'

'Shit! What can we do against that? There's probably only a thousand of us left, and virtually no equipment.'

'What about the Mars base?'

'Totally defensive from what I know. We've got a couple of battle cruisers and some assault craft based there.'

Sacha grinned.

'Well, all's not lost then.'

'I've not been in contact with Mars since they gave me an update of the Annunaki fleet numbers.'

Mark stretched out in his chair.

'I don't even know for sure that the Mars base is still there.'

Sacha leaned forward onto the table and took a gulp of his rum.

'OK, getting back to the point. Where do we go from here?'

'At least we've got transport. That gives us six shuttles now, and you've got some assault craft at London, haven't you, Finney?'

'I don't know, I've not been able to get hold of London.'

Mark stood up abruptly.

'Right, that's it. We don't know shit. We can't work like this. Give it two hours, Finney, then get the guys on the transports. We're going to Sub Sea One.'

Finney stared at Mark.

'Do you even know where it is?'

'Of course I know where it is! At least, I mean … I've got the coordinates for it.'

Finney smiled to himself and then set off to do what he needed to do.

# 51

Sutan was well satisfied with his first two acts of revenge: the annihilation of the resistance at Manassas and the destruction of every capital city on Earth.

Now he would make Dulles rise from the ashes like the proverbial phoenix, under the new name of Tana, in memory of his beloved brother. He had already ordered construction to begin, everything he needed for colonisation had been brought with the fleet, and he was fully determined not to let the grass grow under his feet.

A forty-square-mile area around Dulles was being levelled off and sealed with a concrete-like substance which served as a foundation. On top of this foundation the Annunaki capital city of Tana would be built and colonised. The rest of Earth would be terraformed over a period of time and Earth would become an Annunaki planet. The construction was well planned and from hour to hour the topography of the area was changing dramatically.

Security was no longer a problem. Three of the cruisers were on constant patrol in the skies over Earth. These were backed up by one hundred assault vessels, and numerous shuttle craft manned by Annunaki tactical-response warriors. Three other cruisers guarded the new construction work at Tana, and five more were placed strategically in deep space.

It was certainly looking as if Sutan was capable of

achieving what had always evaded Tannacha: decisive strategy and effective logistics.

There was still some resistance around the planet, but it lacked organisation and as soon as a skirmish started it was crushed with brutal force from above and from warriors on the ground, transported by the shuttles.

The six shuttles docked at Sub Sea One, and a battle-weary bunch of resistance fighters disembarked and headed for the main complex. Mark and Finney set off to find Thourus and obtain any new intelligence that was available, especially regarding the Mars base.

Thourus was a difficult Android to track down, but eventually Mark and Finney caught up with him and the three of them sat down together.

'What's the news on the Mars base, Thourus?'

'The base is fine, Mark. From what I understand, the Annunaki have already searched Mars and found nothing.'

Finney smiled at Thourus, not really knowing whether the smile was wasted or not.

'Well, that's the first bit of good news we've heard for a while. How are you fixed for assault craft, though?'

'Not well at all. There are some that have just come out of the repair workshop, but that's it.'

'How many?'

'Maybe ten at the most. All the other reserves have been used.'

'Where's Sacha got to, Mark?'

'Don't know. Last thing he said to me was, "I'm going scavenging. See you later." Make of that what you will.'

'Thourus, have you heard anything from London?'

'No, London isn't there any more. All the capital cities have been levelled world wide.'

Mark rubbed the side of his head, which was a sure sign of stress with him.

'Shit! This fleet's very different from the first one. They've got more done in a few days than the last fleet managed the whole time they were here.'

Finney stood up.

'OK, so we've got no resources to speak of on Earth. That just leaves what we've got on Mars. Can we contact Mars?'

Thourus interrupted.

'That's not quite true, Finney. We do have a manufacturing facility now attached to Sub Sea One, and it's nearly ready to go into production.'

'What, assault craft? We can make assault craft?'

Mark butted in.

'Can we make cruisers?'

Thourus shook his head.

'No, we can't make cruisers. We lost that ability when we lost the moon base, but once the plant get's going we should be able to produce two assault ships a day.'

'Well, that's better than nothing. At least there's some hope.'

Finney was determined to think positively. He couldn't fail to notice Mark's worrying body language. The last thing they needed now was a stressed-out second in command.

Sacha was having a great time. He had already found the repaired shuttles and now saw to his delight that there were another six waiting in the repair bay. Leading off from the repair bay was a corridor to the manufacturing plant; Sacha whistled when he saw the impressive size of the plant.

There were Androids everywhere. It was like the interior

of an ant hill, full of scurrying activity, and the production line was already up and running with specialised Androids assembling components: one long production line as far as the eye could see.

Sacha wondered where the components were coming from. It looked very much as if everything was prefabricated for ease of assembly. It was certainly a clever operation.

He was right in this. Underneath Sub Sea One was a prefabricating plant for parts. It covered all components for assault craft and shuttles of every size – everything from body parts and electronics to engines.

These would formerly have been shipped to the moon base for final assembly, but now were being constructed in the makeshift assembly line attached to Sub Sea One. It wasn't anywhere near as efficient as the moon base plant, but it was certainly better than nothing. At least now they would eventually be able to put up some kind of fight.

To Mark the next move was obvious. The three of them had to go to the Mars base and meet up with Jumouk and Lee. He knew Sacha would be fine, but Finney was a different story with his morbid fear of flying. He and Finney joined Sacha in the production plant.

'We need to get to the Mars base, lads. We need a plan, so we have to talk to Jumouk and Lee. How about we take an assault vessel each and go for it?'

'Fine by me. Just point me in the direction I need to go and show me the accelerator.'

Mark had forgotten Sacha hadn't had any formal training on flying ESG craft.

'I think we can do a bit better than that. I'll show you the principles of how to fly an assault craft. Honestly, they almost fly themselves once you get used to them. Finney, you've gone very quiet. I know you've been trained to fly.'

'Oh, I can fly all right. I just don't like to.'

'Come on, Finney, don't give me a hard time. You know we need to go.'

'I know. It's not a problem. You just get Sacha sorted out. When do we go?'

'Half an hour should do it.'

'OK, I'll go talk to Thourus and get three assault craft sorted out.'

'Thanks, Finney. I mean it, thanks.'

Mark's relief was obvious. The last thing he needed was trouble from Finney, even though, technically, Finney was the boss.

Mark and Sacha disappeared to find an assault craft for Sacha to practise the basics of flight, under Mark's careful instruction.

The three assault craft traversed the ocean to Western Australia so as not to give away the position of Sub Sea One, and also to have a better chance of breaking Earth's atmosphere without Annunaki intervention. They needn't have worried. The Annunaki were thoroughly preoccupied with the new capital city they were building.

The assault craft broke through the waters off Western Australia unchallenged and sped vertically towards outer space and the Mars base.

The patrolling Annunaki assault ships seemed totally indifferent to the movements of such a small number of craft. This was because all the Annunaki vessels patrolling the skies of Earth and in deep space had the same remit: watch for battle cruisers and ignore everything else for the time being.

Finney had surprised himself. He was actually quite enjoying the flight, even through space. He had come to the conclusion that his fear of flying must have been the result of other people flying him; now he was in control himself, he was more than comfortable with it.

Sacha was still getting used to the controls. He had found when you were actually flying they were very sensitive and keeping in a straight line while on manual control was nearly impossible. Still, he had to admit, it was good fun!

The three assault ships came to rest safely within the Mars base force field and the occupants set off to find Jumouk and Lee. They were met at the entrance to the turbo lifts by Fiona who had been monitoring their approach and landing on the Mars base complex. Sacha smiled warmly at Fiona. He liked her. He liked her a lot.

'Fiona, it is so good to see you again. How are you?'

His Russian charm was evidently not lost on Fiona.

'I'm good, Sacha, thanks. How are you?'

Finney yawned. It was involuntary, but he realised he couldn't have timed it worse.

'Oh my God! I'm so sorry, Fiona. It must be the last few days catching up with me.'

Mark smiled to himself. Wasn't it ironic that even in such dire circumstances humanity could still be so laughably human?

'Hi, Fiona. Look, can you get us to Jumouk and Lee? We've got a lot of information for them.'

'Sure, Mark, just follow me.'

They entered one of the turbo-lifts and sped down into the bowels of the red planet.

# 52

Jumouk listened intently to Mark's version of what had happened on Earth since the arrival of the new Annunaki battle group.

It was now plain to see that the Annunaki had a new agenda, as opposed to a little sport and robbing the planet of its gold supplies. They were now evidently intent on moving from Nibiru, colonising planet Earth, and setting up home there.

The building of Tana, the new city on the Dulles site, was visible evidence of their intentions, and by the look of it the human race was now a mere inconvenience or, at best, a dining option, to be exterminated as and when encountered. Once Earth had been colonised, the Annunaki wouldn't tolerate a human presence on Mars for long.

The situation was indeed looking desperate, and Jumouk struggled to think how to save what Dropas and human population were left, either on Earth or eventually on Mars.

Lee sensed Jumouk's despair, but felt unable to help. He had run out of practicable ideas himself. Perhaps some short-term stuff like more inventive ways of hit and run, but to be utterly frank, with the size of the fleet opposing them and only two battle cruisers and at most a hundred assault craft, what could they do in the long term?

JOHN P. GLEDHILL

\* \* \*

Redemption was to come yet again from an unexpected quarter. Pausanias asked if Jumouk and Lee would be kind enough to join him for a tour of a part of the base they had not yet seen. To Jumouk and Lee this now offered itself as a welcome distraction. Besides, Pausanias seemed always to find ways of surprising them, so they accepted gratefully.

As they drove along corridor after corridor in the small transport, Lee could tell something was troubling Pausanias.

'Is there something wrong, Pausanias? You seem troubled, if you don't mind me saying.'

Jumouk looked quizzically at Lee, almost as if he felt he had somehow overstepped the mark. Pausanias seemed to pick up on Jumouk's concern.

'No, it's fine, Jumouk. Lee's quite right. I haven't been entirely truthful with you both.'

This admission did not come as a great surprise to either of them. Pausanias and the Mars base had been a mystery ever since they had arrived, and trying to get elucidation from Pausanias was like asking questions of a small boy. Revelations had been few and far between. Still, now he had their full attention.

'Unfortunately, circumstances have now overtaken us, and I cannot allow the current situation to continue.'

Lee looked at Jumouk. The tone of Pausanias's voice had changed completely, and his bearing had taken on a totally different character.

Jumouk pursued the subject.

'How do you mean, Pausanias? What situation?'

'Quite simply, the Annunaki cannot be allowed to colonise Earth.'

'Do you have some idea, then, how to stop them?'

The tone in Lee's voice had gone up a note in anticipation.

'We will now intervene and stop them. All will become clear in a moment.'

'We, as in who?'

Lee had just got the question out when the little transport cart came to a halt.

'Follow me, please.'

Pausanias gestured for them to follow him into a turbo-lift. He entered a code into the control panel and the turbo-lift sped off. Lee and Jumouk could both now feel the excitement rising in them as the lift came to a halt. As the doors opened, a cool breeze could be felt, almost as someone had just turned on the cold setting on the air-conditioning control.

The sight that met them when the doors were fully open made Lee glad of the cold blast of air for, hovering in what could only be described as a huge hangar, was a battle cruiser the like of which neither Lee or Jumouk had ever seen. It was vast, dwarfing any battle cruisers the ESG and Dropas had at their disposal.

Jumouk and Lee stood dumbstruck. After a moment Lee blurted out:

'Where the hell did this come from?'

Pausanias said quietly:

'You no doubt have some questions that will need answering, gentlemen.'

This was a massive understatement.

'Does it work?'

It was a stupid question, as Lee realised straight away. Of course it worked!

'Yes, it is in perfect working order, as are the other two on Mars, and the one patrolling under the seas on Earth.'

Lee stopped for a minute as if counting.

'You mean there are four of these beauties?'

'There are four battle cruisers and four hundred predators – what you would call "assault craft".'

'Who *are* you?'

Jumouk was blunt and to the point. The time for playing games was over.

'We are those whom you would call, the people from Atlantis.'

'But ... you're extinct. The Annunaki wiped you out centuries ago.'

'That, as you can clearly see, is not the case. We simply moved to Mars when the continent of Atlantis was destroyed. For centuries we have developed our home on Mars while keeping an eye on the Dropas and human connection on Earth. We were well aware the day would come where you might need our intervention in the fight against the Annunaki. This day has now come.'

Jumouk slowly shook his head. This had come as a total shock to him. The Dropas had always believed that the Annunaki had wiped out the people of Atlantis along with their continent. Here history was being rewritten right before his eyes.

By contrast, Lee was ecstatic. Here was the answer to his prayers. These battle cruisers were obviously far more advanced than either the *Victory* or the *Iron Duke*. He had to get on board to have a look. Then the thought suddenly struck him. What about the crew?

'We'll need to organise crews for them,' he blurted out.

In his excitement he had forgotten about the fully crewed battle cruiser moving somewhere beneath the oceans of Earth.

Pausanias replied calmly:

'All the battle cruisers have a full crew complement, all of whom are experienced in tactical warfare.'

Jumouk was the first to come down to Earth, or Mars, depending on which way you looked at it.

'This does put a different light on things, but it is still going to be far from easy. We'll be outnumbered two to one.'

Pausanias smiled, the first time anyone had seen him do that.

'We will, however, have a huge tactical advantage. Our cruisers are capable of being cloaked and they also have plasma shield technology.'

Lee let out a low-pitched whistle.

'It just gets better and better.'

Then the inevitable question

'Any chance of a look on board?'

Pausanias smiled again.

'I'm afraid that will have to wait until another time, Lee. But I promise you will have the opportunity to have a good look around later. I think Jumouk may want to call a meeting to discuss our next move.'

The meeting was held in one of the main conference rooms. Pausanias had gone all out to impress. Within the lavish surroundings, a first-class buffet had been arranged for the participants to enjoy. Waiters and waitresses were available with chilled water and fruit juice, or tea and coffee.

All the usual suspects were there along with a panel of three Atlantians headed up by Pausanias. The difference this time was that the Atlantians sat at the head of the conference table.

* * *

After everybody had selected their refreshments and taken their places round the conference table, Pausanias rose to speak.

'Thank you for coming, ladies and gentlemen. I am sure everybody is acquainted. However, I would like to introduce the other two members of the Atlantian council of three. On my left, Alcman and on my right, Solon.'

Marie recognised the names of historical characters from ancient Greece. Greek studies had been one of her majors in her early years.

Pausanias went on:

'May I remind you all that questions regarding Atlantis and ourselves can, and will, be answered later. For now though we must deal with the Annunaki threat to Earth, and indeed to ourselves. You all have a brief in front of you which covers our current resources and placements. Any further ideas or contributions to strategy will be welcomed and considered.'

The debate had been going for just short of an hour, and all kinds of ideas had been heard and dismissed, when Sacha, as usual, demonstrated his capacity for original thinking.

'The way I see it is, we want to destroy, or at least see off the Annunaki fleet and forces once and for all. We also want minimal casualties on our side and a planet Earth to return to, not a nuclear waste ground with a half-life of ten thousand years.'

His audience expressed their agreement with enthusiasm. Sacha was well respected following his contribution to the victory at Dulles.

'Now, from what I've heard recently, this base, and

Mars itself, packs a pretty lethal punch. We have to use that in our favour, or we'd be very stupid. So ... we use *Victory* and *Iron Duke* as bait for the Annunaki cruisers in space, we lead them back here and hit them as hard as we can with the weapons on the base and also one of the Atlantian battle cruisers. Along with the *Duke* and the *Victory* that should do some damage.'

Lee interrupted:

'What about the battle cruisers over Dulles?'

'Good point, Lee. We send two of the Atlantian battle cruisers along with the four hundred predators to meet up with the cruiser already on Earth. Everything can be shielded from the Annunaki proximity detectors, right?'

Pausanias nodded in agreement.

'We hit all the Annunaki battle cruisers simultaneously. We synchronise things so that at the same time as the fighting starts up here, we hit Dulles. We'll have split their forces and that'll give us a huge tactical advantage both on Earth and up here.'

Lee was the first one to burst out with applause, closely followed by Mark and Finney. Konoco smiled, amazed at the ingenuity Sacha consistently displayed.

'Shit! That was bloody excellent, Sacha. That's really going to make the bastards think twice!'

Pausanias was deep in conversation with the other two members of the council of three. Then he spoke:

'Thank you, Sacha. Can we please put Sacha's plan to a vote? All those in favour, please raise your hands.'

The 'yes' vote was unanimous.

# 53

Sutan was pleased with the way the building of his new capital city Tana was coming along. From the bridge of his flagship *Orpious* it was an impressive sight.

Tens of thousands of Annunaki workers were busy on the massive construction site. Annunaki workers were considered second class by the warrior-class Annunaki who regarded them as expendable and to be worked as hard as was necessary.

Buildings and infrastructures were appearing at an alarming rate, suggesting that construction would be finished within a month. Fortunately for the Annunaki there had been no interference either from the ESG or the resistance to slow the building work down. That was just the way Sutan liked it and he was determined to keep it that way.

Sutan's new residency and administration building was the first to be completed and he was just getting ready to leave the flagship to inspect it. The supreme commander's shuttle docked by the side of the flagship bridge and opened its doors. Sutan and his entourage boarded the sumptuously fitted-out shuttle craft, and relaxed for the short journey to the new building.

The shuttle craft touched down gently onto the roof of the building and was promptly lowered down two floors on the descending landing platform. This brought Sutan right into his living quarters without his even having to leave the shuttle. This was to provide ease of access and also to foil assassination attempts. The doors of the shuttle opened silently and the departure and arrivals ramp slid silently to the floor of the apartment.

Sutan swaggered down the ramp in full regalia, exulting in the presidential surroundings of his new living area. This was far better than he had been used to on Nibiru or even on his flagship. Most of the furniture and fittings had been looted from what had been Dulles and its surrounding area. Admittedly, everything had been planned down to the last detail and Sutan looked suitably impressed.

The whole apartment was filled with the latest in electronics – visual displays, communications, proximity sensors, all linked to every cruiser in the battle group. Sutan would be able to wage a war from the comfort of his front room. The rest of the building was just as impressive and would become the hub of the Annunaki war machine, controlling Earth and the space around it.

Sutan sent the shuttle back to the flagship. He intended to take a well-earned rest in his new living quarters. If necessary, he could always coordinate anything he needed to do from here.

The only problem with this new building were the electronics. They had still to be synchronised and brought on line, so for practical purposes they were currently ineffective. Sutan hadn't been made aware of this.

As Sutan stretched out on his luxurious chaise-longue, enjoying the array of dubious-looking refreshments laid out for his visit, back on board the flagship the proximity detectors had sparked into a flurry of activity. Two ESG battle cruisers had just appeared from the far side of Mars heading slowly towards Earth.

The commander left in charge of the *Orpious* had been desperately trying to contact Sutan but to no avail. He was, however, in contact with the Annunaki battle cruisers in space and had now given the order to engage the ESG cruisers as Sutan's previous orders had dictated.

The four vast Annunaki battle cruisers patrolling in space needed no encouragement and started off immediately on an intercept course to head off the ESG cruisers. As they got nearer, to their surprise the two vessels appeared to turn tail and head back towards Mars.

This behaviour was so completely at odds with every Annunaki intelligence report which spoke of the brave ESG tenaciously fighting to the last man, that the Annunaki cruisers should probably have paused to report back. They now smelt blood, however, and nothing was going to hold them back.

They bore down on the ESG craft like a pack of rabid dogs. The two ESG battle cruisers turned on their axes and bit back, pulse weapons fire erupting from both ships and hitting the Annunaki craft head on. Unknown to the Annunaki, a cloaked Atlantian battle cruiser had silently slipped past them and was now behind them.

Then, as it uncloaked itself in their rear, its true immensity could be seen, dwarfing the two Annunaki cruisers to the rear of the group. As it fired its beam weapon with the precision of a surgeon handling a scalpel, the Annunaki cruiser farthest from the Atlantians burst into flames, imploding on itself. At the same time, the other Annunaki cruiser, the one farthest from Mars, suffered the same fate from a beam directed from one of the defence banks on Mars.

The two remaining Annunaki cruisers, who had been engaged in a firefight with the ESG cruisers, immediately turned tail and, entering hyper-space, sped away from Mars as fast as they could.

Back on Earth Sutan had heard a commotion outside. Storming over to his main control console, he found that it didn't work. He cursed and headed quickly to a balcony overlooking his new domain.

The sight that met his startled gaze was one he never could have imagined.

Three colossal Atlantian battle cruisers had just uncloaked right next to his battle group and were in the process of decimating his battle cruisers. Atlantian predators were everywhere concentrating their fire on Annunaki assault ships and shuttles. The beam technology and plasma shields were outclassing the Annunaki at every turn.

It wasn't so much a massacre, more like a demonstration of total military superiority. The Atlantians were giving the Annunaki a chance: a chance to leave with minimal losses.

Sutan stood on his balcony screaming at his battle group, screaming for them to go, go and regroup.

The Atlantian battle cruisers were taking multiple hits from the Annunaki banks of pulse weapons, but the plasma shields were simply absorbing the energy and redistributing it for their own use as raw power.

The technologically advanced Atlantian beam weapons were not operating at full power, firing more to disable than destroy, pinpointing weak points on the Annunaki battle cruisers, and rendering them ineffectual, and consequently useless.

Four of the Annunaki battle cruisers and numerous assault craft and shuttles, along with other Annunaki vessels, had now left the fray for the relative safety of deep space, leaving behind only the diehard Annunakis and the disabled craft hanging over Dulles.

Within three hours the whole of the Annunaki battle group had either fled, been disabled or destroyed and what was left had been forced into humiliating surrender. Two Annunaki battle cruisers had been destroyed, three had been totally disabled, and around two hundred assault craft had been destroyed, disabled or surrendered.

The Atlantian losses were minimal. No battle cruiser losses or damage, and a dozen predators destroyed, mainly through pilot error.

Thousands of ESG troops had now been flown down in shuttles from Mars, and the *Victory* and *Iron Duke* were both now in attendance at Dulles. The entire area was a hive of activity as they mopped up the remaining Annunaki warriors and workers. With the odd firefight taking place it was still far from secure.

Sutan and his entourage were in hiding, their plans to colonise Earth in tatters. Sutan was now fighting for his very survival, and a way to rejoin his shattered battle group. They badly needed to get hold of a shuttle and the luck to go with it.

The ESG were already starting to search the buildings that had been completed and they were in grave risk of being discovered. Sutan had already taken the precaution of dressing down, wearing an Annunaki foot warrior's body-suit, so that if they were discovered his rank would not be obvious.

Fortunately for supreme commander Sutan, a planned escape route came with the rank and, more important, the building. He was led by one of the architects that designed the building to a hidden lift shaft within his own sleeping area. It was common for the high command on Nibiru to have well-designed escape routes attached to their living and sleeping areas, such was the distrust that came with rank.

The lift stopped three floors below the ground floor of the building. A series of long corridors stretched out in front of the group of Annunaki refugees. At least now they had the opportunity to get out of the area and avoid capture by the ESG. Two of the entourage had been despatched in the opposite direction by Sutan on an unknown errand.

It had suddenly got better and better for Sutan. The architect informed him that at the end of this tunnel his own personal shuttle was waiting for him in a hidden bunker along with an escort of four Annunaki assault vessels. Sutan was back in business.

# 54

Pausanias had invited Jumouk, Lee and Marie to a meeting on board his flagship *Cronus*, named after the Greek god.

Lee was overawed by the level of technology on board the *Cronus*. It was also so sumptuous and made the ESG battle cruisers look like poor cousins. The conference room they were shown to was considerably smaller than he had imagined. Then he remembered the Atlantian council of three and thought: I guess they probably wouldn't need a very big room then. As they sat down at the conference table, yet again they were waited on by the Atlantian service personnel, with drinks and food. The hospitality was endless.

Jumouk was full of questions for the Atlantians.

'Why were your weapons not on full power. I thought we wanted to destroy the Annunaki battle group?'

Pausanias and his high council clearly had their own agenda.

'Our intention was never to destroy, but to persuade the Annunaki commanders that it would be a futile exercise to try and colonise Earth. The planet must never be terraformed by the Annunaki.'

Jumouk was still unsure.

'I understand the sentiment, but half the battle group is still out there somewhere. How can we be sure they won't come back?'

'I will be talking personally to their supreme commander and assuring him that now the Dropas and humans know of our existence, we will not allow any encroachment on Earth's space again.'

Lee butted into the conversation.

'OK, but how can you be sure they will stick to any agreement?'

Pausanias smiled.

'Lee, my friend, in the space of three hours we disabled or destroyed nearly half their battle group. I think that might have got their attention and convinced them it would be in their best interests to withdraw while they can.'

'I'm sure you're right, Pausanias, but what about the disabled and captured ships and also all the prisoners. There must be tens of thousands of prisoners?'

'If, as they say on Earth, the Annunaki agree to pack up, go home, and never return, they will be welcome to take all their warriors and ships with them.'

Lee had another question.

'What about the devastation on Earth? That is going to take hundreds of years to put right'

'The Atlantian council of three has agreed that we will help rebuild infrastructures and cities. I'm sure our Dropas friends will help as well.'

Jumouk nodded in agreement and Pausanias went on:

'Anyway, these matters are for another day. Are we all agreed then? Provided the Annunaki agree to our terms, we will let them go home peacefully?'

Reluctantly and still with hesitation, Jumouk, Lee and Marie agreed. The situation had changed, with the Atlantians appearing to be calling all the shots, as was their right now.

Marie had been very quiet during the meeting, and Lee began to wonder why.

'Are you OK, Marie?'

Marie nodded.

'Yes. Sorry, Lee. It's just ... something still doesn't feel right and I can't quite put my finger on it.'

'What, is it to do with the Annunaki?'

'I don't know. It's just a feeling. I get them sometimes and the trouble is, I'm usually right.'

The three were now being taken on the guided tour of the Atlantian battle cruiser that Pausanias had promised to Lee. The ship was massive, with guidance aids at regular intervals along all the winding passages and corridors. Pausanias was obviously extremely proud of his grand flagship and they could all understand why. Everything was state of the art, no detail had been missed or excluded. It was so user friendly you couldn't go wrong. The computer systems were programmed with everything you could want to know. If you wanted somewhere to relax, this was it. You would never have guessed that only a few hours before it had taken part in a devastating battle.

Up on the bridge you had an excellent view of what was happening on the ground below. Marie watched the coming and going of the ESG troops as they rounded up the last of the Annunaki prisoners; the remains of smashed assault craft were being cleared up by bulldozers; and piles of debris were being swept away. It was a real clean-up operation.

'Those aren't Annunaki warriors. The prisoners ... their workers, I mean. They're not Annunaki warriors.'

Marie caught everybody by surprise with this remark.

'How do you mean, Marie?'

Lee was puzzled.

'I haven't seen one Annunaki warrior. They're all Annunaki workers.'

She went on excitedly.

'As far as I know, Annunaki workers are expendable, second class, not at all like the warrior class.'

'And your point is?'

'We've just been in a major battle and there's no Annunaki warriors anywhere. Don't you find that strange?'

'I don't see where you're going with this, Marie.'

Jumouk was as puzzled as Lee.

'What about the disabled and captured ships? Where are their crews?'

Lee had an answer for that question.

'Ah, now that I can answer. Fortunately for us they were all abandoned.'

'So all the prisoners we have are second-class workers?'

'I suppose so. I've not checked. I just know we've got a hell of a lot of prisoners.'

Jumouk and Lee were still none the wiser.

'Oh my God! This feels so wrong.'

Marie's instincts were working hard.

'This is a trap. I can feel it.'

Jumouk and Lee were now very concerned.

'How do you mean? How can this be a trap?'

'Put yourself in the Annunaki's shoes. What would you do?'

Lee thought for a second.

'Well, I'd rig the base so, if it was compromised, I could destroy it. A bit like Bill Graham did with the sewer systems.'

'Shit! The base is rigged to self-destruct. That's why the Annunaki left so quickly.'

Marie was right, a device was under the main part of the

base ticking down the hours, minutes and seconds to a cataclysmic explosion that could wipe out half of North America and anything in the skies above it.

Pausanias ordered the immediate withdrawal of all craft and ground troops to a safe distance even as far away as Houston.

Marie had realised this would be a nightmare and could take hours if not days for somebody to find the device and disable it.

Mark, Finney and Sacha were helping to coordinate the prisoner movements when they received the orders to withdraw from the base. Mark couldn't understand it. Why withdraw after such an outstanding victory? Then the message from Maria arrived and it all became clear.

'Listen, guys, there's a self-destruct device here somewhere and we need to find it before it blows.'

Sacha came up with the classic question.

'Where do we start?'

'Not got a clue. Underground?'

'You think? Underground, where?'

Mark was deep in thought when Finney hit on an idea.

'Look, if it was us where would we put it?'

'Underneath the control room?'

'The building you would leave from at the very end.'

Between them they knew now what to look for.

'Which building?'

'It must be one that's complete.'

Finney was first to spot it.

'What about that one? The tall one over there?'

Mark followed the direction of Finney's finger.

'Sweet, that looks like it could fit the bill. Let's give it a try.'

Once inside it became clear that this was a building of some importance. There was a central control room complex, which took up six floors of the building, except nothing seemed to be working.

'It doesn't look like they got anything connected up. This is crap. Nothing works.'

Despite Marks's best efforts nothing did work, and there was no sign of any doomsday device.

'I thought we said *under* the control room?'

Sacha was right. Starting from one corner of the control complex, a flight of stairs led to a complex of basement tunnels three storeys down.

'OK, where now?'

'It's got to be around here somewhere. Let's take a tunnel each, give a loud whistle if you find anything. Let's go.'

Mark was the one who found it. He whistled loudly and the three knelt down to examine the device.

It certainly didn't look like a nuclear device. It was not as big as they had imagined it would be, but it did look complicated. There was no sign of a timing device, although it was hard to make out as most of it appeared to be covered in some kind of shroud.

Mark was in constant contact with Jumouk and Lee on board the Atlantian battle cruiser.

'I think we're going to need someone a bit more specialised for this.'

'What does it look like?'

Mark was stuck for words.

'Like nothing any of us have seen before.'

'OK, hang fire, Pausanias and Marie are on their way down to you. Has it got any kind of timer on it?'

'Not that we can see. There are all sorts of funny gadgets.

Though, having said that, most of it's in some kind of shroud.'

'OK, as I said, Pausanias and Marie should be with you shortly.'

Almost at once Pausanias entered the room and went straight to the device.

'Marie, am I glad to see you two!'

Mark was genuinely relieved.

'It's a matter converter. It takes matter and converts it into antimatter. The longer it runs the more explosive it gets.'

'Can you switch it off or disarm it?'

Marie knew it was a silly question. It was never going to be that simple.

'Unfortunately not. Just looking at the way it's been configured, it's going to have to expend the antimatter before it will stop.'

Finney looked puzzled.

'Expend the antimatter – that means?'

'Blow up, you daft bastard!' muttered Sacha scornfully. 'It's got to blow up to stop, right?'

'Well put, Sacha!'

Mark was being facetious.

'What size of an explosion are we looking at?'

Pausanias was deep in thought.

'As I said, it gets bigger as time goes on and more antimatter is added. Just now, probably enough to wipe out half of continental North America.'

'What sets it off if there's no timer?'

'Eventually enough antimatter will be produced to fill the containment area and particles will seep out past the neutral seal, creating a chain reaction.'

This seemed to be getting worse and worse.

'How long? I mean ... before it blows, and how big an explosion?'

'I don't know. Producing antimatter, it's not an exact science. Once it's full, though, after the explosion you may be sure you won't have a planet.'

'Jesus! what can we do?'

Sacha's face lit up. He had just had an idea.

'Why don't we send it into deep space?'

'First of all, we can't move it without the danger of setting it off, Second, when it did go off the shock wave would send every asteroid in the asteroid belt hurtling at Earth. The ending would be exactly the same. No planet.'

Mark brought things back into focus.

'The first thing we need to figure out is how to move it without its blowing up in our faces. Then we can worry about what we're going to do with it.'

# 55

Jumouk had ordered the two ESG battle cruisers into deep space to monitor the Annunaki battle group that was still threatening Earth.

Sutan had now rejoined his flagship, *Orpious*, and was feeling quite pleased with himself. If he couldn't have Earth, he was quite happy for no one else to have it. He might have lost half his battle group, but the destruction of Earth would be a victory in his eyes.

The campaign against Earth had cost the Annunaki's dearly but, because they hadn't been at war with an adversary for millennia, the cost didn't matter. It was more about the glory. There were other planets in this solar system that could be plundered for raw materials.

The battle group was now under repair to bring it back up to full readiness. Sutan would have liked to have salvaged some of his disabled cruisers, but was well aware that the antimatter device could go off at any time, and he was prepared to sacrifice them in return for the ultimate defeat of Earth.

On board the *Cronus* Jumouk and Lee were pondering the problem of moving the antimatter device. It was Lee who finally came up with a viable solution.

'Why don't we freeze the device to make it more stable?

It can then be moved and freezing might slow down the antimatter production as well.'

Jumouk contacted Pausanias and ran the plan past him. Pausanias was delighted and was very confident it would work. But where would they move it to?

Preparations were already under way to freeze the device. Liquid nitrogen LN2 was on the way and would be used to create a super-freeze state within the holding container in which the device would be placed.

A large, metal, twin-door fridge freezer was selected to contain the device. Inside it was stripped down to the shell and then laid on its back. The LN2 holding containers were placed inside and the doors closed. The device had first been surrounded by LN2 containers to get its temperature down to minus 50 degrees, so it could be moved into the twin-door fridge freezer. Moving it was painstakingly slow, but eventually the device was packed safely into the fridge freezer. Once the temperature had plummeted to minus 50 degrees, the freezer was welded shut. The whole process had taken five hours and had been an enormous strain on everyone involved.

Now there was the problem of what to do with the frozen package. Once again it was Sacha who came to the rescue.

'I know it's not the movies, but why don't we run it into the far side of the sun? There are lots of reactions going on in there all the time, and if we do it on the far side any solar flares caused by the explosion won't affect Earth.'

The plan sounded pretty good to Mark. and he looked across to Pausanias for approval. Pausanias smiled.

'I still can't get over your constant inventiveness, Sacha. That is a brilliant plan, and it might just work.'

'Well, thank you kindly, sir. It's always nice to be appreciated, but shouldn't we get this done sooner rather than later? I'm still feeling quite uncomfortable with this thing sitting here.'

It had been agreed that three shuttles including the fated one would fly to the far side of the sun, and when the timing was right the shuttle would be set on autopilot and sent on its way with the device to its destiny and eventual incineration within the sun's corona.

Arrangements were made to have the freezer taken to its shuttle and carefully placed in the hold. The final question was: who was going to fly the shuttle?

Lee volunteered for the job without hesitation. Even with the high levels of danger and uncertainty, this task could have been made for him.

He boarded the shuttle cautiously. Time was now critical and everyone was getting nervous. The device had been on Earth long enough.

He inspected the freezer briefly. It all looked fine and Lee once again gave thanks for Sacha's ingenuity. Where would they be without him, he wondered?

Safely installed in the pilot's seat, Lee couldn't help feeling a sense of pride, as the three shuttles took off slowly together and began their journey to the sun. As they broke free of Earth's atmosphere, he breathed a sigh of relief.

Two of the Atlantian battle cruisers took up positions to protect the three shuttles from any unwelcome Annunaki attention. As Lee guided the shuttle slowly through space towards the far side of the sun, the cabin began to feel uncomfortably cold even with the climate controls set to high.

Lee was having a lot of time to reflect on events. Ever since the Dropas had made their presence on Earth known, it had been a non-stop, one-thing-after-another, real fight for survival, one that many times Lee hadn't thought mankind would win.

The worst time was when the second battle group had arrived unexpectedly in Earth's space. They had done so much at that point just to survive, and had beaten all the odds against them, only to have to start all over again. Thank God for the Atlantians, he thought! If it wasn't for them humanity would probably be extinct by now and the Annunaki would be lording it over Earth.

He had been so deep in thought that he hadn't noticed that the cabin temperature was rising, but a quick glance out the left-hand-side viewing window explained the increase in cabin temperature.

He'd never quite realised how big the sun was, always just taking it for granted. Seeing it now closer up, it was colossal, a truly magnificent sight filling the whole side of the viewing window and was still burning his eyes even with the solar filters on.

He checked his coordinates and the orbit of Earth. He still had a fair bit of travelling to do to ensure Earth would be safe from the inevitable solar flares after the huge explosion that would be created by the device. Nobody could know for sure exactly what would happen, but this was the only viable option, he knew.

Lee remembered when he had been a very young diplomat serving some time at the Chinese embassy in Scotland. Edinburgh was a beautiful city, and Corstorphine where the embassy was located was only ten minutes from the centre of the capital. The Scots had a perfect expression for situations where the outcome was uncertain: they used to say, 'lucky white heather'. If ever there was a need for lucky white heather it was now.

The calculations for the release of the shuttle to its fiery doom weren't that complex. Just so long as the shuttle exploded on the far side of the sun away from the Earth, everything should be OK.

Lee contacted the other two pilots. It looked as if they were now just about at the right coordinates. He double-checked the figures and began to programme the autopilot. A few minutes later everything was ready. Lee set the delay of ten minutes for the autopilot to kick in and headed for the docking bay, ready to transfer to the other shuttle.

The transfer shuttle docked perfectly with Lee's, and he opened the air-tight doors between the two shuttles, then made his way through to the transfer shuttle, not without giving out a small sigh of relief.

Although it had been a privilege to play such an important role in the salvation of Earth, the pressure and anxiety were now taking their toll. Lee felt absolutely shattered. They would have to linger to make sure the autopilot kicked in when it was supposed to, then they would need to jump into hyper-space without delay, well away from the inevitable cataclysm.

Everything went according to plan. As the shuttle began its final journey to the sun and its inevitable fate, the two remaining shuttles jumped into hyper-space and safety. They emerged from hyper-drive a few seconds later and turned to take up an observation position.

The sun was now just a pinprick in space. Lee activated the observation screen and magnified the picture to maximum. He estimated that within the next minute they should be able to see the results of their endeavours. The sun was now the size of an orange on the screen. Lee and the shuttle pilot hung over the screen not quite knowing what to expect.

Suddenly a white flash crept across the screen and then appeared in the front viewing window, making Lee and the pilot shield their eyes against the glare. As it went dark again, large yellow and orange flashes emanating from the sun could be seen on the observation screen, branching out into space in lashing, whip-like motions.

The predicted solar flares were more massive than had been predicted, but fortunately were not heading in the direction of Earth. They were, however, coming in Lee's direction, travelling at the speed of light and pulling their slower-moving partners, the CMEs, the coronal mass ejections, in lumbering cloud formations behind them.

The solar flares did little damage to the shuttles, which were designed to withstand them, but the CMEs were more dangerous. Depending on their intensity, they could play havoc with the ships' electronics.

Lee was monitoring them closely and, to his horror, saw that they were travelling at forty times the speed they normally should have, which was around 6,000,000 miles an hour. These were travelling at 240,000,000 miles an hour, which would mean that they would be in this area of space within two days. The intensity of these CMEs was generally determined by their speed and would be devastatingly destructive to anything electronic.

Lee guessed that it had been the explosion of the device that was the cause of the unusual solar flare and CMEs' activity. Now all they could do was to make a detour and head back to Earth.

# 56

Jumouk had been monitoring the three shuttles' progress from the bridge of the *Cronus*. As they disappeared around the far side of the sun, the proximity detectors lost sight of them, at which point Pausanias enabled the three-dimensional representation of space around the sun. Sure enough, there were the three shuttles.

As one shuttle began moving towards the sun's corona, the other two suddenly disappeared. The shuttle heading towards the sun was gradually increasing its speed.

On the bridge of the *Cronus* the anticipation was almost physical, as minute after minute passed with still nothing happening.

Jumouk guessed that Lee would now be a safe distance away after being in hyper-drive, and was probably watching as well.

Suddenly and surprisingly a bright flash burst across the bridge, temporarily blinding everybody. As their sight slowly returned, the surface of the sun could be seen to be boiling at the point of the explosion of the device, solar flares angrily spitting into the surrounding space. Whip-like motions flailed into space and beyond. Fortunately, all this activity was in the opposite direction from Earth.

Jumouk was interested to see if the visual representation could pick up the two shuttles that had gone into hyper-drive.

'Pausanias, can you home in on the two shuttles?'

Pausanias made some hand movements and adjustments and sure enough the two shuttles appeared in deep space, sitting all on their own with absolutely nothing near them.

'Well, at least we know Lee's OK.'

'I never had any doubt Lee was the right man for the job. He is a very adaptable and clever human.'

Everyone who had seen the visual representation technology had been amazed by it. Jumouk was trying to guess how it worked, which was nothing unusual. Everyone who had seen it had secretly tried to work it out, but no one had succeeded.

Two or three days were going to have to pass before they could be sure there were no adverse affects on Earth, after the explosion in the sun's corona. However, from all the checks that Pausanias had made it did look as if mankind was in the clear.

All the same Pausanias wanted to wait until he was quite certain that the Earth was going to be safe before he confronted the Annunaki commanders and fleet. To be honest, he didn't even know exactly where the Annunaki fleet was positioned in deep space. All he did know is they didn't present a threat at that moment.

Jumouk was more doubtful. He didn't know why the Annunaki had been so quiet over the past few days. They may just have been waiting patiently, expecting the Earth to rip itself apart in a cataclysmic antimatter explosion, but he wasn't happy not knowing where they were. He kept an eye on the proximity detector but there was no sign of them anywhere.

Pausanias was now quite satisfied. Earth had suffered no

ill effects from the trauma on the sun, and he could now concentrate on finding the whereabouts of the Annunaki fleet.

Ever since Lee had got back from deep space he had been obsessed by the cloud of CMEs travelling into space. They didn't seem to be slowing down or dispersing but just kept going at a constant speed.

He had been monitoring them on the visual depiction technology with, it should be said, Pausanias's blessing. In fact, Pausanias was quite interested in what Lee was doing. The recent events had never been properly tried and tested, and they were producing some interesting results.

Lee stopped what he was doing for a moment and stared intently at the visual depiction, beckoning Pausanias to come over.

'Is that what I think it is?'

Pausanias looked intently at the screen, and after making a few adjustments he nodded.

'Yes, look it's the Annunaki battle group. They've put the sun between us and them, which is why Jumouk couldn't pick them up on the proximity detectors.'

'Can we zoom in closer and get a better look?'

Pausanias wafted his hands around and the image intensified and grew closer.

'I can count five, no six, battle cruisers, that big transport, and, let's see, eight other transports and what … maybe fifty assault ships, plus whatever there is inside the battle cruisers.'

Pausanias nodded in agreement.

'That's just about what we thought what was left.'

By this time Jumouk had joined them.

'How far out are they?'

'They're still a fair way away ... wait a second, Can we just move a tiny bit closer to the sun?'

Lee was looking at the depiction from every angle.

'I thought so. They're right in the path of the CME cloud and it's heading straight for them.'

Pausanias looked at Jumouk. They both still looked bewildered. Lee turned round to them.

'Don't you see? If it was only a normal-strength CME cloud. it wouldn't be a problem. Look ... imagine a large ship at sea. It meets a twenty-foot wave, no problem. Bumpy maybe, but still no problem. But if you multiply that twenty-foot wave by forty and then you get a eight-hundred foot wave, end of game for that ship. It's exactly the same scenario with the CME cloud.'

Enlightenment dawned on the faces of Jumouk and Pausanias.

'You mean the CME cloud is going to destroy them?'

'Well, it's certainly going to give them an extremely hard time. Bear in mind, nothing of this nature has ever been recorded before.'

The irony of the situation wasn't lost on any of them. A bomb that the Annunaki had planted to wipe out mankind was now threatening to do the same instead to the Annunaki.

'What do you want to do about it?'

Jumouk was not sure what answer to expect. After a long pause, Pausanias replied, 'I don't know. Morally, I suppose we should warn them.'

Lee's reaction was immediate.

'We've been fighting them tooth and nail for months now. This is our chance to do away with them once and for all. They'll never come back after this.'

'When will the cloud hit them, then?'

Lee looked at the depiction and began muttering to himself and drumming his fingers.

'Best guess two days but, given time, I can work it out exactly.'

'Do that please, Lee,' Pausanias requested. 'We'll meet up with them and, if there's no change in attitude, we'll leave moments before the cloud strikes, telling them nothing and leaving them to their own devices. Does that sound reasonable?'

'That sounds fair enough.'

'Good, we're all agreed then?'

'Agreed.'

Lee moved over to one of the other consoles to make his calculations. Jumouk and Pausanias sat down together to plan the confrontation with the Annunaki.

Three of the Atlantian battle cruisers appeared out of hyper-space right in front of the Annunaki fleet and opened a communications channel straightaway.

'This is Pausanias, the high commander of the Atlantian fleet, will your commander, please respond?'

The call was put out twice more before a response was received.

'What do you want?'

'As you can see your plan to destroy Earth and its inhabitants has failed. Your device for creating anti-matter out of matter was destroyed. We are now warning you formally that in future your presence in this part of space will not be tolerated, and any incursion will be seen as an act of war which will result in any vessels in this space being destroyed. This is your last opportunity to leave peacefully and not come back.'

Pausanias turned to Lee and asked how much time.

'Four minutes exactly.'

On the main communications console Pausanias continued.

'What is your response?'

Suddenly all hell broke loose. The Annunaki battle group had opened up with everything it had. Pulse weapons fire was intense, smashing into the Atlantian battle cruisers.

Lee gave one word of command and, as suddenly as they had arrived, the three Atlantian battle cruisers were gone.

The Annunakis were delighted that they had finally seen off the Atlantian battle cruisers. Sutan was delighted with himself. So carried away were they that they didn't even see the CME cloud coming.

As soon as Sutan realised what was happening, he ordered every craft into hyper-space. Virtually every system on every craft was failing as they desperately tried to make hyper-space. Air locks opened, weapons shorted out and started to explode. Life support failed.

None, apart from two cruisers and the large transport, ever made it to hyper-space. Those that did make it were damaged almost beyond repair, and faced a very long and arduous trip back to Nibiru.

As the three Atlantian battle cruisers arrived back at Dulles they knew they had seen the last of the Annunaki.

Now came the hard part: counting the cost of the survival of Earth to its inhabitants. At least they would be able to start afresh and had their new friends, the Atlantians and the Dropas.

Earth might after all have a brighter future ahead.